A World Apart

Caro Fraser was educated in Glasgow and the Isle of Man. After attending Watford School of Art she worked as an advertising copywriter for three years, then read Law at King's College, London. She was called to the Bar of Middle Temple in 1979 and worked as a shipping lawyer, before turning to writing. She is the author of eleven other novels, six of which are part of the highly successful, critically acclaimed Caper Court series. She lives in London with her husband, who is a solicitor, and her four children.

A World Apart

CARO FRASER

MICHAEL JOSEPH
an imprint of
PENGUIN BOOKS

MICHAEL JOSEPH

Published by the Penguin Group
Penguin Books Ltd, 80 Strand, London WC2R 0RL, England
Penguin Group (USA) Inc., 375 Hudson Street, New York, New York 10014, USA
Penguin Group (Canada), 90 Eglinton Avenue East, Suite 700, Toronto, Ontario, Canada M4P 2Y3
(a division of Pearson Penguin Canada Inc.)
Penguin Ireland, 25 St Stephen's Green, Dublin 2, Ireland
(a division of Penguin Books Ltd)
Penguin Group (Australia), 250 Camberwell Road,
Camberwell, Victoria 3124, Australia (a division of Pearson Australia Group Pty Ltd)
Penguin Books India Pvt Ltd, 11 Community Centre,
Panchsheel Park, New Delhi – 110 017, India
Penguin Group (NZ), cnr Airborne and Rosedale Roads, Albany,
Auckland 1310, New Zealand (a division of Pearson New Zealand Ltd)
Penguin Books (South Africa) (Pty) Ltd, 24 Sturdee Avenue,
Rosebank 2196, South Africa

Penguin Books Ltd, Registered Offices: 80 Strand, London WC2R 0RL, England

www.penguin.com

First published 2006
I

Set in 14/18.25 pt Monotype Garamond
Typeset by Rowland Phototypesetting Ltd, Bury St Edmunds, Suffolk
Printed in Great Britain by Clays Ltd, St Ives plc

A CIP catalogue record for this book is available from the British Library

ISBN 0–718–14728–6

For Francis, man of ideas

I

Since his retirement Mark's father had, like many men in his situation with agile and curious minds, developed a close relationship with his computer. He talked regularly to Mark on the phone about the fascinating discoveries he made, the interesting sites he visited, and the benefits of the new pieces of software and hardware which he acquired. Mark, who spent a greater part of his working day with computers than he would have liked, found his father's conversational rambles about the internet some-what tedious. But it was communication, father to son, and so he listened patiently.

It was during one of these conversations with his father – he always came on after Mark's mother, who liked to hear about Paula and the boys, and to trade her own bits of news about the doings of family and friends in the town where Mark had grown up – that his father told him about the family photographs. He had begun to go through all the old albums and shoebox-stored collections, assembling the pictures chronologically, scanning them, and putting them on to disk. He said he would be sending some to Mark soon.

'All the ones in that old chest of drawers?' asked Mark. He was suddenly transported, almost to the point of smelling the cedarwood and feeling the grain of the knobs on the drawers, to the spare room in his parents' house in Braintree, and the chest of drawers which stood in the corner next to the window. Its top three drawers contained old clothes – cardigans, old flannel trousers, balled pairs of socks that someone, presumably his mother, imagined might one day come in handy – and the very bottom one was stuffed full of rows of paper photograph wallets. Mark, when he was very young and curious, had spent happy hours going through these packets of photos, re-creating the strange past of his own family. Now, some thirty-five years on, as he sat in his study, he felt a strange lurch of emotion at the memory of them. They connected him with his younger self, and it was a giddy sensation. It passed quickly.

'Those ones,' said his father, 'and the ones in the attic.'

Mark didn't remember any photographs in the attic. 'Well,' he said, 'that sounds like it'll keep you busy.'

He wasn't surprised by this new project of his father's. Last year it had been the family genealogy, which had been interesting enough at first, but had then got a little wearying in the preponderance of detail. Mark, receiving regular updates from his father on the increasingly sprawling family tree, had begun to feel the abundance of for-bears like an oppressive weight. His own existence seemed to dwindle with every new relative or far-flung connection which his father discovered. Those heaps of relatives, those dead strangers tenuously linked to his own present through a murky past. He hadn't liked to tell his father, but it got to the point where it all became irrelevant – it seemed to Mark that you could be related to the entire world, at this rate. And even that possibility in itself was of limited interest. Mark, with his wife and his two teenage sons, had a busy present to concern himself with.

He could understand, though, at his father's age, his preoccupation with his antecedents. The family photo thing was the next logical step, really.

'You'll get a lot of surprises,' said his father with a chuckle. 'I came across some taken when you were at university. You'll like those. The state of you.'

'They should give James and Owen a laugh, at any rate,' said Mark, trying unsuccessfully to recall himself in the late seventies. He'd imagined himself to be the aperçu of cool in those days, so no doubt he'd looked conventionally ridiculous.

'I haven't got round to putting those on disk yet. I've started with the very early ones. There's a lot of material to go at.'

'I'll look forward to seeing them.'

Mark, after a few more familial exchanges, hung up. At least his mother might find this latest computer adventure of his father's a shade more interesting than others. He glanced up, and caught sight of his shadowy reflection in the screen of his switched-off laptop. He still couldn't get used to the way his hair was receding. He always expected it to be a bit further forward. In his mind's eye, in his everyday perception of himself, he had all his hair. So it gave him a bit of a shock to see it further back than it should be. But these things happened at his age, or so he was told. In fact, a lot of changes were supposed to occur at forty-three. Still, when all was said and done – and it wasn't, not by a long chalk, he was young, really – having got to this point in his life, he had reason to be pretty satisfied with himself. His own business, a contented family – by and large; OK, Owen was pretty difficult sometimes, and he occasionally wondered if he and Paula were on the same wavelength, but still – a large house on the outskirts of Harlow, swimming pool, his XJ6 in the garage, Paula's 4×4 standing in the driveway outside, decent holidays each year, a healthy pension fund (which was more than most blokes his age could say). Yeah, so far, so good.

He swivelled in his chair for an uncertain moment. He really badly fancied a drink, but he was trying to cut down. He'd had a medical recently. When the doctor had asked him how much he generally drank in a week, Mark, for some reason connected with bravado and a desire to appear master of his own destiny, had told him the exact truth. The doctor had remarked with a frown that that was a lot of units. Mark had felt instantly humbled. At the end of the examination the doctor gave Mark a brief lecture on the cumulative perils of drinking too much.

Mark picked up the new brochure which had recently been produced to advertise his company's wares. He flicked through the pages of machines designed to aid mankind in its endless task of disposing waste material. Shredders, compactors, balers, crushers ... This new

Kompakter compactor (the name was his partner Gerry's idea) was going to attract a whole new inner urban market. A slimline machine that would boldly go where other waste compactors had never gone before, bringing in a tide of new customers in the shape of high street retailers for whom space was at a premium. As he sat there musing on his business, it suddenly occurred to Mark that the doctor, doubtless accustomed to being lied to on a regular basis by his patients regarding their alcohol consumption, might have assumed that Mark, too, was downscaling. In which case, working on the theory that patients under-exaggerated their drinking by a possible third, he *might* have reckoned Mark's true intake to be in the region of forty units a week. Virtually an alcoholic. So, working on the *same* basis, perhaps Mark could safely disregard the uncomfortable little lecture, which had been intended for someone who was far more of a drinker than Mark, in reality, was.

He got up and went through to the kitchen, took the whisky bottle from the cupboard and poured himself a slug. Paula, who was taking washing from the tumble dryer, glanced at him. Or rather, at the whisky.

'What?' said Mark.

'Nothing.'

The pleasure of that first sip, that glow of warmth, had been stolen. He drank, anyway, then remarked, 'Dad's found himself a new project.'

'Mmm?'

Mark wasn't sure whether she was listening or not,

but he began to tell Paula about the photographs. She interrupted him, her eyes going past him to their younger son, Owen, who had come into the kitchen.

'Did you bring your cricket whites home?'

'No, I forgot.'

'Owen, I told you to bring them home. Well, they won't be clean for the match tomorrow. I can't help it.'

'So? Who cares?' Owen shrugged and shambled to the fridge.

Mark waited for Paula to return her gaze to him, to say, 'What were you saying?' But she went on folding the washing, and said nothing. So Mark resumed his account of his father's project.

'Owen,' said Paula, 'don't start making yourself a snack. Your dinner's going to be ready in ten minutes.'

'I only want a sandwich.'

'If you have a sandwich, you won't eat a proper dinner. Come on, do as I say.'

Mark stood with his whisky, his wife in front of him, his eighteen-year-old son at the fridge behind him. They were talking through him. He might as well be transparent. The trouble with Paula these days was that she was constantly preoccupied. She seemed neither to see nor hear Mark because around her lay a thousand distractions, all demanding her attention.

It hadn't been this way a few months ago. Then she'd had only the family and the household to concern her, plus the three half-days she did in one of Lorna's two dress shops every week. But back in January, Lorna's partner in business had retired, and Lorna had offered Paula a full-time job, managing both shops. It hadn't been an instant decision. Much as the prospect of the job thrilled her, Paula had been beset by anxiety, and had had to talk long and hard about it to Mark. Now, three months on, it was hard to believe that Paula had ever known the meaning of self-doubt. She had thrust herself into the role of the truly modern woman, juggling home and a career. In fact, she made that juggling act a third job in itself. She was constantly busy, absorbed in the process of making the pieces of work and home fit together. It could have been maintained in a state of loose harmony, with the boys doing their own ironing from time to time, and the odd takeaway in the evening, instead of home-cooked meals. But for Paula the bed of life had to be made with hospital corners. To ensure that standards at home and work didn't slip, her days were now rigidly disciplined and compartmentalized. There was a sense of constant frantic energy about the home. She would often be moving from washing machine to tumble dryer, or fridge to cooker, with her mobile phone clamped to her ear. She no longer wore tracksuits or jeans during the day. She got up an hour earlier to wash and blow-dry her hair, and groom herself for her appearance in the shop at nine thirty, and to make sure the household machine was ticking over smoothly. These days she was always smartly dressed, her face made up, nails polished, a woman on the move, flitting expertly through the domestic setting on her way to more important things.

Mark admired the way she handled it all, but somehow he found it both unsexy and unsettling. When he came home in the evenings, he would have liked to find her with her hair tied back, her face bare of make-up, dressed in any old thing, relaxed and with time on her hands. Time for him. He felt marginalized, downsized to accommodate the demands of her new career, with its buying trips and meetings. Once upon a time he had felt that he occupied a central position in her life. These days he felt he was required to fit in with a more important agenda.

The job of managing two clothes shops had subtly altered Paula's perception of herself, and this in turn had led to soft, almost subliminal changes in the balance between herself and Mark. He detected lately a creeping note of exasperation in her manner towards him – although this was possibly no more than a manifestation of feeling harassed all the time – and sex had become less frequent and more perfunctory. The general sense was of a woman with more pressing things to concern herself with. A couple of times over the past few weeks, Mark had thought about sitting her down and talking to her about it, suggesting that maybe she could find more time for him and the boys, and stop putting this job of hers first. But Mark knew what a gigantic non-starter that was. Paula loved her job, and her new perception of herself. She probably even relished, with faint martyrdom, the difficulties involved in running home and work. He could hardly suggest that she should put home and family before her job. That would imply she wasn't coping, that something, somewhere was suffering. Superficially, that wasn't so. Meals were made, clothes were ironed. How could he complain? It wouldn't just be unfair. It would be pointless.

Mark decided to take his drink, and the evening paper, out to the garden. This involved walking past Paula while she was industriously absorbed in folding and sorting his and the boys' underwear. Reproach danced in the air like motes of dust in a sunbeam, each of her brisk movements driving home the point that yes, she was holding down a job in the great wide world, but here she was still toiling tirelessly on the domestic front while he sloped off outside with a drink. Well, he would have offered to help, but he didn't know where things went, which drawers the boys' socks and underwear lived in. Anyway, he knew she didn't want anyone else to help. This was her juggling act. She would catch all the balls, thank you. He walked out into the evening sunshine and sat down at the table on the patio.

He glanced around the garden – two acres in all, with a chap coming in twice a week to keep it looking as lovely as it did – and thought about work the next day. Tomorrow he would be travelling up to Croydon to meet his sales team and fine-tune the marketing plans for this new, slimline compressor. The Kompakter compactor. They should really make market headway with this one.

Mark felt mildly excited at the prospect. The sensation was not a familiar one. Mark, for all the success of his business, was not a driven man. He accepted things as they came to him. Most of his achievements in life seemed to have been by default, instead of intention. He reflected on this truth as he gazed at his domain. Externally he might be perceived as someone who actively achieved things, but Mark felt himself to be a creature of circumstance, from his very beginnings in Braintree in 1962. The course of his early life – his place in the sibling order, only boy, eldest of three; his prep school; his enjoyable years at his minor public school – had been ordained by others. Even in the matter of his university education, at an age where he could have been said to be evincing some self-determination, his role had been largely passive. While his schoolfriends had chosen to study law, or dentistry or engineering – subjects which set them on fixed paths – Mark had, with hesitant consideration, opted for the nebulous disciplines of politics and philosophy. Harmless subjects whose academic resonance had pleased his parents, but which suggested no obvious progression into a particular career or profession.

And the job which he had eventually applied for, which had led so fortuitously to the rewarding present? Even there, he couldn't be accused of embarking on it with any sense of purpose. He had taken a job only because his mother had grown progressively intolerant of his post-university indolence, and he had taken *that* job – as trainee sales rep with a waste-paper recycling firm – because it was the only one available at the Job Centre which paid a decent wage. If anything, the only intentions which Mark had possessed around that time were of the negative variety – as in, he had no intention of remaining a sales rep. But he had. He'd discovered he was good at selling. He had a pleasantly candid manner that suggested a belief in the product. He'd become area manager. He'd done well. All largely due to circumstance. Even the successful business in which he was now a partner – that hadn't been his idea. Gerry had been the dynamic. He had first met Gerry Emden during his early days as a sales rep. Gerry was small and stocky, given to moving at high speeds, and possessed of the energy and ambition which Mark lacked but so admired. He had dark, curling hair and wore large glasses, through which he gazed at the world with a mixture of anxious defiance and childlike hope. An engineer by training, Gerry had briefly been Mark's boss, before leaving to join another firm. They had run into one another again at a conference on hydraulic components a year later, where they bonded over several pints of Sam Smith's bitter, and Mark listened while Gerry had propounded his ideas for world, or at any rate, European domination of the baler/compactor market. It was Gerry who'd had the idea of setting up a business to import ultra-efficient machines from Germany to do jobs which weren't being done in Britain at that time. But Gerry, while an astute businessman, had never been much of a salesman. He had needed Mark's sales know-how, plus the reassurance that he wasn't going it alone. And so Emden Environmental Services had been born, and Mark's fortune with it. But really the company had been Gerry's idea. For which Mark, given the relative wealth which the business had brought both of them, was very grateful.

It occurred to Mark, as he sat sipping his whisky and watching the evening sun glimmer across the sky above Harlow, that he had never truly shaped his own destiny. Fate had simply borne him along on its relentless current. Everything he had achieved up till this moment, he had achieved simply by not saying no. Even marrying Paula had been a reactive, rather than a proactive affair. He hadn't initiated the relationship. Admittedly he'd seen her in the wine bar and fancied her, but she'd started the conversation. Because he was tall and good-looking in a dark, saturnine fashion that made him look more predatory than he actually was, Mark had never been short of girlfriends back then. Women didn't exactly fall over themselves, but he'd never had to make any particular effort. That was the way it had been with Paula. Thereafter, he'd simply gone along with whatever it was she wanted. And he'd been fine with that. Love had grown gradually and naturally between them. The sex was good, which was a manipulating factor in itself. She set the agenda. He let her. And here he was. Father of two sons. They had been Paula's idea, too. He would have been happy to wait a while, but within a year of their marriage Paula had very much wanted to get pregnant, and once James was born, Mark found he enjoyed parenthood. So they'd had Owen. Mark loved his sons with a love that he kept carefully dispassionate, fearing that its expression in excess might render his boys somehow more vulnerable. Not that he was a superstitious man.

A thought occurred to him which had never occurred

to him before. He wondered how differently life might have turned out, if he'd approached it with greater determination and some idea of what he wanted to achieve. It couldn't have been better, could it? No. But different. How? Here his imagination failed. He was struggling with alternatives, starting with his choice of university subjects, when his elder son, James, strolled across the lawn. He was more like his father in looks and physique than Owen, who had his mother's dark blonde hair and compact build. James was tall and rangy, with dark hair and eyes. Mark recognized his younger self in him.

'Off out?'

'Yeah. I'm going round to Lisa's. Catch you later.'

Mark watched him go. Lucky James. He had recently come back from his gap year travels in Thailand and India, working on a hospice project. He had seen more of the world at nineteen than Mark had at forty-three. Mark's travelling experience, leaving aside a school trip to the First World War battlefields, consisted of business trips to Germany and a waste-management exhibition in Vancouver, plus holidays abroad, which didn't count. In fact, the business trips didn't count, either. And Vancouver might as well have been Skegness for all he saw of it.

James had the kind of clear-sighted determination which Mark had never possessed In five months he would be off to art school. He'd wanted to be a designer and illustrator from the age of fourteen. Mark recalled being similarly fired with ambition as a teenager, but it hadn't endured. Exposure to Wilfred Owen and Siegfried Sassoon

– the same year they'd done the battlefields trip – had made him think he would like to be a poet. He'd written many poems as a result. But people didn't become poets, not in Braintree. What a waste. Like that Ian Dury song: 'I could be the driver of an articulated lorry, I could be a poet, I wouldn't need to worry . . .' What a waste.

Then again, probably not. If he'd been meant to be a poet, presumably he would be one by now, not flogging shredders and compactors.

Mark was moved by the sudden depth of his own thoughts. He had never before examined the course of his life with such detachment. The source of his vague and recent sense of dissatisfaction began to crystallize in his mind. When in his life had he done anything with purpose and passion? He thought back across the years and remembered the teenager he had once been. What had become of Mark the poet, the romantic hiding behind the punk facade? What about all the books and music that had been such a part of his life? Where had that all gone? The years had been eaten up by the mundane and the material, selling balers and twiners and paying school fees and buying new cars and taking holidays and building conservatories and playing golf and shopping at weekends and . . . Was that it? Was that all there would be, ever?

He felt a shock of sadness. Suddenly, like a long, sonorous note sounded on a distant horn, yearning welled up in him. Intimations of beauty and romance, elusive and rainbow-hued, swam in his mind, grew gigantic and beautiful. It was a revelatory moment. He saw in an instant of clarity what his life had been lacking, but could not name it. After a few seconds, the feeling began to ebb. His mind tried to hold on to it, like an awakening sleeper clinging to a dream. Then it was gone.

He sat amazed, wondering if this was the way Gaugin had felt before he packed in the stockbroking job. But then, Gaugin seemed to have had some clear idea of the alternatives. What message lay in that visionary moment for Mark Mason? What did he now know? Nothing. Except that there was some song inside him, waiting to be sung.

Thrilled and a little apprehensive, he got up and went inside to lay the table for supper.

2

Mark and his sales team were meeting at the Howard Hotel in Croydon. Such meetings normally took place in head office in Harlow, but head office was being revamped and reorganized, and the south-east London office was small and somewhat cramped, so Mark had booked one of the Howard's conference rooms. Although it was only April, the weather was warm and clear as Mark parked his Jag, hefted his briefcase from the back seat and crossed the tarmac to the hotel entrance. The automatic doors slid open, and the cool air of the lobby's beige interior eddied pleasantly around him. Mark liked hotel lobbies. They were homes, they were comfort zones, and he had known them all his working life. He liked their impersonality, and their genteel artificiality. He liked the acres of carpet, and the charmingly insincere smiles of the receptionists behind their vast, curved desks. He liked the neatly spaced plants that no one cared about, and the muzak that dribbled through the heedless air. He felt at ease in such places, ready to strike deals, shake hands, sit in the squashy armchairs in the bars. He knew where he was, knew the territory.

He paused before the notice board set on an easel at the lobby entrance. 'Dagmar Electronics, Hutchinson Suite;

Achieving High Performance through Strategical Leadership Conference, Churchill Suite; Emden Environmental Services, Easton Suite'. They had called the firm 'Emden' because it was Gerry's surname. The original idea had been to merge Gerry's surname with Mark's, but Mark hadn't liked the sound of 'Emson', nor of 'Maden', and didn't much care whether his name was incorporated in the firm's or not.

Mark glanced around and saw Clive Pinsent, one of the south-east salesmen, sitting at a table near the lifts with some woman. He made his way over. Clive caught sight of his boss and got to his feet, smile at the ready. He was a short, bulky young man, sharply dressed and bristling with energy. He reminded Mark of an alert and ambitious hedgehog.

'Clive.'

'Mark.'

The hands clasped, the smiles tightened. Manly, business-like stuff. Mark glanced at the young woman, who was smiling up at him tentatively.

'You remember Nicky?' said Clive.

This was someone he was meant to know. Blonde, pretty, face vaguely familiar ... Mark was momentarily lost. Mercifully, she stood up and put out her hand. 'Nicky Burgess. I'm not surprised you don't remember me. You only met me in the first round of interviews last September. I think you were abroad when I was actually offered the job.'

Mark shook her hand. The name Nicky Burgess had

floated past his eyes on reports and sales sheets, and he had assumed it belonged to a new male member of the sales team. Stupid, really. So obviously a girl's name. Any man would have called himself Nick. 'Nicky, of course. Good to meet you again.'

Clive's mobile trilled. He fished in his pocket and paced importantly towards the lift, head bent, to take the call. Mark and Nicky sat down and exchanged small talk about their journeys to Croydon. Mark noticed, in a subconscious kind of way, that she was wearing shiny tights, and had nice legs.

Clive tucked his mobile in his pocket and came back to join them. 'That was Neil. He and Steve got lost in the one-way system. Should be here in about five minutes.'

Jim and Craig, the two Midlands sales reps, came across the lobby. There followed more hand-shaking and a little light banter. Mark glanced at his watch. 'Might as well go up, then.'

They went up to the Easton Suite. They snapped open briefcases and arranged papers on the table, and sat down. All except Clive. Clive picked up the carafe of water from the middle of the table and poured himself a glass. Then he walked round the room, whistling below his breath, pausing in front of each one of the prints on the wall, as though actually looking at them. He went to the window and twisted the little rod that opened the slats on the micro blind. He stared across the landscape of car park and urban sprawl.

Mark, sitting idly watching him, was surprised to be

touched by a sudden pity for little Clive, in his double-breasted suit and his sharp shoes, with his cheap tie and his hair in its trendy little sticking-up quiff. That feeling was swiftly followed, quite unexpectedly, by a much larger sense of engulfing pathos, one which seemed to encompass their entire situation: the conference table, the senseless prints on the wall, the nondescript view from the window, their presence here in a hotel that could have been anywhere – Croydon, Inverness, Barking, Luton, Truro; about to have a meeting about waste compactors. A moment of giddiness, similar to the one he had experienced the previous evening when thinking about the chest of drawers in his parents' house, seized Mark and lifted him, and he was frightened.

Panic made him glance in Nicky's direction, as though her female proximity might assuage his anxiety. She was reading through a document, twisting one index finger in her hair. He concentrated in that instant on the coarse texture and blondeness of her hair, and the curve of her finger. Immediately he felt himself calming, coming down. That hadn't been pleasant. That sense of – what? Futility? He closed his eyes for a moment.

Nicky, sensing Mark's gaze upon her, looked up from the document she was reading, and saw that his eyes were closed. She contemplated him for a moment. He was better looking than she remembered from that first interview. How old? Late thirties, maybe older. Mark opened his eyes and her glance slid away.

'Here they are,' said Clive, still at the window. 'That's

Neil's Lexus.' He shook his head, watching. 'He's parked it right in the open. He should have parked next to those trees at the far end. That's where I'd have parked. Always park in the shade. That's what I do.'

So much information, thought Mark, as Clive returned to the table and sat down. Always far more than you needed. Clive's reports were prolix in the extreme. Mark had developed a technique of sifting them. He did the same with Clive's conversation, which could be very boring.

Neil and Steve arrived, and the meeting got under way. Mark forgot his moment of fear. Sitting at the head of the table, six pairs of eyes turned attentively towards him, he had a sense of returning delineation, as though the outline of his personality which seemed to fade through contact with his family was here made bold again. He talked, they listened. He took them through the features of the new Kompakter 5044 compactor/baler, the cubic yardage of the skips it could empty, the cost savings per annum, its portability, its adaptability for special applications, and above all, its dimensions, which would enable it be installed in the tightest locations.

'So this is the market we want to open up,' said Mark. 'Small shopkeepers, premises where space is at a premium. We want to convince them that this is a machine that won't be bulky, that will be easy to install. We want to impress them with the cost-saving benefits, and the space clearance benefits. Point out to them that the space occupied by the 5044 is five times less than the amount of bulky packaging material it can compress.'

They talked about key areas and target locations, and the atmosphere was charged with businesslike enthusiasm.

'You shouldn't have to give the machine itself the hard sell,' said Mark. 'It should sell itself. But you will find certain areas of resistance to overcome that you don't meet with bigger firms, and that means some hard marketing. Many of these small businesses are going to be worried at the thought of the initial financial outlay. The savings – that's what you want to drive home. Space and money. And you have to make the point about the government's new legal requirements on incremental waste disposal. Remind them that these will be coming in early next year. So, moving on to sales areas . . .'

Each manager discussed their separate sales areas. It came to Clive's turn. 'So, Wimbledon, Wandsworth, and taking in Fulham and Chelsea –'

'Hold on,' Nicky interrupted. 'Why Fulham and Chelsea? I didn't think any decisions had been made about the London territory.' F140,238

Clive shot Nicky a hostile glance, then looked to Mark. 'Strictly, they fall within my remit.'

'I don't see why,' said Nicky. 'We're both London sales reps.'

Mark gazed at Clive. The inner London market was going to be competitive, so he could see why Nicky didn't want Clive grabbing the most lucrative areas. His imagination ranged over the prospective customers for this small compactor. Clive, with his tie and his briefcase and his laddish manner, was fine in the wide-open macho world of industrial estates and factory outlets. But the boutiques and bijou emporiums of the West End? No question, Nicky would be better. Mark gave her a quick, speculative glance, one in which sex was the merest undercurrent. She was smart, she had a look of intelligence which Clive, for all his excellent salesmanship, so singularly lacked. She would sell better to this market, in this area, than Clive.

'Let's leave that for the moment,' said Mark. 'This new market we're looking at means we may have to make a new territorial delineation. Don't worry, Clive,' he added, as Clive frowned and opened his mouth to speak again, 'we'll be dealing with this. But for now I'd like to move on to the figures forecast.'

By the time the meeting was over, it was twelve o'clock. Mark and his team repaired to the hotel's Tamworth Bar for a drink. For the men it was pints all round, either lager or bitter; Nicky ordered a Britvic orange with soda. As Mark handed Nicky her drink, she made a remark about the refurbishment of head office, and Mark found himself drawn into a brief, exclusive conversation with her. Up close he could observe that she had nice skin and a pretty smile, and the texture of her hair reminded Mark of wiry candyfloss. Blue eyes, with which she held his a good deal, he noticed. He was conscious of the very maleness of the conversation of the rest of the group, a few feet away. After a few moments, Mark threw out a casual remark to Craig, and the boys at the bar turned enough of their attention to Mark and Nicky to reabsorb them into the group.

Nicky was a smart girl. She knew when her little conversation with Mark was reaching its natural conclusion, and the body language required to bring them both back into the general gathering. She knew, too, that her presence thereafter subtly adulterated the natural blokey spirit of the gathering, lent it a restraint it would not otherwise have had. She liked her fellow sales reps well enough, but she was not a woman who liked to count herself one of the boys. She knew men. She knew men of this type in particular, standing there in their business suits, holding their pints. It wasn't that they didn't like her, or women in general; it was just that they longed to be at their coarse and jocular ease, without the constraints of female society. So she didn't spin out her drink. She let the conversation run on for a little while, even added a couple of jokey remarks, but after fifteen minutes she left them to it.

She headed out to the car park, feeling a little surge of triumph as she recollected the meeting. Little shit-face Clive wasn't going to get the inner London business. She was. She had read it in Mark's eyes. What else had she read there? Hard to tell.

Nicky unlocked her Fiat Punto, swung her briefcase on to the passenger seat, and got in. She sat there for a few moments. She thought, unwillingly, of Darren. She tested the little ache she felt every time she thought of how he was giving her the run-around. Still raw and painful. That was what came of seeing a man five years younger than yourself. Still. She flipped down the visor and glanced in the mirror, flicking her hair, checking her eye make-up. What he needed was to be shown he wasn't the only one who could play the field. She snapped up the visor and put her key in the ignition, reflecting on the chemistry she had felt between herself and Mark Mason. A little fling with the boss could do wonders. Was he up for it? She felt a ripple of anticipation. Nothing like the challenge of a married man. Wouldn't be the first time. At thirty-two, Nicky had been around the block. Mark was attractive, but he had a bit of a safe, careful look about him. Mind you, still waters. It could even help her career along. She quite fancied the idea of being made south-east sales manager. That would really stick it to crappy little Clive.

She revved the engine and drove off.

In the few seconds after Nicky Burgess left the bar, a conversational lull fell. Mark, who had of late grown rusty in the matter of male group dynamics, chose that moment to finish his drink and go to the gents. The minds of the remaining men closed round the space left by Nicky. Either they went for it, or they didn't. It could come up now, or it might come up later after a few more drinks. Either way.

Jim, the biggest and most confident of them – an alpha male, a salesman from his grizzled grey head to his black polished slip-ons, the man with the latest jokes, the juiciest gossip, the best stories – glanced in the direction of the door through which Nicky had just exited. Jim was going to go for it.

'Wouldn't kick her out of bed.'

The rest of the group made either noises or movements suggestive of agreement.

Steve, young, good-looking, and respected beta male, nodded and raised his pint to his lips. 'Nice arse.'

Clive, emboldened by his pint and embittered by the sense that Nicky threatened his position in the sales team, said, 'Bet she gives a great fucking blow-job.'

This was not good. Not good at all. Clive, little Clive, glanced round the group for approval and found none.

The great silverback articulated the displeasure of the rest of the pack. 'Somehow we don't think you've got much to worry about in that direction, Clive,' said Jim, casually caustic. Poor Clive.

'If she's going to shag anyone, it'd probably be the boss,' remarked Neil. 'See the way she was looking at him?'

Mark came out of the gents at that moment. Eyes went in his direction.

'What?' He rejoined the group with an uncertain smile.

'Just talking about Nicky's prospects for promotion. Better than the rest of us, eh, Mark?' said Neil.

'What I'd call upwardly mobile in the company.' This came from Craig, most senior in sales, and went down well. Clive laughed loudest, anxious to restore himself to the group.

Mark was momentarily taken aback by the banter. There

was something he must have missed. In his position as boss, he knew that his immediate obligation was to deflect and disinform. But he could think of nothing to say. He was out of practice.

Neil, his unwitting saviour, suddenly remembered something. 'Here, want to know what some bloke told me the other day? He said, if you want to work out what you'd be called if you were a porn star, you put together the name of your first pet and your mum's maiden name.'

With slow smiles of pleasure the rest of the group took this on, minds veering away, rummaging for putative porn-star aliases.

'Monty Drabble!'

'Buster Pocock – what a stud, eh?'

Much laughter, and more invention.

With relief at the diversion, Mark got the next round in.

There was a buff envelope waiting for Mark on the hall table when he got home at six that evening. He opened it. Mark's father had sent the first batch of photos on CD. Mark went into the kitchen and poured himself a beer. The phone rang. It was Paula.

'I'm going to be at the shop till gone eight tonight. We're stock-taking. Can you get the boys their tea?'

'What is there?'

'I think there's some chicken kievs in the freezer.'

'OK.'

A fractional hesitation. 'How was your day?'

Mark yawned and eyed his beer. 'So-so.' His mind ranged back over the events of the day, and suddenly he found himself thinking of Nicky Burgess. In particular, that panicky moment when the largeness of the universe and the inconsequentiality of his own world had fought a brief battle, and he had found comfort in the way she wound her blonde hair round her finger. 'Got stuck in the one-way system in Croydon. Bloody nightmare.'

'Of course, you had your meeting ... Oh,' Paula suddenly remembered, 'when Owen gets in –'

'I think he's already in.' Mark could hear the thump of music from Owen's room on the floor above.

'Well, if you can get his cricket kit and put it in the wash, it would be a help.'

Mark wondered if he should make a list. He wasn't good at domestic multi-tasking. 'Is that it?'

'Sorry – I didn't think you'd mind especially.' She was piqued. She thought he was being sarcastic.

'I don't. It was just that I thought if there was much more, I'd write it down.'

She took this the same way. 'Oh, for heaven's sake, Mark. It's not as though I'm asking you to do that much! The house doesn't run itself, you know. You should try doing two jobs some time.'

Several possible replies to this ran through Mark's mind, and he articulated none of them. 'I'll see you later,' he said, and put the phone down.

On the way to his study with his beer and the photo CD, Mark paused and went upstairs to Owen's room. He knocked on the door. The music was so loud that the knock went unheard. Mark opened the door and looked in. Owen was working at his desk. He had his A levels coming up. Paula was constantly telling Owen to turn his music down, he couldn't possibly concentrate properly with all that din. But Mark knew this wasn't true. His own A level studies had been conducted to a relentless background of The Smiths.

'Where's your cricket stuff?'

'What?' shouted Owen.

'Where's your cricket stuff?' asked Mark again, a little louder.

'At school.'

Mark nodded. One less chore. He wasn't very good with the washing machine, anyway. 'When do you want tea?'

'Not for a bit.'

Good. Mark closed the door and went back downstairs to his study. He sat down, switched on his laptop and inserted the CD. He brought up on screen the images which his father had selected. Most were familiar to him from the packets of photos in the chest of drawers – snaps of the family on holiday when he and his sisters were children; pictures of his now deceased grandparents at their house in Esher; photos taken at long-past Christmases and birthdays and family gatherings – but he hadn't seen them in some years and they made him smile.

Mark took a sip of his beer and clicked up another

photo. It was of himself. He was sitting on a trike outside the back door of the house in Braintree. It must have been taken when he was about three. The trike itself stirred a vague recollection, as did the green and blue striped T-shirt he was wearing. It was a Ladybird T-shirt. Why did he know that? He had an instant recollection of the little silky label at the back of the neck, with the ladybird logo on it. He had loved those labels, loved the feel of them.

Mark stared at his small self. He clicked to enlarge the picture, and his three-year-old face, with its happy milk-teeth smile, loomed closer. Mark stared into the brown eyes that gazed unblinkingly back at him. Their expression was eager, bright; they looked out on life with hope and expectation. Mark suddenly felt a lump in his throat. The knowledge that this was himself, as he had once been and never would be again, welled up in him. Such a sense of lost beginnings.

'Little guy . . .' he murmured. Little Mark smiled back unafraid, regarding him expectantly. As though there was something Big Mark had to tell him about the years ahead. About the ways things would go. Big Mark stared mutely at the screen. How could he justify to this small person the way things had turned out? The business, the family, the house . . . They were fine, they were good, they were successful achievements. It was just that they weren't what this small boy was looking and hoping for. Had looked and hoped for. Looked and hoped for still. Mark was aware of a dull sense of incomplete achievement. For a perplexing and dizzying moment, it was as though he was being drawn into the being on the computer screen, submerged, bound up with him and his sense of new beginnings. Then, a moment later, his mind withdrew and he was simply sitting there, middle-aged and mildly depressed, looking at a photo of himself as a small boy. He'd been staring too hard, that was all. There was no connection any more. It was just a picture from his past.

He clicked out of the picture, and switched off the laptop. Then he went to the kitchen to look in the freezer for the chicken kievs.

3

Mark talked to Gerry, and they agreed that Nicky Burgess should be responsible for inner London sales of the new 5044. Mark called Nicky to arrange a meeting to discuss sales strategy.

'I'd ask you to come to head office,' said Mark, 'but the place is still chaos. They're installing the new computer system over the next couple of days. Why don't we meet at the London office instead?'

'Fine,' said Nicky, warmly satisfied at having secured the London territory.

'Say Friday, around eleven.'

The suit which Nicky chose to wear that Friday was black and close-fitting. The tights she wore were sheer, smoke-coloured and shiny. She put her hair up. She put on high-heeled shoes. The look was one of ultra-efficiency, combined with subtle sexiness.

She and Mark sat in one of the small meeting rooms in the modest quarters of Emden's office in south-east London. For an hour they sat at opposite sides of the table and discussed strategy and targets. An occasional breeze rattled the blind at the open window. Nicky took off her black jacket and hung it on the back of her chair. The movement caused her to turn and stretch slightly, and Mark's eye was caught, as she had intended it should be, by the swell and curve of her breast beneath her white blouse. It was a modest blouse, white, not especially low-cut.

They continued to talk about key markets and sales tactics. Mark passed a copy of a report to Nicky. Nicky reached for the report, and Mark, without meaning to, caught a glimpse of cleavage. He found himself studying the top of her blonde head as she read the report, and thought normal, indecorous masculine thoughts. These weren't particularly aimed at Nicky, but were of a random sexual nature. He didn't pay much attention to them. They played in the background as the meeting progressed.

They finished a little after half twelve.

'What do you generally do for lunch?' asked Mark, gathering up papers.

'A bloke comes round with sandwiches and soup,' said Nicky.

'I'm sure we can do better than that. Isn't there somewhere decent round here where I can buy you lunch?'

Nicky smiled and reached round for her jacket. She said nothing. Her silence was flirtatious, investing the invitation with unexpected significance.

'There's a little Italian place up the road.'

'Sounds good.'

It was a ten-minute walk to the restaurant, along a main road, dusty and noisy with traffic. Having Nicky strutting daintily along beside him in her high heels, drawing occasional glances from passing van drivers, made Mark feel conspicuously masculine. It was a pleasant and unusual feeling. So much of his time was spent with men – managers, sales reps, accountants, technicians; men of varying shapes, sizes and backgrounds, some dull, some amusing, but all with the same bloke jokes and bloke outlooks. Occasionally Mark hankered for a little intellect, a little elevation of the conversation. Far, far behind him, buried beneath years of machine sales and manufacturing reports and sales forecasts, lay memories of his younger self, of music concerts and theatre trips and books half-read, whisperings of higher things . . . With a woman by his side, Mark felt a strange sense of refinement, as though better things were expected of him, more thought and more care than he normally meted out to men of his acquaintance.

Nicky was excellent company. She was cheerful, a little cheeky, and full of life. The opacity of the boss/employee relationship dissolved. They had a glass of wine with their meal. Away from the restraints of office surroundings, they both felt light and liberated, like children out of school. Mark found her easy to talk to, and didn't automatically ascribe this to the mere fact that they had common work interests. Sitting opposite her in the busy little restaurant, his vanity warmed by her generous eye contact and frequent smiles, he was much enjoying the novelty of giving lunch to a relatively unknown and attractive woman.

'So,' said Nicky, tucking a stray wisp of hair behind one ear, 'tell me everything a good employee should know about her boss. Are you a family man? You look like one.'

Mark wasn't sure that this was flattering. What did family men look like? He imagined someone careworn, slightly rumpled, getting on a bit. 'Do I?'

'Perhaps not in the way you think.' Nicky's eyes narrowed as she smiled. 'But you look like you're married.'

'Yes, I'm married. Two kids.' Mark smiled. 'Boys, James and Owen. James is coming to the end of his gap year and is going to art school in the autumn. Owen's a year younger. He's off to Australia at the end of the summer.'

'And your wife?'

'Paula . . . Oh, Paula's a very busy woman.' Mark stared musingly at his wine glass. 'She manages a couple of clothes shops. It's quite a new venture. Made a big change in her.' He paused for a reflective moment, then his eyes met Nicky's. 'What about you?' He had already noticed that she wore no wedding ring, but that meant nothing these days.

'I was in a relationship till recently, but it broke up. At least,' she said, shrugging and taking a sip of her wine, 'I think it did.'

This was intimate information, more than Mark had expected. 'You think it did?'

'One of those men. Never quite know where you are. Still.'

Nicky smiled. A pretty smile, thought Mark.

Thereafter, no more mention was made of Nicky's ex, nor of Paula.

They talked about work, and then about films, and a little bit about politics. Mark was surprised to find himself quite intently engaged. She was an intelligent girl.

'So, what brought you into the exciting world of waste disposal?' he asked, genuinely curious.

'I was working in the City, market trading. Got made redundant, and answered an advertisement. I suppose I'm a natural salesman. I enjoy it. I like to think I can sell anything.'

'I'm sure you can.' Mark meant nothing by this. They drank their coffee.

'What about you?' asked Nicky.

'Oh, I fell into it, a long time ago.'

'Not that long, surely.'

'Twenty years ago. Seems long enough. I took a job with a recycling firm, by accident more than anything else. Straight out of university, couldn't find anything else to do. It wasn't meant to be permanent. Then I met Gerry, and we started the business.'

'And the rest is history.'

'Soon will be.' Mark regarded his coffee. He felt suddenly in a confiding mood. 'The thing is, lately I keep getting the feeling that there must be more to life.'

'Than waste disposal?' Nicky smiled.

'Yes. Than this. I mean – well – you're young, it doesn't apply to you. But when you hit forty, and you look back and you look ahead, you think – there has to be something else. There must be things you haven't explored.'

'You mean, like travel?'

'No. Things about yourself. About myself. Like I want to find something new and different to do before it's too late. Sorry, this is boring.'

'No, it's not. Just sounds like a conventional mid-life crisis.'

'You're probably right.'

It was a gift attributable to Nicky's warmth of personality that she had managed to create this atmosphere of effortless intimacy. While the entire lunch was quite innocent, she managed to endow many of the little things she did – gestures, movements of her hand, the way she touched her hair as she listened – with a hint of something delectable and unknowable. She had no idea whether this was registering with Mark, either consciously or unconsciously, but by the time Mark had walked her back to the office, then set off back to Harlow in his Jag, a definite friendship had been established.

Nicky might have been disappointed to know the nature of Mark's unconscious response to the events of lunchtime. Driving back to Harlow, he spent a long time thinking about Paula. He had decided he would take her out to dinner tomorrow night, get her to unwind a little. Time, that was what they needed. More time together. The lunch with Nicky had reminded Mark of the pleasure of being in relaxed female company. It seemed a long time since it had been that way with Paula.

He thought of Nicky, too, in an incidental fashion, the way her breasts had looked when she turned and stretched. But nothing serious. Merely a kind of side-current to the more specific thought of making love to Paula, as he intended to this weekend.

He and Paula did indeed go out to dinner the following evening, on Saturday. Mark booked a very expensive restaurant where the well-heeled of Harlow conventionally went on a night out. They booked a taxi, so that there were no concerns about who had to drive. Mark was looking forward to the evening. It appeared that Paula was as well, for she took great care over getting ready. She and Lorna had gone to a health farm for a weekend a month ago, where Paula had had what she referred to as a makeover. She now had a new look. Her appearance was sleek and polished all the time, not just for work. Mark thought he liked it, but wasn't sure.

The evening, however, was not a success. At first things seemed pleasantly relaxed. They talked about the boys, and whether or not they should go away for Christmas. That was fine. Then Paula got on to the subject of the shops, and how much of a strain everything was, and for half an hour or so Mark sat and listened moodily. He tried a couple of times to deflect her, to change the subject, but it didn't work. She expanded the theme to embrace the related topic of how difficult she was finding it to cope at home. Mark was aware that the evening was not taking the direction he had intended. Nonetheless he felt he had to remain involved, to offer some suggestions. He ventured one. Why didn't she cut down on her hours a bit and spend more time at home? They didn't need the money, after all. To which Paula responded that Mark simply didn't understand, money wasn't the point, it was to do with self-esteem. It turned into a kind of an argument. Not a proper one, not a row, but a disagreement that left a certain tension in the air.

They had both had a bit to drink.

The atmosphere on the way home in the taxi was one of faint dejection.

In bed, Mark sought to eclipse the mood of the evening and try again. He offered to massage her shoulders, something Paula usually loved. She lay on her stomach, and he slipped the thin straps of her nightdress from her shoulders, lifted her hair from her neck, and pressed with his thumbs and balls of his hands on to the muscles at the top of her back, kneading her shoulders with his fingers. He felt her relax and soften. She even gave a little groan of pleasure as he worked. But when, after a while, he stopped and moved against her, slipping his hands round to cup her breasts, she turned over restlessly.

'Mark, I'm just really, really tired. I've had such a hard week at the shop. I don't know that I'm up to sex right now.' She stifled a yawn with her hand.

Mark persisted, thinking she would relent. But she moved away from him with even more vehement restlessness. 'Please, Mark. I just want so badly to go to sleep.'

Silence. Mark could feel her mind withdrawing into sleep already. He lay there feeling extremely pissed off. It wasn't as though she would have had to do much, for

God's sake. Just let him. God, what a way of putting it. *Let him.* That was the point. That was the whole problem. Non-participation. Non-interest. Her life was her job, the house, the boys. Not him. Not sex. Not anything that kept things together.

All he wanted was a bit of sex, for God's sake. Was that too much to ask? Apparently so.

He switched off the bedside light and lay there in the dark. He thought about the conversation over dinner and, without intending to, about the conversation he and Nicky Burgess had had over lunch yesterday. When he had talked, Nicky had listened, really listened. She was interested. Paula, he realized, simply didn't seem to be interested in him any more. He felt hurt and lonely.

The next day, after lunch, Mark did some work on his laptop. When he had finished, he played about for a while on the Internet, idly comparing prices of golfing equipment. He could do with some new clubs. After a while he grew bored with this, then remembered his father's photos and clicked on the photo suite. The last picture he had been looking at, the enlarged image of himself on his trike, filled the screen.

Once again, Mark stared in absorption at his childhood face. He thought many thoughts, about then and now. He reflected on the random desires which had filled him of late – desires associated with this song of longing trapped within him. He could connect them to nothing tangible, no ideas or projects.

'What do you think?' he asked Little Mark. 'What do you think I should do?'

Little Mark smiled back.

'Why am I asking you? You don't know the half of it yet,' said Big Mark. 'You haven't the least idea what's coming. Which makes two of us.' He gazed at Little Mark. 'I still pick my nose, you know.' He paused, struck by the odd sense of comfort which it gave him to be talking in this way to his little self. He did it some more, telling Little Mark a few more things he might care to know about his own future.

Then he stopped. Was this daft, or what? No, it was quite enjoyable. He had an idea. He would make Little Mark the background on his computer desktop. So that every time he turned on the laptop, his own three-year-old face would smile out at him. And they could have a chat.

The success of the Kompakter 5044 was important to Emden Environmental Services, and Mark now found it necessary to monitor his sales staff more closely than usual. Over the next couple of weeks he travelled from region to region – something he hadn't done in a few years – and stayed in a variety of anonymous Travelodges and Holiday Inns, where he put on a little extra weight through eating a fried breakfast each morning. Many men might have found their spirits quickly worn down by a succession of these drab and soulless places, but Mark had learned over the years that a proactive approach was necessary to render them endurable. So he made a point of ordering the hotel breakfasts. He employed the trouser press. He filled the kettle and made cups of tea with the bags supplied, and ate the little packets of shortbread. If there was a mini-bar, he helped himself to a couple of beers or Scotches. Even if he didn't use it, he made it his business to ascertain in which cupboard or drawer the hairdryer was hidden. And he watched the pay-per-movie channel, occasionally indulging in a porn film.

He had hoped that Paula might miss him, and that this might engender a little more tenderness and intimacy on his return, but his absences only seemed to provoke her. Paula wanted to know why he couldn't use the hotel laundries, instead of bringing home unwashed shirts and underwear.

'Because I'm never in one place long enough,' said Mark. Which was reasonable. But Paula then got into a state about the amount of extra work it made for her, on top of everything else, and there was no tenderness, no intimacy. Only exasperation and a sense of grievance on either side.

Mark visited the London office. There was Nicky, smiling, fresh, full of positive news about sales in her area. Mark was glad to see her. His communication with her since their lunch had consisted of work-related text messages. Texting was Mark's favourite mode of communication, and he texted his sales team frequently. He liked watching the little envelope dwindle on the screen of his mobile like some wing-heeled messenger when he sent a message, and hearing the reassuring beep that told him he had received one. He liked the jargon and short-hand of texting, the laconic nature of which could render the most mundane message pithy and amusing.

Nicky's messages had a cheerful, bantering tone, not something the male reps ventured with their boss. Mark liked this. He liked being teased. So when he and Nicky met, there was an easy air of familiarity between them. They went out together on one of her sales rounds, and Mark was impressed by her performance. They lunched in a sandwich bar, food on the go, and over coffee they learned a little more about one another.

Nicky made Mark laugh. He made her laugh.

They set off again to new sales destinations and, at the end of the day, after some paperwork back in the cramped office in Lewisham, they went for a drink in a local wine bar.

'Are you heading back to Harlow tonight?' asked Nicky.

'No. I'm staying at that hotel in Croydon, the one we had the meeting at. I have to go to Reigate first thing tomorrow, see how Clive's getting on. Seems to be getting there.'

'This machine sells itself.'

'Maybe. But you should take some credit. You've made amazing progress down here.'

'The size of the market is just so daunting.'

'Don't worry. I'm going to be around to do my bit. I'm quite enjoying being out and about again.'

Nicky had been studying his face while they talked. Mark had high cheekbones, dark brows which almost met in the middle, and brown, sad eyes. He looked like he had a decent body, but you never knew with guys over forty. You could only guess. He seemed fit enough. Nice hands. Long fingers. She thought of those fingers touching her, how those hands would feel on her body.

They had finished their drinks. Mark knew he should go. But he also knew that he would happily sit talking to Nicky all evening. And he suspected Nicky would be content to stay, too. There was nothing so bad about this. Not really. They were work colleagues.

'There's a restaurant upstairs,' he said. 'We could have dinner. I'd rather eat here than at the Howard. Or are you busy?'

'No. I'd like that.' She sounded cheerful and matter-of-fact, which made Mark feel better.

They had dinner and some more wine, and talked and talked. They explored what was now jocularly referred to as Mark's mid-life crisis.

'You need to rediscover something you used to enjoy, something you haven't done for years. Some lost passion,' said Nicky.

'I don't think I ever had passions.'

'A hobby, then.'

Mark thought for a moment. 'I used to write poems. When I was a teenager. I really enjoyed that.' He smiled diffidently. 'The usual adolescent angst. But it made me feel good, writing them.'

'Well, then.'

'No.' He sighed. 'I don't think that would do it for me.

I couldn't think of anything to write now. Anyway, I have the feeling it's got to be something bolder than that.'

'Climb Everest. Take up sailing.'

'That's the trouble. I'm so bloody lazy. I think I want to do something life-changing, but I probably haven't got the energy. Come on, let's change the subject. I'm bored with me.'

It made Mark feel good to be able to talk so easily with Nicky. As easily as he talked to Paula. More so, in some ways. Plus, it was interesting getting to know someone new. He tried not to dwell on how attractive he was beginning to find her. Not just the superficial prettiness, blonde hair, nice breasts, all that. But her voice, her mannerisms, the way she lifted her head when she laughed. She laughed often.

They had walked to the wine bar. At the end of the evening they strolled back to the office where their cars were parked.

Nicky took her keys from her bag. 'Thanks for dinner.'

'Any time. You saved me from a boring evening in Croydon.'

Nicky opened the door of her car. 'See you when you're next in London.'

'I'll probably be down again next week.'

Mark got into his Jag and watched as Nicky drove off into the night. A nice evening. Nice girl. If things had been otherwise . . . *Come on, mate. You'd love to. You know you would.* He tried to subdue his fairly natural inclinations. She was an attractive young woman who happened to work for him, and he was a married, middle-aged man who shouldn't be thinking this way. She wouldn't like it. She saw him as a friend. They got on well together. That was all.

He drove carefully to Croydon, knowing he was a bit over the limit, and thought of nothing but how much he'd like to sleep with Nicky Burgess, and how he probably shouldn't make the mistake of seeing her out of office hours again.

The next day, around ten, while he was sitting in the crawl of M25 traffic, his phone beeped. Mark fished it from his pocket and opened the text. It was from Nicky.

'Thnks 4 dinner. See Times, p11'

At lunchtime Mark picked up a copy of *The Times*, and turned to page eleven. It featured a long article about men in mid-life crisis. He smiled. Then he read it. None of it seemed to apply even remotely to his own increasingly confused state of mind, but that wasn't the point. The point was that Nicky had been thinking about him. That knowledge pleased him. He felt a small and guilty thrill of intimate connection.

He sent her a brief, jokey text by way of reply. She texted back. This went on throughout the day, the messages consisting of nothing more than a running joke on the subject.

Nicky received the latest of Mark's messages towards the end of the afternoon. She read it with amusement. Amazing how much could be accomplished through a few mobile phone exchanges. She knew her tactic now must be to remain silent, to send no more messages today. He would be faintly disappointed. That was just how she wanted it.

4

Mark was having breakfast with James. His eldest son, now on the cusp of manhood, seemed to Mark to inhabit a closed world. His comings and goings were mysterious, his friendships and destinations remote. Just a couple of years ago James had been a mere boy, with insecurities and needs connected to childhood. Now he was grown up, coming into his inheritance – cars, girlfriends, staying out all night, drinking with friends – a young man in possession of the realities of life without yet having to take them too seriously.

Once this had been Mark's world – just the other day, it seemed – but it was his no longer. Mark had known this for some time, but James's occupancy of it sharpened his awareness of the fact. He felt edged aside. Saddened. He dwelt now in the realm of the middle-aged man, and twilight glimmered on its dim horizon.

'Fancy a game of golf this weekend?' Mark asked James.

James shook his head. 'Can't, Dad. I'm going down to Brighton with some friends. Thanks, anyway.'

'Anyone I know?'

James got up and took his plate and coffee mug to the sink. 'Don't think so.' Possibly from some sense of compunction, he asked his father, 'How's work these days?'

Being nice to the old man, thought Mark.

'Yeah, it's good. We've got a new machine, opening up urban markets, bringing in quite a lot of business.'

James was not remotely interested. 'Good.' He nodded. 'Anyway, got to go. See ya.'

James was working in a friend's recording studio for the remaining months of his gap year. Mark had no idea what he did there.

Paula came into the kitchen with the morning post. She handed Mark some letters and a small packet.

'Can you run Owen into school today?'

'I thought he took the bus.'

'He does. But he's got to take his portfolio plus all that stuff for his DT coursework. I can't possibly run him. I've got new stock coming in first thing.' She fastened on her earrings, then poured herself a swift cup of coffee. She never sat down to breakfast these days.

'Fine. I'm not going in this morning, anyway. I thought I'd work from home. The office is still chaos.'

She gave him a brief, diving kiss, took a couple of sips of coffee and picked up her bag. 'See you this evening.'

'Bye.'

Mark glanced at the letters she had handed him and put them aside. The packet, he knew, was the next instalment of photos from his father on CD. He would look at it later. He glanced at the kitchen clock and went to call to Owen.

He helped Owen put his materials into the car, then drove him to school.

'Fancy a game of golf on Saturday?' asked Mark, as they approached the school gates.

'Can't,' said Owen. 'I've got a match.'

'Right.'

'Sorry, Dad.'

Mark realized he must have looked a little forlorn at being rejected by a second son. 'Not to worry. How about Sunday?'

'Yeah, Sunday would be cool.' Owen retrieved his materials from the boot of the car, and Mark watched him carry them carefully through the gates into school. Mark remembered taking Owen to nursery school, helping him carry a precariously glued-together model crane which Owen had made at home. How many years ago that must have been. It seemed only yesterday.

Mark spent the morning on the phone and working on his laptop. Towards lunchtime he took a break. He inserted the new CD which his father had sent him, and brought up the images on the screen.

These were pictures from his teenage years, and were less familiar than those of his early childhood. One was a picture taken at a birthday party. His. Which one? He studied his grinning self, surrounded by friends, and searched for clues. His seventeenth, in all probability. He was wearing that electric blue mohair jumper his mother had knitted for him, and those skinny Levis. How cool had that been? That was Liam on the right, who'd left

49

after the first year in sixth form, and Mark hadn't seen much of him thereafter. So, yes, it must be his seventeenth. Then he remembered. That had been the year his parents had given him his music centre. God, how he'd wanted that. How he'd cherished it. He'd taken it to university, setting up the speakers above his bed in the hall of residence, then to his first flat.

And at that very party, his seventeenth, he'd had it proudly blasting out the music. The Clash single, 'White Man in Hammersmith Palais', that his sister had given him. They'd played it over and over. Mark had a sudden yearning to hear that song again. 'If Adolf Hitler flew in today, they'd send a limousine anyway . . .' What a great, great song. It held so much of summer, so much that was long ago.

And in that instant of recollection, in the same moment that he clicked up the next photo, he felt as though a hand had crept round his heart and was slowly squeezing it. The memories pearled, forced out like blood. Sandra. There she was, with him, in the back garden in Braintree. Blonde, beautiful. It had lasted six weeks. She'd come and gone like summer itself. Chucked him for that bloke who was a lifeguard at the local swimming pool. How he had loved her, before, during and after. Now he couldn't even remember her surname.

Sandra, Sandra.

Sensory overload, emotions and sensual recollections piling up. Above all, the recall of something he would have thought impossible. The memory of infatuation. The feel of it. The depth of it. Being taken over, mind and body, by the image of another. Longings both substantial and insubstantial. He had given them form by writing poems to her, for her, about her. Remember those? Sandra.

How could it be that he hadn't thought about her in twenty-five years?

For a long time Mark sat there, mustering every neuro-biological impulse to recreate the feelings of that time, reliving, at a shallow remove, the euphoric self-knowledge that young love brings. He remembered their first kiss in the alleyway down the side of the cinema, and his fingers, tentative and longing, on the swell of her young breast under her jumper. The recollection made him almost dizzy with anguish. Those first kisses. In many ways they had been the height of sensual perfection. It came to Mark that it was now two decades since he'd experienced the mind-blowing pleasure of kissing a woman for the first time. It was practically a violation of his human rights. This almost formless thought, in the nanosecond it took to race through his mind, was the first sideways step from fidelity. Small, but significant.

Emotion. That was what was lost and forgotten in his life. The romantic depth charge that might or might not go off. Being with someone else, wanting that someone else, and creating out of your own passion a whole new entity. It wasn't Sandra he recalled with such longing – she was now nothing more than a construct, a sixteen-year-old blonde catalyst – but the feeling that went with her.

What was that feeling? Love? No. He couldn't say his present existence lacked love. It didn't. He loved his sons. They loved him back, in the careless way that children do. He and Paula loved one another. Of course they did. It was taken for granted. But where was the passion? Every aspect of his life was predictable and accepted, from his relationship with Paula, with its sour edge of late, to the rote of meetings and sales targets and compactors, balers, shredders . . . What could he look forward to in life that would ever bring him alive, make him feel the ecstasy and despair of that summer and Sandra? Nothing.

The force of his anguish at this realization almost made him panic. He clicked on quickly to the next photo, one of his sister and Patch, a long-dead terrier, on the beach at Whitstable. He wouldn't think about Sandra, or anything that had happened long ago. It wasn't relevant. Not now.

When Mark switched the computer off five minutes later, he noticed his hands were still shaking slightly, and he wondered if he might not be coming down with something.

Thoughts come unbidden, and the mind at rest wanders where it will. That night, prompted possibly by the photograph of Sandra, Mark dreamed, vividly and in the early hours, of Nicky. It was a dream of such powerful and tender eroticism that he woke in the pale, real light of ten to seven, with a heart suffused with longing and an erection of tremendous rigidity.

While his body quickly came to terms with reality, Mark's mind was more deeply affected. Throughout the day the shadow of the dream lingered. His perception of Nicky Burgess was subtly altered, sexually and romantically. When he thought about her, it was with a new and significant intensity. Over the weekend, while he was shopping with Paula, playing golf with Owen, combing the Sunday papers, she hovered at the back of his mind.

The following week he went to London again, and this time he found himself dry-mouthed and excited as he parked his car in the forecourt of the Lewisham office.

Nicky, of course, knew nothing of Mark's dream and its epiphanic effects. It was only after they had finished closing a contract at a large retail premises in central London, and were having lunch in a sandwich bar, that she detected the change in him. Nothing that was outwardly visible, no alteration in the way he looked at her or spoke to her. It was simply as though some layer of him had been stripped away, leaving his emotions closer to the surface. Beneath the casual smiles, the commonplace conversational exchanges, she could sense and smell his desire, his infatuation.

Mark had no idea that he had given anything away. His radar was no longer finely attuned. His neurological signal paths were cluttered with sensual impedimenta. He was busy absorbing the look of her skin, her hair, her eyes, the sound of her voice. Busy bringing infatuation into existence.

They visited more premises in the afternoon, then went back to the office, where they worked separately for a while. At the end of the day, Mark suggested a drink at the wine bar they had gone to the previous week.

It was Mark's new air of restraint, Nicky decided, that was the biggest giveaway. Last time they met he had been entirely at ease, talking freely and self-deprecatingly, laughing easily and often. This evening he was less relaxed, held in check by his own awareness of his new feelings.

This, in turn, gave Nicky a sense of slight ascendancy, and afforded her the opportunity to manipulate. She endowed every casual gesture and glance with a conscious sensuality, while keeping the conversation light and amiable. She stroked the stem of her glass with slow and idle fingers. She parted her lips as she smiled and let his gaze hold hers for a significant fraction longer than usual. She was gratified by the response which she saw in Mark's eyes – a response of which he was entirely unaware, convinced that his infatuation was his own secret, hidden in the depths of his heart.

Had it not been for Nicky's own stratagem, that secret might have remained hidden. Mark was not by nature an adulterous man. He knew a couple of men who regularly had extramarital affairs, and neither romance nor infatuation ever seemed to be involved. More a kind of sexual pragmatism. He was not that kind of man. Nicky was not that kind of girl.

'We could do dinner again, if you like,' said Nicky,

when their glasses were empty. She had been waiting for Mark to suggest this, but the wait had gone on too long. Her smile was friendly, open. Disingenuous.

'I have to get back to Harlow tonight.'

The truth was, he felt that the excitement of his feelings when he was with Nicky had robbed their relationship of its ease and comfort. He desired her, he wanted to breathe the same air as she did, but he wasn't happy any more.

'Fine.' Her smile didn't falter. She picked up her bag and they left.

What occurred in the car park wasn't by his design, or hers. Nicky pressed the remote on her key to unlock the door of her car, and Mark reached out to open it at the same time as she did. His hand rested on hers, and then he was close against her, and she turned. Had he read anything but desire in her eyes, Mark might not have kissed her. But her lips were parted, her look startled but softly expectant, and he had no choice. It wasn't even a matter of choice. He had to kiss her. For the sake of his long-gone seventeen-year-old self, for the sake of Sandra, and every other girl he'd known and longed for, he had to. He did. Gently and tentatively, but with growing conviction. And it was exactly as thrilling and arousing as any first kiss had been years ago. More so, because he knew he shouldn't be doing this.

When it was over, Mark was instinctively apologetic. 'Perhaps that wasn't a good idea.'

Her arm was still around his neck, her face close to his.

Mark held her, uncertain. Thoughts of Paula – not Paula *per se*, but a consciousness of her existence in all this – pressed in on him.

'I think it was the best idea you've had all evening.' She put her mouth to his again and they kissed at length. This time it was passionate and consuming, bodies pressed together, hands everywhere – in hair, on breasts and thighs, as they sought out one another with their limbs and mouths. Mark was intoxicated. Desire so gripped him that he stepped outside himself. He was not the old Mark. Or anything. His thoughts flew wildly in the direction of hotel rooms, some destination for the consummation of this mutual passion.

'We could –' He stopped. Not just to get his breath. To articulate his desires seemed sordid.

'What?'

'Find somewhere. Go somewhere.'

Mark was aware of the rise and fall of her breasts as she looked into his eyes. She shook her head. 'I don't want you just to make love to me once and then forget about me.'

That is what Nicky said. What she was *thinking* was that there was no way she was going to make it easy for him, going to some hotel and sleeping with him right off, just like that. Not that she wouldn't have minded. It was weeks since Darren had disappeared, and she did quite fancy Mark. He was a good kisser. He might be great to go to bed with. But there was more at stake here.

'I wouldn't. How could –?'

Nicky stopped him. She drew her body away from his, took her arm from round his neck. 'Mark, it's not like that. I'm not like that. Don't get the wrong idea. I really, really like you. I'm not sorry this happened. But I'm not just going to jump into bed with you.'

'I'm sorry. I didn't mean —' He cast around, perplexed, wordless.

'Apart from anything, you're my boss.' She studied him candidly, then sighed. 'Maybe you were right. Maybe this wasn't a good idea. I'd best be getting back.'

She opened the door of her car and slipped inside. As she started the engine, she glanced up and gave Mark a gentle, significant look, touched with regret. She drove off into the night, leaving Mark standing there, raw with desire and blocked by confusion, as intended.

Mark returned home. He slept. He worked. He spoke to his family as they came and went. The currents of life drifted around him, vexing and insubstantial. His dreams and desires grew, filling his mind, filling the days, becoming more real than real life.

He didn't speak to Nicky. He didn't text her, nor she him. He alternated between the mortifying conviction that he had behaved grossly, and the passionate certainty, remembering the way she had returned his kiss — especially the second time — that she felt as he did.

He thought constantly of Nicky. He even felt a little deranged. He fantasized about her, though he found it difficult to remember her features clearly — his mental image of her was like a photograph that had been too well-thumbed.

Perhaps it was the extent of the fantasizing that brought him back down to earth, hard and sharp. Perhaps it was guilt. Or foreboding. Whatever it was, one evening he decided to have a talk with Paula. It suddenly seemed more vital than ever that they try to reconnect, to restore some intimacy and tenderness.

They had finished supper. Mark said, 'Listen, we need to talk about a couple of things.'

'Mmm?' Paula, who had had a glass or two of wine and appeared as relaxed as she ever did these days, was leafing through a magazine.

'I just get the feeling we lead such separate lives right now. We don't seem to – well, have time for one another.'

Paula drew her gaze reluctantly from the magazine to meet his. 'Is this your roundabout way of saying you don't get your shirts ironed regularly?'

'No!'

'Don't look like that. I wasn't being serious.'

'Oh.' Mark was nonplussed. Already this conversation had been steered towards the domestic agenda. 'I didn't mean that at all. You run the house amazingly. I don't know how you do it. With the job and everything.'

'Nice to be appreciated.' Paula flicked a page of her magazine.

'It's just that our lives seem to be running on parallel lines, never meeting. It was different before you started working at the shops –'

'Oh, here we go.'

'No, listen. I'm not having a go. I think it's great that you work. It's just that everything's changed. I can't explain . . .' He reached out for her hand. 'D'you know how long it is, for instance, since we had sex?' He asked the question quietly, beseechingly.

Paula flipped the magazine shut. 'I'm sorry. I know that's my fault. I just don't feel in the mood much these days. Maybe I'm tired or something. It'll pass. You know I've had phases like this before.'

'I thought, maybe if we went through the motions, it might get things going –' He was only being half-serious, but she didn't take it that way.

'You want me to have sex even when I don't want to, just to keep you happy?'

'Why do you have to put it like that? I'm trying to talk to you. Trying to explain that I feel something's wrong, and we should do something about it. I don't know the answers. I just know that, as a man, it's difficult to . . .' He tailed off. What was the point of this? He could tell from her eyes that the thoughts which danced behind them were not even remotely sympathetic to his.

'It's not just about sex, is it? It's to do with my job, and everything that goes with it. You've been like this since I took over the shops. You don't like it. You don't like the fact that my attention isn't solely concentrated on you and the boys any more. Look, I'm sorry if I get tired. I'm sorry if I'm not there in fishnet stockings and suspenders for you every night. But I need something for *me*, and this job makes me feel important. So don't start trying to make me feel guilty about it.'

'Don't I make you feel important?' He asked this curiously, wistfully, his fingers stroking hers.

'Not really, no. Not in the right way. I'm talking about a sense of identity, Mark. With the job, other people don't just see me as your wife and the boys' mother. They see me . . .'

Mark switched off. She wanted to blather on about work and identity and self-esteem, when for him it was simply about sex, and seeing someone else smile because you made them smile. He didn't care if the meals weren't there on time, which they were, or his shirts weren't ironed, which they were. She didn't understand this. She didn't seem to see that something had been lost between them. Maybe it wasn't there to be found. Maybe if he were to try telling her everything that was really going on inside his head, about Nicky, and his sense of free-falling through these middle years of his life . . . As his fingers stroked hers absently, his eyes were drawn to her nails. They were longer than she usually grew them, slightly obscenely curved, and painted a dusky red. Sexy, but strange.

'Your nails look different.'

'What?' He had interrupted Paula mid-flow. She drew her hand away.

'Let's have a look.' He tried to take her hand again, but she wouldn't let him.

'They're false, if you must know. I hate my nails. I always have. They're so brittle, and I can't keep them looking nice. It's important in the job to have decent hands. Lorna suggested getting some false ones.'

'I liked your hands the way they were.'

'Oh, well.' Defensive and distant, Paula got up to clear the supper plates away.

'Strange.'

'Not really.'

There wasn't much more to be said. Mark rose and went through to his study. He switched on his laptop and up came chubby Little Mark on the desktop. Big Mark met his smile with a sigh.

'What a great success that was, little guy. No sex, please, I'm knackered. You know, a hundred years ago I could just have demanded my conjugal rights. What d'you think about that? D'you think that's the answer?'

Little Mark laughed back at him.

It wasn't simply about sex. Paula had been right about that. Though kissing Nicky had driven that issue to the forefront. God, had it ever. What was it about Nicky? He scarcely knew her, yet she was so much in his thoughts. The idea of sleeping with her obsessed him. That abortive attempt at a discussion with Paula had nothing to do with any of it. This was something outside and beyond him, and he might as well just give in to it. An affair with the female member of his sales team. It couldn't be as simple and mundane as that. Could it? He stared at the screen, excited, nonplussed.

Little Mark just sat there on his trike, supplying no answers.

5

The refurbishment of the Harlow head office was finally complete, and a meeting of the sales team was scheduled to discuss the progress of sales of the Kompakter 5044. The run-up to this meeting was torture for Mark. He wanted badly to see Nicky, and yet dreaded it, too. He couldn't fathom the source of these conflicting feelings. He was in too much turmoil to rationalize anything.

Nicky's feelings were rather different. For a start, she wasn't infatuated with Mark. Merely flattered, and a little excited by the idea of a nascent affair. She felt a gentle frisson every time she thought of kissing Mark. And there was the additional stimulus of uncertainty. Mark was a married man. Just because he had kissed her, and kissed her in such a way, didn't necessarily guarantee anything.

Today she would find out. Today she dressed in a closely cut suit, no blouse or top underneath, her Wonder-bra pushing up her cleavage to just above the top button – not too much, just enough. Skirt a couple of inches above her knees, nice glossy tights again. He seemed to like her legs. Hair down, make-up discreet, kitten heels. Demure capability.

She smoothed her hands over her hips as she stood in front of the mirror, lifted her chin and looked herself in the eye. Darren – Darren no longer seen or heard from – had damaged her pride, but this thing with the boss was going to go some way to repairing it.

The Emden sales team sat round the long oval table in the meeting room. The scent of newness filled the air. Carpet tiles, shelving, overhead lighting, state-of-the-art flat-screen computer monitors – everything exhaled the toxic aroma of workplace efficiency. Much money had been spent on the rearrangement and redecoration, and its effect on everyone at the meeting was rejuvenating. Especially Nicky. Did she ever feel fresh and ready. She sat with Clive on one side of her, Jim on the other, filled with such an exultant, powerful sense of her own femininity that it seemed to rival the odour of the new paintwork

Enter Mark.

He was looking good that day, tall and authoritative, with the aura of possibility visible only to Nicky's eye, and she experienced a tremor of pleasure. Mark said good morning, and everyone replied. As he sat down, nobody could know the trepidation he felt. He glanced around, casually letting his gaze travel in Nicky's direction. The expression in her eyes, as she raised them to his, was one of cool submissiveness. The faintest of smiles touched the corner of her mouth as she looked away. He got the message. His heart expanded, exploded with pleasure, arousal and delight stirred his loins. He felt connected, confident. He could soar through this meeting with wings.

It helped, too, that the meeting was such a positive one. The Kompakter 5044 was a runaway success. It was burning up the inner urban market. Everyone had achieved their sales targets. Mark spoke of the amount of business being generated within the London area.

Clive took the opportunity to whinge. Why, in that case, couldn't he have a slice of the London market, instead of being relegated to the outlying suburbs, where there was less take-up for the smaller machine? It had traditionally been his beat, before Nicky arrived.

A glance at Nicky. Heads turning. Nicky threw a scornful glance at Clive.

'Because,' said Mark, 'we don't need anyone else to cover that market.'

'But you said yourself the response was unprecedented. What's wrong with putting me in there as well? I want to be out there selling, Mark.'

'Nicky's got most of it covered. And I've been helping her out.' Jim, apparently lost in idle thought, flicked his pencil, causing it to roll a little way across the table. Neil, sitting opposite, grinned and folded his arms. Nicky crossed her legs. Clive, trying to appear aggressive and salesman-like on the strength of his last remark, frowned like an upset gnome.

'I've quite enjoyed being active in the field again,' continued Mark unwittingly.

Jim's eyes raked the ceiling in heavy appreciation, and Neil squared his shoulders and gazed at the table. The others looked at Mark with interest.

'Good to keep your hand in,' said Craig.

Mark nodded.

'Keep on top of things,' added Jim.

'Exactly,' said Mark. 'So I'll be taking up any slack in the London area, Clive.'

Neil picked up his tumbler and took a drink of water, just in time.

Mark had no idea that his two fleeting visits to the London office had generated wisps of gossip. Nicky knew. It was the one aspect of all this which made her uncomfortable. Already marginalized in the sales team by the mere fact that she wore a skirt, the rumours set her at an even further remove. She was acutely aware at this moment of the ribald and very masculine amusement which rippled through the sales team. It diminished Mark. She didn't like it. The thought flickered through her mind that this might not be worth it.

Mark sensed nothing. As boss, he wasn't part of the group, wasn't attuned to the subtle signals and exchanged glances. So he carried the meeting to its conclusion in a state of innocence.

Everyone stood up, pushing back chairs, picking up papers and briefcases and heading for the door. Mark said, 'Nicky, can I have a quick word?'

Nicky paused reluctantly. She really wished Mark hadn't chosen to do it like this. Jim passed her and gave her a smile. Nicky kept her face expressionless.

The door closed. Mark and Nicky were left alone.

'I need to talk to you,' said Mark.

'You're making it a bit obvious.'

'What? Making what obvious?'

Nicky gestured towards the door. 'That lot. They're talking. They think there's something going on.'

'Why?'

'You know what offices are like. You've worked in one for long enough.'

Mark thought about this, and dismissed it. His voice was low and urgent. 'I need to see you. I can't stop thinking about you.'

'That sounds unhealthy.' She smiled nonetheless.

Mark gazed at her, loving the way her smile pushed her lower lip out a little, plump and provocative, while her eyes remained cool and thoughtful. He had a dizzying vision of ripping her clothes off there and then, bending her backwards over the oval meeting table. That, and more.

'Can I see you after work?' he asked.

She gave a pretty, troubled frown. 'Mark, I'm not sure that's a good idea.'

'I know. It probably isn't. Frankly, I don't care. Please.' His eyes burned with an expression of unmistakable longing, and Nicky felt both flattered and aroused. He really had got it bad.

'All right, then.'

'We can't meet around here. I could come into London.'

'Fine.'

'We'll have dinner. I'll book somewhere and text you.'

She nodded and moved to the door.

'See you later.'

When she had gone, Mark sat down in the empty meeting room. He was certain that what he was doing was wrong, and reckless, and he didn't remotely care. They were going to meet that evening. He didn't look ahead, didn't even want to peer into that tantalizing unknown. He just wanted to harness this elation to the present, to absorb the reality of what he was about – he hoped – to embark on. This was nothing to do with Paula. This was nothing to do with his marriage or his home life. It was to do with him. It was to do with everything he owed himself. A last chance, an extension of his being, something above and beyond the existence to which he was bound. Where it would lead him, he had no idea.

Once again, for a few brief seconds, he had that sensation of soaring, then gliding, on wings of possibility, sustained by currents of desire. And it was wonderful.

Mark rang Paula and told her he was having dinner with a client. He and Nicky dined at a restaurant in the West End. The conversation was as fluid and amusing as always. Gradually, as the evening wore on, the mood deepened and intensified. A note of sexuality crept in, light at first. By the end of the meal it was wine-dark and heavy. Each could feel it in the other. The recollection of their last kiss cast a sensual shadow. They went to Mark's car. Inside they fell upon one another. As he kissed her, caressing her body beneath her clothes, Mark felt senseless with longing and excitement. Could they go back to hers?

Breathless exchanges, punctuated with fevered kisses, established that they could.

They drove to Camberwell. Nicky's flatmate was out. But not for long. Mark and Nicky were in mid-grapple on the sofa when the flatmate came in. Nicky and Mark disentangled themselves, and Nicky introduced Meg. Meg said 'hi' and gave Mark a look of smiling curiosity. She went through to her room.

Nicky took Mark to her bedroom and they picked up where they'd left off. Again, not for long. Mark, lying next to Nicky on her bed, was at the trouser-removing stage.

'I'm sorry,' he said.

'What?' The word was no more than a ragged gasp, so reduced by desire was Nicky. She was down to her Wonderbra and knickers.

The sound of someone moving about in the next room was obvious. Not just footsteps, but objects, pieces of furniture. There was the sound of a chair being dragged at length across the floor.

'What the hell's she doing?' asked Mark.

'She's got a studio next door. Meg's an artist. Sometimes she paints at nights. She's probably setting some things up.'

'Christ.' Mark, leaning on one elbow, shirt on the floor and trousers unzipped, closed his eyes and leaned his head on his forearm.

'What's the matter?' asked Nicky.

'Nothing.'

'What is it?' Passion was now lace-edged with irritation.

68

'I can't. Like this, I mean. With her next door. I feel like someone's going to come in.'

'No one's going to come in.'

He lay there for a moment. 'It's no good.'

Nicky unhooked her Wonderbra and led Mark's hand to her breast. 'Come on. Ignore her. Come here, baby.'

She did her best, with her tongue in his mouth, to revive the moment, to regenerate their passion. For a few moments it seemed to be working, then Mark rolled on to his back.

'Christ. Christ, I'm sorry.'

She gave him a reflective glance. They said this often happened to guys in their forties. Never happened with Darren. He had a prick like iron. She wouldn't think of Darren. Not at this moment. There were still things that could be done. She bent her head.

Mark closed his eyes and tried to concentrate on what she was doing to him, but it was worse than ever. Why? Why was this happening? He raged internally. Sounds came from Meg's studio next door. Music. Mark groaned. Nicky detached herself.

'Don't worry,' she said. 'It doesn't matter.'

'But it does!' He turned and looked at Nicky. She masked her exasperation with a smile of pitying gentleness, and this made him feel even worse. 'It's not you,' he said, and stroked her hair. 'I want you so much. You've no idea.'

He's going to tell me this has never happened before, thought Nicky.

'This has never happened to me before. It must be the set-up, your flatmate coming in. I'm really, really sorry. I don't know what's going on.' He gave a sigh of anguish. 'Maybe I just want you too much.'

Nicky wanted to smack him one. She could scream with frustration. She wondered about trying again. But an obstinately flaccid penis was about the most tedious object a girl could encounter, and she couldn't be bothered. Mark's plaintive air of failure was enough of a turn-off. She pulled the sheet up, feeling slightly chilly.

'It doesn't matter, Mark. Really.'

Mark wondered if there were many worse scenarios in life than this one. Let down by your prick, that faithful ally and constant companion. The one time it really matters, and there's nothing you can do about it.

'You say that, but it does. I just don't want you to feel it's anything to do with you. You're so lovely. I want you so much, believe me.'

'Don't beat yourself up about it. It's not important.'

She hated mouthing these maternal irrelevancies. Of course it was important. Why would they be here, otherwise? The last thing she needed was to have Mark reassuring her that it wasn't her fault. She knew perfectly well it wasn't. Like most women, she'd been here before, though not that often. Certainly not with Darren. She added, 'Maybe if we just lie here for a while. You know. Have a talk.' But she knew from experience that if someone wasn't going to get a hard-on at this point in the proceedings, they never would. Not without an uphill struggle, and she wasn't prepared to put in the kind of effort that your average call girl normally got tremendously well paid for.

'No,' said Mark. 'This is stupid. And pathetic. I'd better go.'

She lay with the sheet up to her chin and watched as Mark stumbled into his trousers and put on his shirt. Yeah, he did have a nice body, if a bit on the slack side. She felt bored and a little tired.

Mark, when dressed, leaned over the bed and looked down at her. With her mascara slightly smudged and that sheet below her soft, naked shoulders, she looked adorable. He felt totally useless. He couldn't go without trying to set this right, redeem something. He sat down on the edge of the bed. Nicky suppressed a sigh. He was going to talk. She just wished he would go. Perhaps Mark sensed this. He decided against saying anything. He stroked her shoulder and stood up.

'Wrong place, wrong time.' He bent and kissed her gently. 'I'm going to make it right. I promise.'

Nicky smiled, bemused.

It was as though a storm raged in Mark's head as he drove home. His very sense of manhood was afflicted. He blamed many things. He blamed his age. He blamed an excess of unassuaged sexual longing. He blamed the obtrusive sounds from Nicky's flatmate's room, evidence of an alien, proximate presence. That might not have been a turn-off when you were nineteen, but it certainly was when you were forty-three. He even blamed, randomly and rather spitefully, his dick, whose propensity to have a mind of its own had never manifested itself so negatively before. That those wayward tendencies of youth could turn to such flagging unenthusiasm.

But he himself had been far from unenthusiastic. That was the trouble. Maybe if he hadn't built it up so much beforehand, he could have performed.

He tried not to rerun the scene in his head, but he couldn't help it. Each time he thought about his failure, his mortification intensified. Then, after a while, it began to lessen. He considered the situation objectively. Twenty years ago he might have just bailed out altogether. But that wasn't going to happen. This was his big adventure, and it deserved better than this.

He drove along, thinking. The more he thought, the clearer it became. Tonight had been all wrong. Passionate fumblings in a car, followed by a quick screw (theoretically) at her flat? That wasn't what it was all about. This relationship was meant to add a new dimension to his entire existence, to let him revisit those lost places of his youth, to kindle rediscovered emotions.

He would not let Nicky down.

He would not let the little guy on the desktop down.

He would find a new and better context for this adventure.

6

A text message is the modern billet-doux. What a wealth of feeling its little electronic heart can enfold – the ambiguities of desire contracted into cryptic titillation, tender longings cupped in a tiny paraphrase, the language of the poets reduced to acronym and curtation.

Of late the beeping text tone on Mark's mobile phone, once the harbinger of nothing more interesting than a message from Gerry or his sales team, or perhaps a smutty text joke, now set his heart on fire. Always, always there was the possibility that the message might be from Nicky.

He was finishing breakfast the following morning when the message tone on his mobile beeped. He picked it up from where it lay next to his keys and wallet. The little black envelope winked tantalizingly at him.

Mark pressed the button, and Nicky's name came up. Love and dread flooded his heart in equal measure. He hesitated, then opened the message.

'I wont give up if you wont x'

Mark couldn't have been more joyously reassured if he had received a seven-page missive penned in violet ink on scented notepaper and bound with a ribbon tied in a lover's knot.

Paula was clearing away breakfast dishes. 'Who's texting you at this time?'

'Just one of the sales team. Have you finished in the bathroom?'

'It's all yours.'

Mark slipped his mobile into his dressing-gown pocket and went upstairs. He had no idea what to text by way of reply. He keyed in several messages, but they all struck the wrong note, and he sent none of them. He waited until Paula had left for work, then went into his office and called Nicky on her mobile.

'I want to forget last night ever happened. Do you still want to see me?'

'Of course I do.'

This was true. Nicky was a kind-hearted girl who didn't like men to feel bad about themselves. Besides, she didn't like to leave a thing unaccomplished. He wasn't the first bloke to get off to a false start, and to be fair to him, he was over forty. She was pretty confident they'd get it together. The point was, she really, really liked Mark. He turned her on, they had a laugh together, he was interesting to talk to, and he did a lot for her ego. Apart from anything, Nicky liked to have a romance on the go. It kept life interesting.

'It wasn't the best set-up last night,' Nicky added.

'No. I want to change all that.'

Nicky wasn't quite sure what he meant. At that moment she was trying to negotiate a parking space outside retail premises in Peckham, hoping to catch

74

the owner before the day got busy, and it wasn't easy with her mobile clamped to her ear. 'Listen, I have to go. Call me.'

Mark hung up the phone and went to shower. He stood there, letting the hot water course over his body, mind vacant, which was the way he wanted it. If he thought backwards, he was faced with last night and its humiliation; if he thought ahead, he saw only indecision and futile longing. When he went to the bedroom to dress he found that, unusually for Paula, the bed was unmade. He shook out the duvet, then smoothed it down and plumped up the pillows. On the cabinet next to Paula's side of the bed lay the glasses she wore to read last thing at night. The sight of them was intensely evocative, summoning up her presence. He gazed slowly around. They had shared this room for ten years now. Their belongings hung behind the wardrobe doors, and lay in the drawers. There reposed in the silence of this room a sense of communion which he had always taken for granted.

Now he was actively contemplating – no, had already tried to accomplish – a betrayal of their marriage. He should feel ashamed. That was what he told himself, and so he tried. But shame would not be readily activated. Nor guilt, the more familiar emotion. The fact was, this wasn't about him and Paula. What Mark wanted was for his marriage to remain intact, untouched. He wished no one any harm. He simply wanted to arrest his everyday life as it slid into middle age, to know romance and passion before it was too late, without reproach or difficulty. How hard was that? He needed to create a parallel universe. That was how hard it was.

Mark dressed and went downstairs. He poured himself another cup of coffee and went through to his office to fetch his laptop and some papers. A pile of magazines lay on the window sill beyond his desk, recent copies of periodicals – the *Economist*, the *Spectator*. No one else in the house read them. He picked up the most recent *Spectator* and flipped through it as he drank his coffee. He read the problem page at the back and then glanced idly through the classifieds, pondering the offers of tutorial services, booksearches, relaxation therapy, villas in Tuscany – and paused at the section headed 'Accommodation Offered'. There was only one advertisement in the section. He read it.

Marylebone Village WI.
Exceptional two-roomed sunny,
south-facing study/bedroom suite
in quiet Georgian house.
Would suit non-smoking
professional. Mon-Fri let only.
£500 p. c. m. No other bills.
Call 020 7262 0215.

Idly he tried to picture these sunny, south-facing rooms and wondered what kind of person would end up renting them. As he did so, a lateral thought occurred to him. He raised his eyes from the page. It could be done. A parallel universe. A little flat somewhere. A hideaway. Discreet, private, no need to encounter hotel receptionists at three in the afternoon. A place of intimacy where the fact or thought of other people needn't intrude. A context for an illicit affair. Another life.

Mark picked up his laptop, and left the house. As he drove into work his mind was busy with the idea, ranging over the technicalities, the possibilities, the problems. What kind of place and where? A flat, a decent one, would be expensive. Mark's earnings from the business were pretty healthy, but would they run to that? And how would he slip it past Paula? He envisaged himself going through the process of finding a suitable place, taking out a lease, negotiating landlords and deposits . . .

By the time he reached work, Mark had come to the conclusion that his original idyllic notion was in fact burdensome and fraught with problems. He might be his own boss, but even he could only manage a couple of afternoons a week, if that. The whole thing was too much to justify a few hours of passion with Nicky every now and again.

The little bluebird of fantasy fluttered sadly back to earth.

He didn't discard the idea entirely, however. His mind returned to it two or three times during the day, but there was no way he could ever see it working. He came round, despondently, to the idea that they would have to make do with hotels. Which had the advantage of being practical, if nothing else. Getting away in the afternoons wasn't difficult for either of them. Nicky built her week around a number of clients, seeing them whenever it was convenient. And he – well, it was his firm, he could come and go as he pleased. Salesmen and saleswomen – always out and about. He tried to imagine being with Nicky in such a setting. Checking in – together or separately? – crossing the lobby, the hum of the lift, stepping into one of those bleak, impersonal boxes filled with the lonely, departed smell of other people, the preamble, talking, touching, making love on questionable beds. And knew he would hate it.

It was not the kind of parallel universe he wanted or intended.

Later that evening, after supper, he went through to his office. The magazine from the morning still lay open on his desk. He was about to put it aside and get on with some work, but found himself glancing once more at the little advertisement. He read it through again. Possibilities suddenly flickered and kindled. Now he thought about it, wasn't this perhaps more the kind of thing he wanted? A couple of rooms. Not expensive. Not like renting a flat, with all the attendant expense and complication. Five hundred a month. He could easily manage that on a cash basis, without Paula having any idea. And if that proved too complicated, maybe he could do it above board and justify it on the basis that it would save hotel bills when he had to be in London? He could foresee problems there, though. And there were other obvious drawbacks. What was the implication of the Monday–Friday let? That the owners of the house were in residence all the time, or that they only came back at the weekends? He had no idea. Someone else's house. Very probably the thing was a complete non-starter. And Marylebone Village? Where the hell was that? He had a vague idea of the district of Marylebone, somewhere near Oxford Street, but he'd never thought of it as a village.

He hesitated. Where was the harm in ringing? The more he looked at it, the more Mark found something mysteriously attractive about this artless little advertisement, sitting all alone in its section, like a sign. A portent. He had to start somewhere. He might as well see. His heart took a little leaping stumble. He closed the door, then picked up the phone and rang the number. After three rings, a woman's voice answered.

The next day Mark and Gerry were lunching with the firm's accountant. Throughout the two-hour meeting Mark had to work hard to tether his mind to the conversation. He kept restlessly revisiting the thing he had done, unsure whether it was ridiculous folly or sublime inspiration.

He had to talk to Nicky. After lunch he rang her mobile.

'Where are you?' he asked.

'In the office.'

'Any chance of meeting up at the end of the day?'

'Yeah, go on.' Nicky was feeling randy and unfulfilled. She'd also been giving a little thought to Mark's problem of the previous night. He was a sensitive type, the kind who would agonize over things unless reassured fast. The best thing to do would be to take up where they'd left off, before he got it into his head that they were never going to make it. It was handy that Meg would be away for the next couple of nights. She decided not to mention that. Not at this point.

'Where d'you want to meet?' asked Mark.

'Why don't you come to my place around half six?'

Mark hesitated. Recollections of his failure smarted. But he agreed.

He rang Paula at five thirty.

'I'm going to be late tonight. Gerry and I are taking our accountant out for a drink.'

'How late?'

'Nine? Half nine?'

'I won't do dinner till you get in.'

'Don't wait for me. I'll probably grab a bite while I'm out.' He wanted to take Nicky somewhere for supper. It was one of the things he liked most about their relationship. Their affair. Sitting opposite her in a restaurant, somewhere discreet and quiet, watching her face, talking and listening. Those occasions had such containment, such a rounded sense of clandestine intimacy, yet were still entirely blameless. Just two people being together, talking.

Whatever Mark had expected when he pressed the bell of Nicky's flat, it wasn't the sight of Nicky clad only in lacy black underwear of the most scanty dimensions, and high heels. His breath caught in his throat. She stood before him, smiling, hardly Nicky at all – rather the fulfilment of a schoolboy fantasy, a construct of blonde sexuality that would have aroused any man. He closed the door behind him and approached her slowly, feeling his way into her semi-naked embrace.

'Meg's away,' she murmured as she touched her cheek to his, dropping a shivering kiss upon his ear. 'No one's going to interrupt this time. Let's pick up where we left off.'

He kissed her for some minutes, touching her all over, skimming the black lace froth of her underwear with his fingers. They went through to her bedroom. She knelt on the bed in a position of provocative supplication and he stood there, allowing himself to be undressed. The pace was quite different from the night before, when all had been feverish lust, communication confined to gasps and grapplings. This time he could watch her face, her fingers, and he felt rigid with promise and confidence.

He stood above her, closed his eyes to the feel of her hands. This time, no question.

Twenty gratifying minutes later, Mark was lying listening to the slowing beat of his heart, Nicky cupped against him in the embrace of his arm. Her chest rose and fell to her rapid breathing. He touched her skin with his fingers. It was damp and hot. He leaned up on one elbow and gazed at her, at her blonde hair against the pillow, her drowsy smile as her eyes met his.

'Fantastic,' she said.

Mark felt like a praised schoolboy. 'You are.'

They played around with words in happy post-coital intimacy for a while. Then Mark said, 'D'you know what I did today?'

'What?' She traced her finger down the line of hair from his chest to his navel.

'I set about finding a place for us.'

Nicky's mind darted around this statement, unsure what to make of it. 'A place?'

He turned his head on the pillow to look at her. 'Somewhere for us to be together.'

A little warning note sounded in Nicky's brain. Heavy, it said. This sounds heavy.

'What's wrong with here?' She was careful to smile.

Mark reflected. How to explain to her . . . There was silence between them for a few moments. Nicky's brain was sliding into self-protect mode, her senses hardening imperceptibly against what she suspected was a step too far in this relationship. Mark's mind was in a hazier realm, seeking words to convey his wish to transport her, together with his feelings, to some place where he could indulge them both. Failing to find them, he settled for a mundane explanation.

'This is fine, for now. Being here with you. But I want there to be more than just snatched moments. OK, your flatmate's away tonight, but mostly she's around. Besides, evenings are difficult for me.' He would rather make no specific mention of Paula, if he could help it. 'If we had a place to go to, to be together, everything would be much easier, much better.' He kissed her forehead. 'I'm down here a lot, in London, doing business. It makes sense. We could find time during the day. Time for this.'

'It's a weird idea,' said Nicky. 'I mean . . .'

What did she mean? As far as she was concerned, the existing set-up was OK. She had no problems with being Mark's bit on the side. As long as she was in control and having fun. But the idea of some kind of love nest . . . It made too much of the whole thing.

'Look,' said Mark, 'it's not something you really have to think about. I'm doing it. I'm finding myself somewhere in London during the week, and if we can spend some time there, then great. I think you'll find it will all work out.'

She shrugged. Then she kissed him, and diverted his mind to other things.

It was ten o'clock when Mark got home, famished. By the time he and Nicky had exhausted themselves with sex, it had been too late to go out, and Nicky didn't have any food in, beyond a couple of bio-yogurts and a box of Special K.

He found a piece of cold chicken in the fridge and slammed a potato in the microwave to bake. Paula came downstairs, fresh from her bath.

She glanced at the plate of cold chicken. 'I thought you said you were having something to eat while you were out?' She sat down, placing a pot of clear liquid on the table.

Mark stood by the microwave, sipping a beer.

'What? No . . . We were going to, but by the time we left the pub it was a bit late. Have you had supper?'

'Ages ago.'

Mark brought his supper to the table and sat down. 'How was your day?' he asked, with greater brightness and interest than was customary.

'Hectic. One of the girls in the High Street shop was off sick, and we had a delivery of new summer stock, so I've been rushed off my feet.' She pushed the butter towards Mark, giving him a curious glance. The smell of cigarette smoke which usually hung around him after an evening in the pub was absent.

'Don't you want any salad with that?'

'No thanks.'

She watched him take a sip of his beer. She knew her husband well. He hadn't been near a pub. She could tell he hadn't had a drink all evening.

'So, who were you and Gerry out with?'

'The accountant. Wally. Big guy. You met him at the firm's Christmas do.'

'Oh, right.'

Paula pushed up the sleeve of her bathrobe, extended her left hand, and dipped the tips of her fingers into the pot of clear liquid.

'What the hell is that?' asked Mark, watching.

'Acetone.'

'What's it for? It stinks.'

'Takes my nails off.'

Paula sat, fingertips immersed, not looking at her husband. Should she say something? Challenge him on his account of the evening? A little chill had settled on her insides, and she was trying to will it away.

As he ate, Mark kept glancing at Paula's hand. After a few moments she lifted it from the liquid, and on to the towel in her lap. She bent her head, picking at the inner corner of one her curved false nails, lifted it, and peeled the nail slowly off.

'Christ.' Mark stared. 'Paula, that's disgusting.'

'No, it's not. They're just bits of plastic.'

Mark watched as she dropped the nail on to the towel, then started on the next one. He put his knife and fork together and pushed his plate away. Plastic or not, there was something essentially nauseating about the sight. It was too real. He swallowed the remains of his beer, then stood up and took his plate to the sink.

Paula glanced across at him as he bent over the dish-washer. Where had he been? With whom? Questions of enquiry and investigation unfolded in her mind like tickertape, but she couldn't bring herself to utter them.

An hour later, Paula came to bed. Mark was lying on his side, head propped on one elbow, reading a golf magazine. Paula slid in next to him and kissed his shoulder. Then she flicked off the switch on her bedside light.

Mark looked round. 'Aren't you going to read?'

Paula turned on her side and slid a hand round his body, caressing his chest. 'I don't feel like it tonight.' She drew her body close against his. She was trying to shut away the knowledge of his lie, and that very act had brought on a profound insecurity and need. She had always trusted Mark, her sense of connection and intimacy with him was such that she didn't believe he would ever be unfaithful to her. But she was aware that recently events – the house, the job – had eroded that intimacy. She would not contemplate where he had been and what he had been doing. She would simply set it right.

Mark closed his magazine and turned to her with a small sigh. He rubbed her shoulder lightly and kissed her face. 'I thought you said you were really tired?'

'I am. But not too tired.'

As her hands began their familiar and practised routine, Mark felt an instant of misgiving. He and Nicky had made love twice this evening, which he'd thought was pretty good going. But three times? Mark kissed his wife and caressed her body, closing his eyes and pretending it was Nicky. He felt ashamed and guilty, but it was the only way he could respond.

And so they made love.

For Mark it was a miracle, and a matter of no small pride, that he managed it at all. Afterwards, Paula said nothing. Not about the remoteness, or the half-heartedness, or the fact that she thought she had detected on her husband's skin the very faintest atoms of the scent of someone else.

7

The next day Mark left Harlow at eleven, and joined the traffic crawl through the outskirts of London, arriving in Marylebone just before twelve thirty. He was half an hour late for his appointment to view the rooms. He sat resignedly at the Lisson Grove traffic lights, and he wondered why on earth he was doing this. If it hadn't taken him so long to get here, he'd have had half a mind to turn round. He stared out at the unprepossessing shops and buildings flanking the Marylebone Road. A village? He should have realized that was just a piece of pretentiousness, the sort of thing you'd expect from the back pages of the *Spectator*.

The lights changed, the traffic crept forward. Mark glanced down at the *A–Z* lying open on the seat next to him, and indicated left. A few hundred yards on he hung another left, leaving the main road, and turned into a long side street. According to the *A–Z*, Lucas Grove was at the other end. He drove slowly for a hundred yards or so past grocery shops and dry-cleaners and a wine bar, took the first right, and found himself at one end of a very small street, flanked by neat Georgian houses. The London traffic still rumbled far out on the Marylebone Road, but its voice was muted and distant. Mark parked at the corner. He counted the doors down. That would be it, the one with the red door, with the lamp post outside. He sat in the car for a few moments, absorbing the atmosphere. The street was utterly still. No one came out of any house, or went into one. A cat sat on one of the doorsteps, licking its paws in the sunshine. A slight breeze stirred the leaves of the trees which grew at intervals along the flagged pavements. An old man in Arab dress walked the slow length of the street, then disappeared round a corner.

This is mad, thought Mark. His hand reached out to the ignition. He couldn't see himself renting rooms in this odd little backwater, bringing Nicky back here for evenings and/or afternoons of illicit passion. He glanced again at the red door, and his hand hesitated. He wanted to see the sunny rooms. He wanted to set eyes on Mrs Kendal, she of the voice like the slow ripping of lace. The entire set-up was clearly all wrong, but it seemed to Mark that it would be rude just to drive away, to leave this small adventure without any kind of proper conclusion. He was here now.

He got out of the car, walked the few yards down the street, and rang the bell of number eleven. As he stood on the doorstep, Mark noticed that the flowers in the window boxes had shrivelled and died, giving the house a faintly neglected air. After a few seconds a woman opened the door. She was tall, slender to the point of gauntness. She wore baggy linen trousers and a burgundy silk camisole top. Her long hair, tied up in a straggling knot, was a bizarre shade of pinkish red, threaded with silver. Mark guessed her to be in her mid-fifties. Her face was fine-boned, the clear skin etched with lines round large, deep-set blue eyes and down the sides of her wide mouth. The effect was of a child looking out, surprised and expectant, from the face of middle age.

'Mrs Kendal? I'm Mark Mason. I'm sorry I'm so late.'

'Oh . . . Yes.' Mrs Kendal put out her hand to shake his. Her fingers were cold, heavy with silver rings. 'Come in.'

The hallway was long and high-ceilinged, and painted a stark shade of mustard. A large rectangular mirror hung on one wall, its pewter frame stuffed with postcards and business cards, a straw hat perched on one corner. Against the opposite wall, stacked on the polished wood floor, were two Wine Society cases, a sprawl of mail lying on top of them. Music ricocheted down the hallway from the kitchen.

Without any preamble or small-talk, Mrs Kendal strode past him to the stairs. 'Come up. I'll show you the rooms.' Her movements were brisk and leggy, at odds with her actressy voice and fragile look. Mark noticed, as he followed her upstairs, that she was barefoot. Her feet looked leathery and strong, the nails unpainted.

As they went upstairs, Mark was struck by the atmosphere of the house. It spoke of something that was not quite neglect – more a loss of interest, of enthusiasm grown tired. The bright colours of the paintwork had lost their vibrancy. The bold, beautiful pictures and mirrors were lightly filmed with dust. Rugs, lamps and furniture glimpsed through doorways had the faded look of expensive chic of a different, fashionable day. Not so long ago, but long enough. Life and style had burned themselves out in this house, like a woman worn out with trying.

Mrs Kendal spoke to Mark over her shoulder as they climbed. 'My job's taking me abroad for the next few months. Luxembourg. I'll be commuting there and back every Monday and Friday. So' – Mrs Kendal paused on the first floor landing – 'whoever rents the rooms will really be doing a bit of house-sitting.'

She set off again up the next flight of stairs. 'The rooms are right at the top of the house.' They reached the next, smaller landing, and Mrs Kendal opened a door and gestured for Mark to go in ahead of her.

The bedroom was small and light, painted a cool shade of blue, furnished with a double bed and a few pieces of neat white furniture. The curtains at the window were of blue raw silk, and the same material covered a number of cushions on the large bed. The effect was clean and spare. 'And this' – Mrs Kendal moved ahead of Mark to open an adjoining door – 'is the sitting room, or living room, whatever you want to call it.'

This room was longer, with two windows facing out on to the street. The walls were a soft crimson, almost the same colour as Mrs Kendal's camisole top, the ceiling and woodwork a creamy white, like the curtains. The furnishings were an eclectic mix of old and new – a deep, old sofa with a high back, piled with cushions, a large rosewood table near the window, bookcases, Chinese rugs scattered on the dark polished floor, a small, stern fireplace with nothing in it – and, quite unlike the bedroom, had an extraordinary air of personality about it, as though its invisible owner had stepped out for a moment. Mark crossed to the window and looked down at the street. He could see his Jag parked at the corner.

What the hell was he doing here?

Alice Kendal was wondering much the same thing. This tall, dark man had so far said nothing – about himself, or his purpose here. He had given no indication why he was interested in renting two rooms in Marylebone from Monday to Friday. She watched him as he stood at the window. Despite his dark good looks, he had a peculiar air of purposelessness about him, almost as though he lacked definition. A businessman? He looked to be, from the suit and tie. She waited.

Mark turned from the window and caught Mrs Kendal's eye. Her appraising look turned to a quick smile. Mark returned the smile and then moved around the room, glancing at the pictures.

'It's a bit of a hotchpotch,' said Mrs Kendal. 'My mother used to live with me, and these were her rooms. She died a little over a year ago.' She glanced at Mark. 'I hope that doesn't bother you. I didn't really see the need to change things. I redecorated the bedroom, but this room is much as it was. Some of the older pieces of furniture are rather fine, actually.' She ran a hand lightly over the rosewood table.

Mark said nothing. He was wondering whether he cared that these rooms had belonged to Mrs Kendal's dead mother. Why should he care? Unable to read his silence, Mrs Kendal went briskly back through the bedroom to the landing, and opened the door to a small bathroom. Mark looked in, nodded. Spick and span.

She closed the door. 'I suppose you must be wondering about cooking, and so on . . .'

Nothing of the kind had crossed Mark's mind. It was busy dealing with a hazy vision of himself and Nicky here in these rooms on the quiet top floor, making love in the afternoon.

'Of course, you'd use the kitchen downstairs. It's quite big, plenty of room to eat there in the evenings.'

Her tone had dwindled into vagueness. She set off downstairs. Mark wondered whether she'd already written him off as an unsuitable prospect.

'Have many people replied to the advertisement?' asked Mark, more by way of conversation than interest.

'Two, apart from you.' They reached the hall. 'Coffee?'

This was his moment to make a graceful exit, if he wanted. He wasn't at all sure if the place was right. He'd envisaged something more impersonal. This place was full of the scent and colour of other people's lives. Maybe an anonymous service flat would be better. But he hesitated, and then said yes, he would like a coffee. He was still curious, though about what, he wasn't quite sure.

The kitchen was L-shaped, with a large dining area overlooking a small garden. 'Have a seat,' said Mrs Kendal, as she prepared the coffee. Mark sat at the big round table at the far end of the kitchen. He felt the need to make conversation.

'What kind of work do you do in Luxembourg?'

'I teach businessmen how to speak.'

Images of inarticulation rose in Mark's mind, rows of men in suits with muffled voices and baffled faces. 'To speak?'

'Express themselves. Communicate. I work on their image and presentation skills, teach them how to conduct meetings and address conferences, that kind of thing.'

She brought the coffee over and sat down. 'So – you haven't said why you're interested in the rooms.'

Mark realized that he had come with no prepared story. He reached for an approximation of the truth.

'I'm looking for an escape.'

Mrs Kendal stirred her coffee. 'An escape? From what?' She pulled a couple of clips from her pink hair, which was coming loose, bound it up again, and replaced the clips. The gesture caused her to lift her chin, and Mark saw from her high cheekbones and full mouth that she must once have been beautiful. Still was, in a weathered fashion.

'Reality.' The sensation that filled Mark, seeming to expand his inner being, was close to excitement. He could say anything he liked. There were no conformities. The process of reinvention which had begun with turning himself into someone's lover could be taken to wherever he wished, here in this strange house, in the company of this unknown woman.

Mrs Kendal nodded, gazing at him, trying to fill in the blanks. There were probably any number of questions she should be asking him, but she couldn't think of them. He didn't look like a rogue or a chancer. Above all, she was impatient to get this business with the rooms sorted out.

'The point is, I need someone who can pay the rent and look after the place while I'm not here. I don't honestly mind what you're escaping from. But I'll need references, obviously, and a month's rent in advance.'

Mark nodded. References hadn't crossed his mind. But this was just a game he could walk away from. He might as well play it while he was here. 'Are you offering me the rooms?'

'If you want them.'

'How do you decide if someone's going to be a suitable tenant on such a short acquaintance?'

'Gut feeling. You don't look like the kind of person who's going to sell the furniture.' She contemplated him. 'So – are you interested in taking them?'

'What about the other two people?'

She made a dismissive gesture. 'One was a student, studying in town during the week, off home at the weekends, daddy paying the rent. I don't want a student. The other was a politician. I hate fucking politicians.'

The obscenity sounded strange in her dry, delicate voice. They eyed one another for a few seconds. Mark smiled. He found the situation exhilarating. She didn't know who he was, where he came from, what his situation was, and she didn't care. In the space of a few seconds, he made up his mind.

'Yes. I think the rooms are just what I want. I can pay you rent in advance, and I can give you references.' This one he hadn't yet quite sorted out, but he would. 'And I promise not to sell the furniture.'

She glanced at her watch. 'When can you let me have them? I'll need to check them out before you sign the tenancy agreement.'

'I'll send them tomorrow.'

'When would you want to move in?'

'Next week? I could come over at the weekend to sign things and pick up the keys.'

'Fine.' She stood up. Mark hastily finished his coffee.

Mrs Kendal smiled. 'That was very quick and painless. Do you think it's meant to be?'

'I don't know. I've never done this before.'

They walked to the front door.

'Thanks for showing me the rooms, Mrs Kendal.'

'Thanks for taking them. I hope it's going to work out. And I'm Alice.'

'Thank you, Alice.'

'A pleasure, Mark.'

He shook her hand and left.

'What? So this is a reference for James, when he starts art school?'

'No, he's already got references. But I'm paying for the rooms, so my name's going on the tenancy agreement as well, and I need something to say I'm wonderfully solvent and trustworthy.' The lie slid out easily.

Gerry's eyes blinked behind his glasses. His face wore its customary preoccupied look. 'Oh – OK. Fine. I'll let you have it first thing in the morning.'

'Thanks.'

Mark left Gerry's office, experiencing only a tiny quake of anxiety. That was one reference sorted out. For the other, he'd ask the family GP.

Mark rang the health centre on his mobile on his way home later that afternoon, and arranged the second reference. He considered the rest of the practicalities as he drove. He'd already worked out that he would arrange for a sum from his drawings from the partnership to be paid to a separate account every month to cover the rent, and reduce the monthly sum that went into his and Paula's joint current account accordingly. As far as the firm was concerned, it would be rent for James's flat. In the meantime, he could pay Alice Kendal five hundred in cash up front. The chances of Paula noticing were practically non-existent. Throughout their married life all bills, accounts, insurance, mortgage payments, all that kind of stuff, had been his provenance. She very rarely looked at the statements. As long as there was enough money sloshing around in the current account, she didn't pay much attention. There was nothing more to it, really. The simplicity with which it was all being accomplished amazed Mark. He thought of the rooms, and of being there with Nicky for snatched hours on summer afternoons, soundproofed from reality, talking and making love. A separate world, clinging like a crystal drop on the edge of reality, pure romance and passion, all that his starved soul required.

When would he tell Nicky? Not yet. Not till he had the keys, and felt in possession. Then he would take her to the rooms. And there would be seclusion, another world.

'Why do you have to go up to London on a Saturday?'

'Just to finalize something with a client. I'll only be a couple of hours.' Mark slipped on his jacket, patting the inside pocket where he had put the envelope containing five hundred in cash.

Paula said nothing for a few moments, busy with the meringues she was making for a dinner party that evening. Then she said, 'I need you back by six. Evelyn and Trevor are coming at seven.'

'I told you. I'll only be a couple of hours.' He crossed the kitchen and kissed her face lightly. 'You've got a bit of a tan. Have you been sunbathing?'

'I've been on the sunbed a couple of times.'

Mark digested this information. Aspects of Paula seemed to be shifting into uncharted realms these days. She had never been into things like false nails and sunbeds in the past. He wondered if all the new pieces would fit together into some person from whom he felt such distance that there would be no guilt. It would help, certainly. He tried not to think about guilt, or betrayal, or falsehoods.

'I'll see you later.'

Paula plugged in the electric whisk and set to work on the egg whites. She glanced up and looked out through the kitchen window as Mark's car turned out of the driveway and into the road, then sped out of sight. Her heart felt heavy and painful. She didn't really believe him. There could be no earthly reason why he should need to see a client on a Saturday. It was like the other night, when he'd said he'd been out for a drink and clearly hadn't.

She didn't want to believe anything bad about her husband. Everybody did things out of character, everyone kept things from other people. Possibly there was an explanation, one she didn't need to know about. Possibly she was entirely misreading two innocent occurrences. Possibly she was completely wrong.

Possibly he was seeing someone.

That was stupid. Mark wasn't that kind of man. In just about everything he was transparently honest. She knew him.

But we don't know everyone the way we think we do – do we? Otherwise why ever be suspicious? Paula had to acknowledge this truth.

She drew in her breath in a trembling sigh and switched off the whisk. She sat down at the kitchen table, trying to rationalize the feelings that darted and swarmed within her. She couldn't believe Mark was seeing someone. He couldn't smile at her and make love to her and behave normally, and all the time have some secret that took him away and beyond her. She knew his nature. Against this she stacked the knowledge that it happened – it happened to lots of women that their husbands, their faithful, taken-for-granted men, after many years of marriage, suddenly and unexpectedly went off with someone else. A younger woman, someone prettier, or sexier, or newer, or . . . whatever. It happened to others. It could happen to her. Mark was at that age, an age considered dangerous for men.

Swiftly projecting ahead to further possibilities she encountered fear, the floundering, trembling sense of fear of the unknown. Rejection, being left alone, divorced, spent, cast off. Shadowy images of life by herself . . .

She told herself to get a grip.

She couldn't be sure. Two things, and they didn't necessarily add up to much. No point in getting in a state. She would have to do a little work. She would have to do what suspicious wives did, much though she disliked the idea. Check the texts on his mobile phone, watch for clues. If Mark was having an affair – and he wasn't necessarily – then she would find out, one way or another.

'That's handy.' Alice Kendal counted out the cash from one hand to the other. 'You could have written a cheque, if you'd wanted.'

He looked at Alice as she counted the money. Her appearance was different from his last visit. She was wearing make-up, her large eyes smudged with some dark stuff, and her hair hung round her face in little shining waves, as though she'd been braiding it. Her long cotton dress was sleeveless, and rings of bracelets adorned both arms. On her upper arms they dented the soft, slack flesh.

She put the money into her bag. 'I'm just on my way out. Have you brought any things?'

'Things?'

'Moving-in things.'

Mark hesitated. 'No. No, I'll bring what I need when I move in properly during the week.'

Alice Kendal seemed accepting of this. 'I've told the neighbours that someone will be coming in and out during the week. The couple at number nine both work. You won't see much of them. Sometimes they're abroad for whole weeks at a time. An old fellow called Ronnie lives at number thirteen. I doubt if you'll see much of him either, though he does like to chat if he gets the chance.'

Mark hadn't given any thought to neighbours. He wondered to what extent his comings-and-goings were likely to be reported back to Alice, and whether he cared.

'I have to be honest. I'm not going to be here all day, every day. This is going to be very much a base for when I happen to be in London. That's all.'

'Mark, that's entirely your affair. I'm just glad of the rent, and the fact that someone's going to be around. Whenever. So.'

Mark glanced at his watch. 'I'd better be getting back.' He was about to say something about his wife and the dinner party, then remembered. Man of mystery.

'To Harlow?'

This startled Mark. 'How did you know?'

Alice's wide mouth stretched in a smile. 'The references. Your company partner. Your doctor.'

How bloody stupid not to think of that. So much for mysterious.

'I can understand anyone wanting to escape from the reality of recycling cardboard,' she added.

Mark felt defensive. 'It's quite a profitable business. Actually, it's the reality of overnight stays in hotels I want to get away from. Nothing more.'

'Whatever.' She waved a hand. She really wasn't interested. 'Anyway, look . . . I might not see you for a bit. You here in the week, I mean, me back at weekends. You can always leave me a note, if there's anything I need to know. Or give me a call. I've put my mobile number on a list with some others I thought you might find useful. It's in the kitchen, with stuff about the boiler and the cooker and so on.' She handed him the keys. 'Big silver one and the Yale for the front door. That one's the back door. Can be a bit stiff. Come and I'll show you the burglar alarm.'

She led him out to the hall and showed him the code to switch the alarm on and off. 'My daughter Lizzie has spare keys. She lives in Kensington – for the moment, at least. She may pop in from time to time. Her number's on the list.'

Mark nodded and put the keys in his pocket. 'Right.'

'I think that's everything you need to know. Like I say, call if you have any problems.'

'I will. Thanks.'

They shook hands. 'I hope it's the escape you want,' said Alice.

Mark just smiled.

He went back to his car. He felt somewhat mundane now, in Alice Kendal's eyes. He was who he was, a man who sold machinery for a living and wanted rooms in the week for some unstated, but probably guessed-at purpose. He got into the car, and as he pulled his seat-belt across he felt the small, secret weight of the keys to number eleven, Lucas Grove, against his hip. It made him smile. It didn't matter what Alice Kendal thought. As long as he had keys to his new and secret world, for just a couple of hours a week, he could be a different man entirely.

8

Mark rang Nicky on her mobile on Monday morning.

'How's your week looking?' he asked.

'Not bad. I've got six clients to see between now and Wednesday. Not as busy as it was a couple of weeks ago.'

'Interest's peaked. The figures are looking better than anyone expected.'

'Bonuses all round.'

'How would you like to receive a special bonus from the boss later on this week, in person?'

Nicky winced. An age thing, no doubt. All those *Carry On* films. 'Cheesy.'

'It was a bit. Sorry. Anyway, some afternoon this week.'

'Afternoon?'

'I told you. I've found a place in town, somewhere we can go whenever we want. Do whatever we want.'

'Your little love nest?' Nicky had to laugh. It was the best defence. It really seemed a bit OTT, all this. Getting a flat, just for the odd quickie now and again. Made her wonder where he thought all this was going.

'What about Wednesday?'

'Yeah, I can pencil you in.' Her voice held a smile. 'What's it like, this place?'

'You'll see.'

'Is it a flat, or what?'

Mark realized that a couple of rooms in a house in Marylebone didn't quite sound right. 'I said, you'll see. I'll call you on Wednesday.'

Mark put the phone down, touched with misgiving. How would the set-up appear to Nicky? Odd, perhaps. A couple of top floor rooms in some stranger's house.

Nicky dropped her mobile into her bag. How much was he spending on this? She pictured some smart little service flat up west, Chelsea Cloisters perhaps. Discreet, upmarket. He could probably afford it. The firm was doing well. Maybe this was all part of his middle-aged scenario. Wife and family safely tucked away, mistress on the side in town. You had to laugh. She wondered for the briefest of moments what it would be like to be set up in some ritzy little flat by some rich guy, being visited a couple of times a week, no need to work, having money spent on you. No, not really her scene, being a kept woman. Anyway, Mark wasn't rich. Not properly. And she didn't envisage this as some long-term thing.

She turned her attention to her schedule for the day ahead.

There were moments when Mark felt baffled by what he had done. It was as though he had become two people: the Mark I of old, of always, prosperous partner in Emden Environmental Services, husband to Paula, father of James and Owen . . . and Mark II, a separate being altogether. Mark II was having this affair. Mark II had rented the rooms. Perhaps this was why guilt seemed in such short supply. The new Mark's doings did not impinge on the life of the old Mark. It was as though a new identity had sprung out of the little guy on the desktop, fulfilling long-forgotten dreams.

He thought often about the rooms, imagining them utterly still and unoccupied, in the silence of the house in Marylebone.

When Wednesday came, Mark was consumed by the prospect of seeing Nicky. He had made an appointment to see a client near Waterloo at eleven, and then drove to Marylebone and parked in Lucas Grove. He sat in his car and stared at the house, trying to see it through Nicky's eyes. He took from his pocket the slip of paper on which he'd written the alarm code, and checked it. Then he got out and went up the steps, unlocked the front door with the unfamiliar keys, and let himself in.

He closed the door, switched off the alarm, and stood in the silence for a few moments, waiting for the sensation of trespassing to subside. A couple of letters lay on the floor, and he picked these up and laid them on the hall table. He went down the hall and into the kitchen. Alice Kendal seemed to have made no particular effort to tidy up before leaving. A breadboard covered with crumbs lay next to unwashed breakfast dishes by the sink, which looked like it could do with a good clean. After a moment's thought, Mark decided this did not necessarily have anything to do with him.

He went upstairs to the top of the house. On the way

he noticed that all the doors to the other rooms in the house were closed. He wondered if Alice Kendal had decided to be cautious, and locked them. He didn't stop to test any of the handles. He had no particular curiosity about the life which lay behind them. He opened the door on the second floor and stood in the cool blue of the bedroom, and felt a tremble of anticipatory excitement. Outside the sun slipped in and out of lazy white clouds, and patches of sunlight came and went across the floor. He went through to the other room. He looked about him for some moments, refreshing his memory of the room's contents and its peculiar charm, then sat down slowly in one of the high-backed chairs. He couldn't see any use for this room for Nicky and himself. All they needed was the bed next door, and the long hours of the afternoon.

He took his mobile from his pocket and tapped in Nicky's number.

'Hi, it's me.'

'Hi.'

'Where are you?' He could hear voices and noise in the background.

'A shop in Ladbroke Grove. We're installing a machine. Where are you?'

'I'm here, waiting for you. What time can you get away?'

'About an hour. What's the plan?'

Mark glanced at his watch. Almost half twelve. 'Meet me for lunch. We'll take it from there.'

'Where?'

Mark hesitated. He didn't know any restaurants in the area. 'Here.' He would make lunch here. That way she could get used to the set-up. They both could. He gave her the address.

Mark clicked his phone off and sat gazing through the window at the clouds and the sky. He felt oddly serene, shorn of the preoccupations and cares of his everyday existence. Here he would regenerate those pure passions he had felt when he was a teenager and a poet. The romance of desire. The desire for romance. He thought about Nicky, about their last encounter, and her black underwear, and closed his eyes.

Food. Lunch. He would have to go out and see what shops there were nearby. He got up and went downstairs, set the alarm, and went out, locking the door. He walked to the corner and back towards the row of shops he had driven past. He recalled seeing a delicatessen.

Mark bought bread and olives, pâté and tomatoes, and some wine. When he got back, he decided he couldn't prepare lunch without cleaning up a little. He wiped the crumbs from the bread board, and stacked the mugs and plates in the dishwasher, then gave the sink a cursory scrub. He cleared the Sunday papers from the kitchen table, and then investigated the whereabouts of cutlery, plates and glasses. He was struck by how similarly Paula and Alice Kendal organized their cupboards and drawers. Perhaps all women followed the same rough pattern. He had no experience of other women's domestic arrangements. He expected his fleeting thoughts of Paula to give way to guilt, but they didn't. She was remote, part of another existence.

When he had put the wine and food in the fridge, Mark stood and looked around. His gaze strayed to the double doors at the far end of the kitchen, and the garden beyond. It wasn't the warmest of May days – in fact, there was quite a breeze – but it was still nice enough to sit outside. A table and chairs stood on the flagstoned patio just beyond the back door. Mark felt in his pocket for the keys to unlock the doors, then thought of Ronnie next door. The last thing he wanted was a chat over the fence. He changed his mind about eating outside. Instead, he sat down and picked up one of the Sunday supplements while he waited for Nicky.

She sent a text around half one, its little beep startling Mark in the silence of the kitchen.

'Machine stuck. Will be late.'

She arrived a little after two. The boredom and annoy-ance which had grown in Mark over the past hour and a half vanished in a flash when the doorbell rang, and she was standing there on the doorstep. She gave Mark a casual smile when he opened the door, as though they did this every day. She stepped inside, looking around. 'Does this place belong to some friend of yours, then?'

'No. I'm renting it. A bit of it.'

'Weird.' She checked her reflection in the hall mirror. 'Not quite what I expected.'

'Well . . . Anyway, I've got lunch, if you'd like some.' He led her down the hall to the kitchen.

'I had a sandwich on the way.' She made an apologetic face. 'I was starving. I'd've fallen apart if I didn't have something. The machine got stuck in the back alley behind the shop. Took the lads bloody ages to shift it.'

'You could have left them to it.'

'I wanted make sure they actually got the thing in.'

Mark opened the fridge. 'Have some wine, anyway.'

'Thanks.' Nicky sat down at the table, glancing round the kitchen. 'This is nice. Very spacious.' She looked towards the garden. 'Why don't we sit outside?'

'There's a nosy neighbour. I haven't met him, and I don't particularly want to. Not today.' He put two glasses on the table and bent to kiss her. Ten minutes ago he had been hungry. Now his hunger had vanished. He would share the wine with her, then they would go upstairs.

Nicky sighed. 'I've had a horrible morning. And I came on today.' She caught his look. 'My period.'

'Right.' The things you didn't bargain for. The irritation he had felt before her arrival flickered up again. Oh, well. Not the kind of thing she could have texted him, exactly. He was happy she was here, that they could spend some time together. Still, it did change the agenda somewhat.

'Are you annoyed?'

'No, no. I'm just trying to find a corkscrew.' Mark rummaged in the drawer which should, to all appearances, contain such a thing. Then he tried the cutlery drawer. Then all the other drawers. 'This is ridiculous. She must have one somewhere.' In exasperation he tried a couple of cupboards, then roamed around, scanning the worktops and shelves.

'She? Who's she?'

Mark glanced at Nicky, who was sitting cross-legged, showing a silky length of thigh, picking at the varnish on one of her nails. She looked unself-consciously and cheaply sexy, stirring strange emotions within him. He turned away.

'The woman who owns the house. Mrs Kendal.' He began poking about again. 'This is fucking ridiculous. Everyone has a corkscrew.'

'Don't fuss. I don't care about the wine.'

Mark did. Nicky got up and wandered about. 'So where is she now? I don't understand the set-up.'

'She's away. She doesn't live here during the week. That's why I rented the place.'

'What, the whole house?

'No, I told you. Just a couple of rooms. I don't bloody believe this.'

'Don't get in a strop. Where are they?'

'What?'

'These rooms.'

'Top floor.'

Mark had discovered another cupboard beneath the cooker, which looked promising, containing wire racks. It had suddenly become the most important thing in the world, that he should find a corkscrew. But the wire racks contained nothing except old herb jars and stuff like Marmite and mustard. He swore as he got to his feet. Looking around, he found no Nicky.

He went out into the hall and called to her.

'I'm up here.' Her voice floated down from above. 'Exploring.'

Mark went upstairs after her. She had opened the door to one of the rooms on the first floor. Alice Kendal hadn't locked them after all.

'Don't go in there,' said Mark.

'Why not?' Nicky was looking around what appeared to be some kind of study, lined with books on one wall, a cluttered desk with a computer monitor at the window.

'It's not my house. I've only rented two rooms.'

She did as she was told. Mark closed the door behind them. Nicky carried on up the next flight of stairs and Mark followed her, watching her softly swaying backside. As they reached the top, he reached out a caressing hand to stroke one buttock, and she turned willingly into his arms, embracing him on the landing, smiling. 'I told you – I'm off limits.'

He kissed her long and hard. 'I just want to hold you.'

He took her into the bedroom, and lay down with her on the bed, running his hand over her breasts as he kissed her. He felt seventeen again, randy as hell.

Nicky sat up. 'I want to look round.'

She got off the bed and went to the window, then turned and gazed round the bedroom. She said nothing. She glanced at the adjoining door. 'What's through here?'

'Another room. Part of the deal. Not important. Come back here.'

But Nicky went through to the sitting room. Mark

lay back on the bed and stared at the ceiling. Today of all days. He counted up. This time next week – should be all right by then. A week, a whole week's wait before he could make love to her. Still, now that she was here, the uncertainty of the last few days seemed to be steadying. She seemed all right with the place. Accepting, at any rate. Amused, even. He waited for her to come back.

In the the next room, Nicky gazed around. A bedsit in Marylebone. Was he weird, or what? The bedroom was all right, but this room felt like someone had died in it. And someone else's house. It was all too domestic, the smell of other people in the air. She was never going to be all right with this, but she didn't know how she could tell him. She went to the window and looked out. So quiet, just faint traffic noise and the hollow, high drone of jet planes far away. It reminded her of being off school, in bed and unwell. Depressing. Very.

She went back to Mark and lay down next to him. She didn't mind resting here for a couple of hours, anyway. She was knackered, and her lower back ached. She turned on her stomach and asked Mark to rub the base of her spine. He was happy to do so. They lay and talked. Nicky asked Mark a question that set him off about his childhood in Braintree. He seemed happy talking about that, but she quickly grew bored. She turned the conversation back to the here and now.

'What made you decide to rent *this* place, exactly?'
'I don't know. I liked it. Why? Don't you?'

'It's strange. Someone else's house. Not what I expected.'

'I didn't want somewhere impersonal. I wanted something that we could turn into our own.' Nicky met this with silence. 'Like that little place Glenda Jackson and George Segal had in *A Touch of Class*.'

'What's that?'

'A film.'

'Don't know it.'

'It was on television a while ago.' Nicky said nothing. 'Will it do?' asked Mark. 'Will you want to come here, to be with me, to make love?' He was unbuttoning the top of her blouse, kissing her skin.

'Mmm, perhaps.' Nicky was deliberately non-committal. Mark thought she was deliberately teasing.

The truth was that Nicky's interest, always a short-span affair, was fading. Mark had started off as her boss, a bit aloof and unobtainable, powerful, and that had been attractive. An affair had looked like fun. But by going to these lengths, he had taken the amusement out of it. She felt she could do anything she liked with him, and that was boring. Nicky liked a little uncertainty.

But she gave nothing away. She lay with him and talked, kissed, dawdling the afternoon away.

Around four, Nicky said, 'I should be going. I still have that paperwork to do back at the office.' She sat up, smoothing her hair.

Mark felt anxious, filled with a vague dissatisfaction. Things hadn't been as he'd hoped. There was a distance about Nicky, and all through the last couple of hours he felt he had been trying unsuccessfully to re-establish the happy intimacy they'd shared on other occasions. They hadn't laughed much today. Maybe that was to do with Nicky's mood. Maybe it was to do with this place.

In the hall, just before she left, he tried again. He took her in his arms. 'I want this to be special, and it will be, I promise.' He kissed her. 'Next week? Another afternoon?'

She returned his kiss. 'I might get used to it. OK.'

'God, I'd see you every day, if I could.' He pressed her close, seeking some return of passion, of true feeling. But Nicky just smiled. 'I'll call you,' said Mark, and nearly added 'I love you.' Because he was beginning to think maybe he did. He wanted to be in love. But he held the words back.

When she had gone, he felt a little strange. Purposeless, unfulfilled. He went into the kitchen. The bottle of wine still stood unopened on the table. Mark put it back in the fridge, along with the untouched food. He walked to the end of the kitchen and looked out across the garden. What was it he felt? Lonely. Yes. Lonely and uncertain. He should be happy, but somehow he wasn't.

He set the alarm, locked the door carefully, and drove home. Which took two dispiriting, crawling hours.

That evening, Nicky met two girlfriends for a drink after work. They went to a wine bar. It was hectic and crowded, and Nicky wasn't feeling great. She decided she'd rather go home and take a couple of paracetamol and lie in front of the telly with a hot-water bottle on her stomach. On the way out she had to ease her way past a group of young men at the end of the bar near the door. One of them said her name and touched her elbow.

She turned, and there was Darren.

'Hi, babe,' he said.

Nicky's heart began to hammer, but she kept her expression cool and contained. 'Hi,' she replied. She turned as if to carry on out of the wine bar. She kept walking, through the door and out on to the pavement. Dusk was beginning to fall. Darren was right behind her.

'Nicks, hold on.' This time he grabbed her arm, but lightly.

She turned and looked at him.

'I haven't seen you in weeks.' Darren stood stocky and confident, giving her his best Robbie Williams smile.

'Whose fault is that, then?'

'I'm sorry. I've been meaning to call. I've been busy. Had to go off on a couple of trips. How've you been?'

'Yeah, fine.' The proximity of his square, muscular presence, that cocky smile, those lovely eyes, were all doing things to her, but she wasn't going to let him see it. She willed a little surge of self-righteous anger. 'Listen, Darren, great to see you, but I can't hang around.' She turned and walked.

'Hold on, hold on . . .' Darren was up beside her. 'Listen, babe, don't be like that. I know I should've rung, but I wasn't back twelve hours and my boss was sending me off again. It's not been a great couple of months.'

'Tell me about it.'

'I will, if you'll let me.' His eyes held hers. 'Fancy going somewhere?'

'Now? What about your friends?' She nodded in the direction of the wine bar.

'I'd rather be with you. Come on. What d'you say? I've really missed you.'

She felt herself relenting. 'All you had to do was ring, you know.'

'Forgive me for being a bastard. Please?' He smiled, pretending to plead. It did for her. Maybe he really had been busy the last month or so.

Catching sight of a yellow taxi light, Darren put his fingers to his mouth and whistled. 'Come on. I'll take you for a meal, make it up to you.' The taxi drew up, and Nicky and Darren got in.

Hours later, Nicky lay alone in bed, gazing into space and thinking. The delicious, bruising taste of Darren's kisses was still fresh in her mind and her mouth. He was right. He was such a bastard, and he was so lovely, and she would always forgive him. That was the worst of it. The warm, expansive feeling she got thinking about him made her feel helpless and happy. Not that she'd let him see. She'd played it cool, kept him at a distance. That was good.

He'd asked to see her tomorrow night, and she'd said no. Nor would she see him the next night, nor at the weekend. The effort involved in this kind of thing was enormous. But it would be worth it. Darren didn't like 'no'. What man did? He'd said he would call again on Saturday and change her mind. Maybe he would. She smiled in the dark.

In her mind, or at the back of it, Mark had dwindled to a grey and nameless shape. Her middle-aged boss with whom she'd made a mistake. He didn't matter. Back to Darren, and all the things he'd said this evening. He'd admitted he'd seen someone else. He'd been wrong, and he knew it now. He was really sorry. He was glad he was telling her. The last few days he'd been meaning to ring her, but he was worried he might have blown his chances. Fingers laced through hers, face leaning across the table towards hers. If they got back together, he'd said, things would be different. Seeing her this evening had been the best thing that could've happened. Then the kiss, the first of many.

If they got back together again. Oh, they would; she would make sure of it. In happy certainty, she drifted into sleep.

9

It seemed to Mark that some kind of momentum had been lost. He wanted to text Nicky, or call her, but he sensed a lack of connection.

How right he was. Darren had called Nicky on Saturday, taken her out that evening, and spent all of Sunday with her. Poor Mark.

On Monday, after a hopeless weekend of thinking about her and longing to see her, to re-establish his intimate and secret world, Mark rang Nicky. Perhaps in his subconscious he detected some weakness in his position, because he used the half-yearly sales figures as a pretext for the call. She sounded friendly and businesslike, and Mark felt happier as the conversation progressed.

Nicky was relieved that Mark ostensibly wanted to talk work. But she knew what was coming. Their relationship. Their affair. She dreaded telling him it was over before it had even got started. She couldn't do it over the phone. All the trouble he'd gone to. Why hadn't he been able to play it cool, take it for what it was, a bit of fun? Instead, she had to go to the bother of feeling guilty, when she shouldn't have to.

When the sales figures were out of the way, Mark

said, 'You've no idea how much I've been missing you. I thought about you all weekend.'

'Mmm.'

'I can't wait to see you on Wednesday.'

Nicky hesitated fractionally, then said, 'What about tomorrow? Let's do tomorrow instead.'

Mark was so surprised and pleased that he failed to detect the prevarication in her voice. He thought she couldn't wait. 'Fantastic. The sooner the better. Come to the house ar –'

'No, not there. I want to talk. Let's meet for lunch.'

Silence settled in the space that followed her words. Mark wasn't sure what to make of this. 'Whatever you say.'

'Remember that place you took me to, the Italian place up the road from our office?'

The lightness of her tone – which cost Nicky some effort – deluded Mark. 'Nice idea. Back to where we started. We can go to the house later.'

Nicky clenched her teeth against the awfulness of his misconception. She simply said, 'See you at one,' and clicked her phone off. Then she let out a long, slow breath. It might be a good idea to start looking round for another job. She'd had enough of waste compactors, anyway. Not really a girl's world.

'The thing is, I'm getting back with my boyfriend.'

Mark had wondered, fearfully, what was coming. From the moment he had picked Nicky up from the Lewisham office, he had sensed her wariness, and the awful, gentle reluctance in her manner. But now as they sat in the restaurant, and her pretty lips parted, and her eyes looked sorrowfully into his, and the words came out, he felt his heart cave in. He gazed at her miserably.

'I see. Right.' He picked up his glass and took an untasting sip. A long pause. 'When did this all happen?'

'At the weekend.' Mark's stark, unhappy expression genuinely touched Nicky; she felt bad and glad at once. 'I'm sorry. I didn't want to hurt you.' He remained silent. 'I'm not sure it was a very good idea, anyway – you and me.'

'Didn't you? I thought you did. You behaved as though you did, a couple of weeks ago.' Mark could see no dignified path to take. So he spoke as he felt.

Nicky could afford to be forbearing. 'Mark, I really, really like you. But to be honest, you and me getting together had a lot to do with me breaking up with Darren. I was feeling pretty vulnerable and – well, you know, you're a very attractive man, so I let something happen that probably shouldn't have.'

Mark sat in silence for some moments, refusing to meet her suppliant gaze. His edifice of romance, of love, was in ashes. 'Would it make any difference,' asked Mark at last, raising his eyes to hers, 'if I told you I was in love with you? If I tried to explain how much you mean to me?' He knew it was hopeless even as he spoke.

Nicky shook her head. 'I love Darren. I really want to make it work with him.'

Mark could stand it no more. He thought he was going to cry. He stood up. 'You stay. Put it on the firm's account – the bill.'

'Mark –'

But he was gone, out the door.

Nicky sat there for a few moments, relieved, but feeling bad for Mark. In love. Or so he thought. That was awful. She glanced absently at the menu in front of her. They hadn't even got as far as ordering. No doubt the delicate thing to do, in the circumstances, would be to pay for the wine and leave, but she was hungry. So she signalled to the waiter, and ordered some lunch.

When she got back to the office, Nicky wrote Mark a note. It said,

Dear Mark,

   I don't want you to think that what happened
between us didn't mean anything. It did. It meant a lot.
I am really, really fond of you. We've had good fun
together, but it's probably for the best that it's over. I'm
looking around for another job, so you won't have to
worry on that score. Please believe me when I say that I
never meant to hurt you.
Love,
Nicky

She marked it 'private and personal' and got a courier to deliver it to the Harlow office late in the afternoon.

Mark's heart rose in senseless hope when he saw the envelope with her handwriting on it. He read the trivial contents and felt no better. Miserably he returned the note to its envelope and put it in his jacket pocket. Which was where Paula found it that evening, when she was looking for his mobile phone to scan his text messages.

Paula was sitting at the kitchen table when Mark got back from the gym. She heard the front door close, and her heart began to thud in the heavy, dreadful way it had when she'd first read the note. Since finding it she had read it several times, working past the contents to the spiky, confident handwriting, then back to the contents to sift every word for the fullest understanding of what had been going on.

The note lay in its envelope on the table before her. She could have concealed her knowledge of the note and taken a circuitous route to the facts by process of a painful cross-examination, but she preferred the shortcut. Straight to the truth. The note told her only the basics. That Mark had been having an affair with someone in the firm, someone called Nicky. And that it was over. Paula had wondered, through the cloud of her pain, how much difference this last fact made, and had decided – none.

Mark dropped his bag in the hall and came into the kitchen. He had begun to say something, and then saw the envelope lying on the table before Paula. He saw his name written in Nicky's hand, and went cold. His eyes slid to Paula's face. It was stony, her eyes burning, the little flames of panic that had been leaping inside her now banked down low. She would not show her anguish and fear. She couldn't afford to. She had to find out how far this affair had taken him from her.

Mark sat down. He reached out and drew the envelope slowly towards him. 'You went through my jacket.'

'Yes, I went through your jacket. For weeks now I've been wondering what's been going on. You're not very good at deception. Or loyalty. Or keeping your women.'

Mark shut his eyes. He had thought, earlier this evening, that nothing worse lay beyond the flat, dull misery he felt at the loss of Nicky. Well, here it was. Here it was.

Mark opened his eyes. 'I don't know what to say.' And that was very true. The situation was beyond any utterance.

'How much did she mean to you, Mark? Were you going to replace me with her? If she hadn't dumped you, what were you going to do? When was I supposed to find out?'

'You weren't. I mean, this has nothing to do with you.'

'What?' Paula found it hard to articulate, gasping with disbelief. 'Nothing to do with *me*?'

'Not in the way you mean. Not like that. I never meant anything beyond –' Mark stopped, and stared helplessly at his wife.

'Who was she? Someone in the firm, I gather. Some secretary? Someone half your age?'

'She works in sales. Look, it wasn't –'

'How old is she?'

'I don't know. It doesn't matter. It's over. It never really began. It wasn't something I went looking for. It just happened.' Was this a lie? He no longer knew.

'These things don't just happen, Mark! You *make* them happen! Why? Wasn't I enough for you? Does our marriage mean so little that you can just do something like this, and to hell with the consequences?' Paula's eyes had begun to fill with tears. Mark's heart contracted with pain.

'Don't,' he said. 'Don't. I wish I could make you understand why I did it. It was stupid. It was to recapture something. Something I thought I'd –'

Something I thought I would never know again, that I would grow old without tasting again, that the little guy on the desktop might never otherwise . . .

'How can you sit there spouting that – that *crap*, without one word of apology! As though it just happened and you couldn't help it! You started an affair because you *wanted* to, because you don't place any value on our marriage, or us, or this family at all!'

'I do! I didn't want to hurt you. I didn't want it to make any difference to us. I love you. Believe me, I really do.'

If these words brought Paula any relief, she couldn't acknowledge it properly. Anger displaced any incipient fear.

'No, Mark! No, you don't! If you loved me, you wouldn't have done it. Don't you see that? You're just a cheat and a liar, and I don't want to live with that! I can't live with that!'

'No, please . . . Listen –'

And then for over half an hour they argued and wept and he pleaded and she threw out every bitter, hateful feeling she'd been harbouring, until the air was full and poisoned. The grievances of how hard she had worked, running the shops, running the house, cooking and washing and looking after the boys, while he and his bit on the side went off and screwed in some hotel somewhere.

'Where did it happen, Mark? Here? Did you bring her here?'

'Of course I didn't!' Mark's mind flew to the top floor of number eleven, Lucas Grove, and the cloud-scudding sky beyond the window, and his hand rubbing the small of Nicky's back in the silence of the afternoon. They hadn't even made love there. How pointless. The whole thing. Pointless. On some level beneath the present wretchedness, he felt sad. 'You may not believe this, or want to believe it,' said Mark heavily, 'but I only slept with her once. Once. I swear to God I've never been unfaithful to you apart from that one time.' Not for want of trying.

Paula stared at him with red-rimmed, accusing eyes; her tears had dried up. 'I don't believe you. And even if I did, it wouldn't make any difference. I hate you for doing this to me, to our family. I don't want to live with you. I don't want you in this house.' She hadn't known she would say this. In the instant of saying it, she felt convinced it was right. She had to.

'Paula, it's over. I regret it. If I could do anything to –'

'You can. You can go upstairs and pack a suitcase, and

get out. If she doesn't want you any more, guess what? Neither do I.'

Paula stood up and went to the sink to fill the kettle. She had taken a stance, and even though she couldn't work out at this moment whether it was the right one, her misery was briefly assuaged by her sense of strength.

Mark sat listening to the drumming of the water. He looked down, his fingers still on the envelope. He picked it up and ripped it in two, then crossed the kitchen to drop it in the bin.

Paula had her back to him as she plugged in the kettle. He touched her shoulder and she shrugged it away. 'Can't we try and sort this out? I don't want to leave, Paula.'

'You should have thought about that when you started your little fling.'

'Does it occur to you,' Mark asked quietly, 'that part of the reason I did this stupid thing was because everything – everything between you and me seems to have gone cold, lately? There's no warmth. Every bit of your emotional energy goes on the shops and your busy life. I know how proud you are of the way you run the house, and all our lives, but we need more than to be just managed.'

She turned. Mark almost flinched at the look on her face. 'Are you telling me this was my fault? That I'm to blame for your scummy little affair? You bastard!' She launched herself at him physically, and Mark retreated. She was really hurting him. He held his hands up as he backed towards the kitchen door, and she stopped, breathing hard against her fierce sobs.

'Get out of this house *now*!' she screamed. 'I don't want to see you, I don't want to speak to you, I just want you to *go*!'

So Mark went. He didn't see any alternative. He went to the bedroom, stuffed a few things in an overnight bag, went back downstairs, tried to plead with Paula again, and gave up. He left the house and got into his car, unable at that moment to compute his feelings.

James opened his bedroom door. So did Owen. James saw the look of anxiety and fear on his younger brother's face. They went downstairs. Their mother was sitting on a kitchen chair in her dressing gown, weeping. They stood there, guilty and uncertain in their masculinity. Then James crossed the kitchen and put an arm about his mother's shoulders.

Mark sat in his car for some moments. He turned to look at the house, trying to comprehend his position. He could perfectly well understand Paula's point of view, her sense that she'd been done some terrible wrong. But he still couldn't feel any connection between his feelings for Nicky and any aspect of his domestic life. It seemed absurd that she was throwing him out.

Maybe I'm a psychopath, thought Mark. Unable to empathize with the feelings of others. Though he did. He felt for Paula in the awfulness of what he'd done to her. He just knew that whatever he'd felt for Nicky – still felt – had grown out of some other part of him that was nothing to do with all this.

Where was he meant to go? There was a hotel three or four miles away, one of those Travelodge things, but the thought of spending the night in a beige box, waking to anonymity, was unexpectedly horrible.

Lucas Grove. He was paying for the place, and the very fact of it was, as much as the affair with Nicky, a product of this other self whose dreams and desires he had been so selfishly trying to fulfil. He would go there and think, and try to sort this hellish mess out in the morning.

He switched on the ignition. The rising note of the engine, the familiar glow of the dashboard, and the bright banter of the evening talk-show host that sprang up from the radio brought momentary comfort. He set off towards London, cocooned in the warmth and security of his car, music and voices around him, the motorway ahead of him, heading for exile.

He woke next morning to an unfamiliar light, soft and blue through the curtains of the little bedroom. Mixed with his disorientation was a momentary and pleasurable amnesia, a limbo of nothingness. It didn't last. It quickly gave way to a bleak recollection of the way in which he had well and truly screwed things up.

To stop himself thinking about Nicky and about Paula, and in the hope that activity might shift the weight of misery within him, he got out of bed. He looked round the little bedroom. He pulled on the T-shirt and sweat pants in which he had left the marital home last night, had a pee in the bathroom across the landing, and went downstairs.

The house felt more foreign than it ever had so far. Letters lay on the mat, and he dutifully picked them up and placed them on the hall table. In the kitchen he made himself some instant coffee, which he had to drink black, and found some stale-ish bread in the bread bin, which he toasted.

He ate his toast, standing at the French windows at the end of the kitchen in a house he did not know, looking out over the garden into which he had never stepped. A circle of thoughts turned slowly in his head. He was tempted to look in at the Lewisham office. He was in London, wasn't he? Life had to go on. There was business to attend to. He knew the real reason he was thinking this way. Nicky might be there. He just wanted to see her, to look at her, even if it turned the knife in his wounded heart. They might be able to talk, maybe she'd had second thoughts . . . Futile, futile.

He stopped this train of thought and switched to another. The important thing was to sort out this mess with Paula. Maybe sleeping on it had helped her calm down a bit. The very act of kicking him out had probably been therapeutic. He doubted if she'd want to go beyond that. The truth was, he couldn't see very far into her heart these days. It was some time since he'd tried to fathom her feelings. Time spent together seemed to consist largely of exchanges of information. Dispatches from foreign territory.

Mark turned and padded out of the kitchen and upstairs. Repairing the damage he had done would be a brick-by-brick job, but surely he could do it. He needed to make her see that this whole thing had really had nothing to do with her. Only with him, and this blank space in his heart. How would he explain that?

She would have left for work by now. He would have to wait until this evening. The day stretched ahead of him, a wasted, loveless terrain which held nothing he cared about. Except Paula and the boys, and that wasn't the way he meant. His heart literally ached, a raw pulse.

The only thing to do was to go back to Harlow, to head office, and there don the guise of Mark I and spend the day in a semblance of work. At least in the office he might not feel so middle-aged and discarded.

When he drove up to the house a little before six, Paula still wasn't home. He let himself in and paced around. There was no sign that she had taken steps to make his removal permanent. His clothes still hung in the wardrobe and lay in the drawers. In this serenity and normality he saw Paula relenting.

He was wrong.

Paula came back half an hour later. Everything about her was quite different from the previous evening, the loose, unhappy ends all ravelled up and tucked away. She looked made-up, blow-dried, attractive and efficient. She didn't seem surprised to find Mark in the kitchen, drinking a coffee and reading the paper. Her gaze seemed to hover around him, rather than be directed at him.

Paula had spent much of last night, and all of today, considering her position. Now that she had taken her stance as the wronged wife who had kicked her husband out, she intended to conduct herself with aloof composure. She could think of no appropriate alternative. She was too unhappy.

She crossed the kitchen without a word. Mark had thought all day about what he was going to say, and now he began.

'Paula, can we talk this over properly? I think we have to. I did a crass and stupid thing. It meant absolutely nothing.' This was so far from the truth that it didn't matter. 'Please give me a chance to set things right.'

She turned, drying her hands. Her expression was light and unconcerned. 'No.'

It took a moment for her reply to sink in. 'No – as in, I can't set things right? Or as in, you don't want me to?'

'Either. Both. I'm really not bothered.'

Mark rose. 'Oh, come on, Paula. We're not the first couple to whom this has happened. We need to talk about it.'

'No, Mark, we don't. I said all there is to say last night. I don't want you here right now. I don't really know why you came back, unless it was to get your things.' Paula was so much in character now that she couldn't have let his entreaties make any difference to her, even if she'd wanted to.

'So – what? Is this meant to be permanent? Is that what you're saying?' In his helplessness Mark grew heated. This was not the way it was meant to go.

'I don't know. I'll have to see. But for the time being, I want a separation.'

'But – but why? What good is it going to do? How can we possibly sort this out in an adult fashion if you kick me out?'

Paula leaned back against the sink. 'What makes you think I'm so keen to sort it out?'

'I don't understand what you're saying.'

'You've had your little affair. I found out. Bad luck for you. Why should I forgive and forget, let you come back and carry on as before? I don't just stand still for you, Mark. Not any more.'

'I know you don't. I –'

'You know nothing of the kind. Do you want to know what gets me most? It's that for the last five months I've been working – out there, in here, keeping things going, doing what I thought I had to, while you've been having a lovely, romantic time with some tart in your sales team. I really feel I've been missing out, Mark. Don't you? Don't you think I have?'

'Paula, I haven't a clue what you mean about missing out, but the fact is you don't need that job. You don't need to put yourself under that kind of pressure. Don't pretend there's any point to it. It's not like we need the money.'

'Mark, you don't get it at all, do you? It's not about

money! I do that job to make my life more interesting, to make *myself* more interesting! For you – so that I'm some-one with a life beyond the shirts and the meals, so that I don't go nuts with the boredom of thankless housework and meal-making, so that I'll have things to talk about – things beyond this house and all the domestic trivia that all the other housewives I know are preoccupied with! That's why I do it! And what a bloody waste of time it's turned out to be.' Mark said nothing. 'I want a separa-tion because I want to see if life is worth living without you. You seem to have been prepared to take that risk about me.'

'It wasn't like that. Believe me, the last thing I wanted to risk was you, or our marriage.'

'Well, hey – that's what happens when you sleep with other women. So, off you go. Get your stuff, and piss off.'

Paula went to the fridge to prepare supper for herself and the boys.

Mark felt rigid with anger and humiliation. There was no point in having another stand-up row, not with her in this mood. OK, if that was what she wanted, fine. She was probably just doing this to see if he really would take her at her word. He went upstairs, found a suitcase, and began to fill it, thrusting things in. He went to his study and unplugged his laptop, and sorted out essential items to take with him. Coming out of the study, he met James on the landing. James's eyes went to the suitcase.

'Hey, Dad.' The greeting was cautious, casual. Mark instinctively sensed the small boy terror lying beneath it.

'Has your mother spoken to you?' said Mark, in reply to all the unanswered questions his son wasn't throwing at him.

'Sort of. She said you'd had a row.'

'Did she say what it was about?' The idea that James and Owen knew what he had been doing flooded Mark's heart with shame.

'No.' There was a silence. 'It must be a really big deal.' Another silence. 'Mum was pretty upset last night.'

'She had a right to be. Anyway . . . she seems to think I should move out for a bit.'

'Have you been having an affair? Is that what it's about?'

Mark was trapped. 'It was hardly that. But yes. You could say so.'

The expression in his son's eyes was unfathomable. Contempt? Curiosity? Both.

James said nothing. He moved past Mark and went downstairs.

Mark stood there, examining the farther reaches of his behaviour. That which had been precious and personal only a few days ago was now at large, roaming through the family domain, big and bad and serious.

He would have to speak to Owen. He put down the suitcase and went to Owen's room, but it was empty. Tuesday night. Cricket nets. Mark wondered whether he should go to the school and seek Owen out, tell him before James did. No point.

I am the outsider, thought Mark. Bring on the dancing horses. Echo and the Bunnymen.

10

And so Mark went to Marylebone. This would have to be his home for as long as it took to sort things out with Paula. What would happen when the weekend came and Alice Kendal came back and found him there? Maybe it wouldn't happen. He still had the hopeful notion that he could talk Paula down over the next few days; he didn't believe she wanted the family fractured in this way, the boys unhappy.

How would she have reacted, after all, if he'd left of his own accord, if he'd jumped rather than been pushed? She would be in pieces. Wouldn't she? Recalling Paula's steely composure earlier this evening, Mark felt a startling, unsettling uncertainty.

For the first time since he had visited the house, Mark went into the sitting room next to the bedroom. He placed his laptop on the rosewood table near the window and searched for a plug. Then he pulled up a chair and sat down. For a long time he sat looking out of the window, watching dusk gather in the London sky.

He pondered his predicament, wondering how he had come to this moment. Love, in theory, should be an infinitely expandable commodity, so that the love felt for one person didn't diminish in proportion to the love borne for another. But it didn't work like that. Everything came at the expense of something else. He let his mind dwell upon Nicky. He tried to cut through the pain of rejection to make a forensic examination of the state of his feelings. He was no longer sure whether it was Nicky he had been in love with, or with the idea of love itself.

He settled for the latter. What did he know of Nicky, really, except that she made him feel the way Sandra had made him feel twenty-five years ago? That was what he'd loved. Her mouth, for instance, that thing that happened to her upper lip when she smiled – it hadn't been her mouth he'd loved, but what it did to his heart. Effect, not cause. He didn't really know Nicky at all.

He sat thinking over all these things, until the light outside had faded to the translucent blue-grey of early night and he could hardly make out the dim shapes of the furniture in the room. Despite the knowledge of the turmoil he had brought to his marriage and his family, here, locked away at the top of this house, he felt a certain sad peace.

At length Mark roused himself. He opened his laptop and switched it on. Everything around him was so still that he could hear the whispering rush and drone as the computer came glowing into life. A few flickering seconds, and there he was on his trike, on the screen, Ladybird T-shirt and all. Mark addressed the round, expectant face. His voice sounded dry and strange in the darkness.

'This was not what I intended, little guy. The parallel universe wasn't supposed to touch the real one.'

How stupid had that idea been? Husbands had affairs and their wives found out. He had barely had time to taste the fruits of an affair before Paula made her discovery. Worlds colliding. Secrets uncovered. His existence and identity adrift: wife, home and family untethered and beyond his control. And here he was in two rooms in a house in Marylebone, watching the night come down, with only small prototype Mark for company.

Talk about a parallel universe.

Morning dawned in Lucas Grove. Mark's installation was becoming a little more permanent. A few of his clothes hung in the wardrobe, his shaving things were in place in the bathroom, and he knew exactly how little there was by way of breakfast when he went down to the kitchen. Black coffee, and nothing else. He'd finished the bread yesterday.

But the sun was shining outside, and Mark's spirits were not as low as they might have been. This isolation was tranquillizing. It wasn't as though he had to rush into work. He dressed himself in a T-shirt and some chinos, rather crumpled from his angry packing last night, and stepped out into the light, bright air to hunt down breakfast.

A couple of blocks away he found a sandwich bar, and next to it a small newsagent's which stocked a selection of Arab and international newspapers. He bought a *Guardian*, and sat down at one of the little pavement tables outside the cafe. He ordered a latte and a bacon sandwich.

He opened the paper to read it, but found he spent more time watching the people passing by. It was quarter to nine. Most of them were on their way to work. He drank his coffee and ate his sandwich with a bizarre feeling of dislocation.

He rang work on his mobile and told them he'd be in later in the morning. Back at the house he showered, changed into a suit and open-necked shirt, and straightened the bed. As he shook out and smoothed down the duvet, Mark paused. Nicky had come here just once, and never would again. His heart opened like a parachute and sank slowly to earth. He realized now, thinking back to last week, that Nicky hadn't wanted any of this. What on earth had he been thinking of, renting these rooms?

Still, they had their uses, if not quite the ones he had envisaged.

He locked the house and went to his car, and discovered he'd been given a parking ticket for parking in the residents' bay without a permit. The idea that he would have to ask Alice Kendal how to go about getting a parking permit slipped into his mind for the merest nanosecond, before he dismissed it. He wasn't going to be here that long.

Was he?

Almost as soon as he walked into the shiny new reception area of Emden Environmental Services, Mark could sense the awareness. The knowledge. He caught it in the glance of Stella the receptionist, as she lifted her eyes to his.

'Morning, Mr Mason.'

'Morning.'

He passed on down the short corridor and into the open-plan office. People looked at him. He greeted them, and they returned the greeting.

'Morning.'

'Morning.'

Nothing untoward there. Yet they knew something.

Mark felt the eyes follow him as he went into his office and closed the door.

He wondered how they knew. And what, exactly. That Paula had kicked him out? That he'd had an affair with Nicky? Both? Or had rumour taken some other strange, unaccountable form? He stood for a lonely moment, then went out and headed for Gerry's office.

Gerry was on the phone. Mark sat down and waited.

Gerry put the phone down at last, looked at Mark, and immediately assumed an expression in which compassion and reproach were exquisitely blended.

'What the hell have you been up to?'

'I don't know,' replied Mark. 'What's Paula been saying?'

'I haven't spoken to her directly. She talked to Sam yesterday.' Samantha being Gerry's wife, and close friend of Paula's. 'I know she kicked you out.'

'Is that all you know?'

'Paula said she found out you'd been having an affair. With someone here.' Gerry inclined his head in the general direction of the office. 'There's talk out there that you've been seeing that girl from the sales team. I don't know where that lot get their information from, though.' He held Mark's gaze. 'I take it it's true, then?'

Mark sighed. 'Only up to a point. The thing is, I never intended –' He stopped. Explaining was useless.

Nothing was said for a moment or two.

'Yeah, well, it happens, I suppose,' said Gerry at last. 'I'm surprised, though. Sorry, too. Sam and I are fond of you and Paula.'

'It's not the end of the bloody world, Gerry.'

Gerry raised his hands. 'OK, if you say so. It's your marriage.'

'We'll sort it out.'

'Will you? That's not the way Paula was telling it to Sam.'

'She's still in a state about things.'

Another silence, then Gerry asked, 'So, it's not serious with you and this girl?'

Mark didn't know how to answer this honestly. No, there was nothing serious, not between him and Nicky. But something serious had occurred, in his life and in his heart. And it was still unresolved.

He shook his head. 'It's been blown out of all proportion. The whole thing.'

'Come on, Mark. An affair's an affair. What's proportion got to do with it? Paula's got every right to feel the way she does.'

'Yeah, I know.'

'I'm not judging you. Your private life is your concern.

Not the best thing to have happen in the office, though. Where do things stand with this girl – what's her name?'

'Nicky Burgess.'

'Right. It doesn't look too good within the firm. You do see that?'

'She's already told me she'll be leaving.'

'Good. Or maybe not so good. Losing decent sales staff.'

Mark looked past Gerry at the world beyond the window. He tracked the path of a plane flying soundless and tiny across the sky, and was suddenly visited by that same feeling he had experienced at the outset of that Croydon meeting a couple of months ago, a rising sense of panic. He gazed around Gerry's office, and each detail – carpet, desk, plants, files, computer, even the year planner on Gerry's wall – seemed pathetic and futile. The world of Emden Environmental Services was numbing in its smallness, its uselessness. His heart started to pound.

He stood up and walked around Gerry's office, staring at his own feet. After a moment the nihilistic sensation began to dwindle, and was replaced by an intense and immediate desire to be somewhere far away from these premises and these people, including Gerry. He turned to meet Gerry's gaze.

'I want to take some time off.'

Gerry looked disconcerted. 'What – like a holiday?'

'A period of extended leave, I believe they call it. I honestly don't think I can handle things here right now.'

'What makes you think *I* can? This is a partnership, you

know. A business. The sales side can't just run itself. How long are you talking about, for God's sake?'

'I don't know – a couple of months.' Mark had no idea what he meant, what he wanted the time for. He just didn't want to be part of this world, not for a while at least.

'A couple of months? You can't just disappear and leave me to handle everything for that length of time!'

'I don't intend to disappear. I just need to be away from – all this. I've fucked up of late, Gerry. You said it yourself. Home and work.' He met Gerry's indignant, anxious gaze. 'Don't worry. I've got my mobile, and my laptop. I'm not talking about vanishing off the face of the planet.'

'You'd better not be. I don't know about this. I really don't.'

A silence.

'Just some time,' said Mark, 'to sort myself out.'

Gerry shrugged. 'I can't stop you.'

'You can, actually.'

'Yeah, well.'

'Nothing in my department will suffer, I promise. Craig can look after things in the short term. He doesn't need to be out in the field right now. He can see to the admin. Look, anyway . . . it may not be more than a week or two. I don't know. I have to see how things go with Paula.'

'If I were you, I'd do some serious grovelling.' Gerry glanced up at Mark. 'Where are you staying, anyhow?'

'I've got somewhere. I don't plan to be there for long. I'll straighten things out.'

Mark spent the rest of the day making sure that Craig would be able to handle things for the next few weeks. Craig, in the course of discussions, revealed that Nicky had handed her notice in. She would be leaving at the end of next month. Nothing was said about why. Mark felt an inner blush at the thought of ribald comment rife among the rest of the sales team. He wanted to be far, far away from all this.

He went back home at the end of the day, and saw Paula's car in the driveway. In the hallway stood two large suitcases. He stared at these for a few seconds, wondering if Paula was going off somewhere, before he realized they must contain his own clothing. A lot of it. Possibly all of it. He noticed his golf clubs standing next to them.

This didn't augur well for further attempts at reconciliation.

He went into the kitchen. Paula was out in the garden, taking washing from the line. Mark went out.

'I take it those are my things in the hall?'

Paula glanced at him, carried on folding a pillowcase. 'I thought I'd save you the time.'

'Look, why is it so important that I leave? Don't you think we have a better chance of sorting this thing out if we're living under the same roof?'

'You keep talking about sorting things out, as though

it's just a bit of a mess you've made that can be tidied up, and everything will be neat and orderly again.' As she spoke she snapped pegs deftly from clothes, flipping and folding, laundry in one basket, pegs in another.

'That's largely how I see it, Paula. I don't see why we have to treat this as some marriage-wrecking event.'

'An event?' She turned and stared at him, her face cold and hard. 'An event? Mark, this is not something that just came along, that just happened! You did it. Do you understand? You did this. You betrayed my trust.'

'I know. And I'm sorry. I want to make it better.'

'You still miss the point, Mark. Maybe I don't.'

'Oh, come on.'

The last of the washing off the line, she hefted the laden basket on to one hip and headed for the house. Mark followed, not enjoying the submissive, beseeching figure he was forced to cut. 'Has it crossed your mind that I might not want to move out?' he asked. 'That you can't exactly force me out of my own home?'

'Yes. In which case, if you won't go, I'll leave myself.' She set the basket down on the kitchen table.

'Why are you making such a big fucking deal out of getting me out of the house?'

'Because I don't want to live with you, Mark. After what you did, I can't stand the sight of you. And,' Paula added, 'because it's my prerogative.'

'What? To destroy our marriage?'

'As I recall, that was your idea.'

'I give up. I give up. If that's the way you want to play

it, I'll get out for good. Where are the boys? Someone needs to explain to them what's going on.'

'They know. I told them.'

'I still need to talk to them.'

'James is out. Owen's upstairs.'

Paula watched him leave the kitchen. She felt a moment's misgiving, a slight buckling of the resolve she had been forging since the night she had confronted Mark with the letter. But there was no way back from her position. Not at the moment. She wasn't even sure if she wanted a way back. She wasn't sure about anything at all.

Owen was in his room, the music blasting. Mark knocked on the door, to give Owen time to stop posing in front of the mirror with his air guitar.

After a few seconds Owen's head appeared. 'Yeah?'

'Can I have a word?'

Mark went in and closed the door. He asked Owen to turn the music off, and they sat awkwardly next to one another on Owen's bed. In the course of the stumbling, inconclusive father-and-son conversation which followed, Mark attempted to tell Owen how things were with his mother, which Owen already knew, while Owen nodded and articulated a few inchoate mumbles designed to get rid of his father and the embarrassment of this discussion.

'Nobody's perfect,' said Mark, by way of winding up. 'I know what I did was wrong, but your mother doesn't seem in the mood to forgive me right now.' He laid a hand on Owen's shoulder. 'Don't worry. I'm around. This will sort itself out. I promise. We'll have some games of golf, talk a bit. OK?'

'Mmm.'

Mark picked up a CD case from the floor. Libertines, eh? Good band. Not as good as The Streets, though.'

Owen nodded, saying nothing.

Mark stood up. He recalled his own feelings when his father used to come on like some trendy old sod. How had he got here from there without even noticing? His heart was leaden. 'I'll give you and James a call at the weekend. See if we can't get together. OK?'

'OK.'

Mark went down to the hall. He stood looking at the suitcases for a moment, then picked them up and took them to the car.

When he came back, Paula was standing in the hall. Although she had maintained throughout the packing of his cases the same sense of righteous resolution which had fortified her for the past two days, the sight of Mark carrying them to the car made her feel unexpectedly and horribly bereft. She didn't want to acknowledge this. So she brought up a mental picture of him in bed with his piece from the sales team, and it acted like a pilot light on her anger.

'This seems stupid,' said Mark. 'It really does.'

'Maybe to you.'

'What good is it going to do?'

'I don't know. All I know right now is that I don't want to see you or be with you.'

There was nothing more to be said. Mark got into his car and drove away.

Paula turned and went back into the house, fighting down her sense of loneliness and rejection. She was appalled that she should feel this way. She had every right to send him packing. He had committed his sin, and he needed to be banished and punished. She tried to resurrect her sense of cool, drawing on the insouciance portrayed by women in her circumstances in films and books. She was an independent woman, after all, with a life of her own to lead. She could do without him.

When he arrived at the house in Marylebone, Mark remembered the ticket he'd got that morning and parked at a meter round the corner. This was going to get prohibitively expensive, he thought, as he fed in the pound coins. He took his cases from the car and into the house. He carried them upstairs and slung them on the bed. He was confused and depressed. This was the lowest he'd been in a long time.

He went through to the next room, seeking the odd, consoling peace he had found there last night, and glanced around. So, this was home for however long – always assuming Alice Kendal accepted the situation. That was something they had to talk about. He took his mobile from his pocket and searched for her number.

As he did so, the house phone began to ring. The sound emanated from at least three different points in the house, and one of them was this room. He hadn't noticed the telephone before. It was on a table by the fireplace. Mark hesitated. Should he answer it? Alice Kendal probably had the answerphone on somewhere.

But the phone continued to ring, so he went across the room and picked it up.

'Hello?'

He recognized the husky, delicate voice immediately. 'Mark, is that you? It's Alice Kendal. I tried all day yesterday and today. Just wanted to see how things were.'

'Well, fine . . .'

'Only I was a little worried.'

Mark paused. 'Why?'

'There didn't seem to be much – much evidence of you around when I was back at the weekend. I do want you treat the place as your home while I'm not there. I can't think what you were living on last week. The fridge was absolutely bare.'

'I haven't been here much, to be honest. Actually' – Mark sat down in an armchair – 'that was something I wanted to talk to you about. Strangely enough, I was about to ring you when you called.'

'Oh?'

'You see, my circumstances have changed somewhat. On the domestic front. I need somewhere to live on a permanent basis.'

There was a silence. Then Alice Kendal said slowly, 'Well, I don't really think so, Mark. We have an arrangement . . .'

'No, fine, I do understand. I'm sorry to have –'

'Hold on a minute. Hold on.'

Mark held on.

'I don't want to see you in difficulties. On the other hand, I hadn't intended anything more than a Monday to Friday tenant.' There was another silence as she pondered. She sighed. Mark felt the wretchedness of his situation, this imposition. 'Look, you can stay this weekend, and we can discuss it then.'

'Thank you. The last thing I want is to cause you problems.'

'No, well . . . We'll talk later. Bye.'

Nobody wanted him. He sat by the phone in the silent room. Perhaps taking time away from the office wasn't the best idea. At least there he possessed some significance.

Significance. He considered this. He had read recently about status anxiety, people's need to define themselves in the eyes of others. That was why he was thinking this way. Here he was – Mark, the rejected and dejected, craving the feeble comfort of finding substance in the one role left to him. The boss. Pathetic. That was exactly what he had to fight against. Hadn't all this come about through his longing to find a new definition, to fulfil some deep, unexpressed personal desire? A love affair, it seemed, was not the solution. Shorn of his marriage, his home, his children, and divested of his workplace significance, what in the world was he?

It seemed to Mark that his identity was slowly vanishing, like smoke through a keyhole.

11

Mark ate a solitary meal in a little local restaurant that evening, and the next day went to the supermarket. He hadn't done this for a long time. The contemplation of his requirements involved a consideration of how he proposed to spend his time in his bedsitting limbo in Marylebone. He had no idea. So he furnished himself with adjustable, staple commodities. Waiting at the checkout in Waitrose, Mark's thoughts strayed to the evening. He added a bottle of wine from a nearby shelf to his basket, and experienced a small surge of self-pity.

As he was unloading his purchases at home, Mark recalled that there was nothing in Alice Kendal's kitchen with which to open a bottle of wine.

So Mark went out into the wide world to buy a corkscrew.

The area seemed to possess plenty of pubs, newsagents and seedy supermarkets, but nothing in the nature of a hardware shop. After walking in a westerly direction for ten minutes or so, Mark emerged in what he found to be Marylebone High Street. It was narrow and busy, with an eccentric, haphazard air which Mark found very pleasant. He began to see why the area called itself a village. He strolled the length of one side of the street, stopping to gaze in the windows of the patisseries, bookshops and boutiques. He crossed over and walked back up, passing shops full of pretty pastel linens, smart florists and a couple of small galleries, but nothing that seemed to promise a corkscrew.

The cookware shop took him by surprise. It was large and lovely, its windows displaying polished wooden bowls, elegant glassware, and various kitchen implements of utilitarian chic. Mark pushed open the plate-glass doors and went in. He wandered the aisles. Surely, among the copper saucepans and espresso machines and Sabatier knives, there must lurk something as mundane as a corkscrew.

A girl approached him. She wore a nondescript black top and trousers, and over this a very large apron.

'Can I help you?'

Mark found he was enjoying browsing among the ceramic dishes and pastry cutters. He didn't want immediately to be directed to the corkscrews. He wanted to come upon them unawares.

'No, I'm fine, thank you,' he replied. The girl drifted away.

Eventually he found them next to tin openers and cheese slicers. There were a few different kinds, from the absurdly elaborate and expensive to the simple and efficient. Mark opted for a cheap and amusing one, which consisted of a little wooden tube with a hole at one end which unscrewed to reveal the corkscrew, which in turn fitted together with the wooden tube to form the handle. It was only one pound fifty.

As he paid for the corkscrew, Mark noticed an area at the end of the shop with tables and chairs where coffee was sold. He was hungry, so bought himself a coffee and a muffin. He sat down at a table and gazed into his coffee, contemplating yet again the predicament of his marriage. He had been thinking about the situation so much that the various elements were now beginning to possess a strangely elusive quality, like the scattered fragments of a dream. It was as though the immediate present – the corkscrew and the smell of the coffee as he sat in the cookshop, the High Street outside, the house in Lucas Grove – had grown more important. Which was absurd, because the reality of his life lay back there, bound up in Paula and the boys and his home. This was merely a brief spell in a foreign realm.

'Did you find what you wanted?' The girl in the over-sized apron was picking up empty cups from the adjacent table.

Mark glanced at her. She had a thin face, with wide brows and mouth, and wispy, brown hair that grazed her cheekbones as she leaned forward to wipe the table. Her arms were very skinny.

'Yes, thanks.' He smiled.

She returned the smile, then went away.

Mark tried to focus again on thoughts of Paula, and what to do next. His mind went blank. Then his mobile trilled and he fished it from his trouser pocket. It was Clive, het up about machines which hadn't been delivered. He was at the premises in Camberwell now. Couldn't

Craig deal with it? No, it appeared Craig couldn't. Mark spent the next ten minutes trying to resolve Clive's difficulty. It was very much like being at the office, only without the various resources he had there at his disposal.

In the end he realized he would have to go back to his rooms and dig up certain information from his laptop.

He switched off his mobile. The thin girl was there again. 'Would you like another coffee?'

'No, thanks. I'm just off.'

Mark set off up the High Street, trying to retrace his steps, getting lost once or twice, until he recognized the church in a small, sequestered square just south of Lucas Grove. He saw a traffic warden, and immediately remembered his car.

Bugger, bugger . . . He went to the car and, sure enough, he had a ticket. The only answer was to find a car park in the area, or else be clamped or towed away.

Mark got into his car and drove around the streets until he found an NCP car park in Welbeck Street. The rates, for someone who wanted to keep his car there on a semi-permanent basis, were astronomical. For the moment, however, there was nothing else he could do. Mark left the car there and walked back, thoroughly pissed off.

He spent the next two hours sitting in the rooms at the top of the house, trying to sort out the problem in Camberwell. By three o'clock Clive and his customers were in a better frame of mind. Mark sat by the open window, contemplating his laptop. What on earth had made him suppose he could distance himself from the business? He had just needed to be away from the place, the people, the claustrophobic pressure and futility . . . So how was he going to do this?

Confused and miserable, Mark clicked out of the program he had been running. The familiar form of Trikeboy came up on the desktop. Mark didn't like the image any more. It had taken on a strange, smiling malevolence, as though Little Mark had decided to surprise Big Mark out of his apologetic complacency for the ordinariness of the life that was to come, and had engineered the recent train of events with the mute malice of a ventriloquist's dummy.

Mark dug around in the overnight bag he had packed on the first night of his banishment, and found the discs his father had sent him. He slipped in a CD and went through the pictures of his youth until he found one from his university days. Himself and his friend Brian at a college disco, Christmas '82. The year of The Jam. *Beat Surrender.* He was wearing a combat jacket and his Levi's 501 originals, the jeans with the red stitching on the seams. God, he'd been proud of those. There he was with the bottoms turned up and his loafers on, pretty pissed by the looks of things. But happy. Happy and pissed and carefree. He saved the image as the background to his desktop.

That was more like it. It fitted better with his present sense of dislocation and vague defiance. Defiance? Well, he was at odds with whatever world he'd belonged to for the past twenty years. He stared at the picture, humming *A Town Like Malice* under his breath, feeling a shot of the old fire in his limbs. Brian, last heard of working as a social worker in Finchley. They'd had some laughs together back then. Good days. Times when he had felt properly himself, touched by music, not fettered by any real responsibilities. Those clothes, that hair. Eccentric, in the true sense of the word.

And here he was once again, outside the circle.

That evening he settled down in the kitchen to watch television and eat supper, feeling lonely. The idea of ringing up friends in Harlow had crossed his mind, but that would mean talking about the situation with Paula – word would have got round – and that was the last thing he wanted to do. He was the guilty party. He felt ostracized by his own behaviour. He couldn't talk to Gerry. The business stood between them, and Mark wanted no part of that at this moment.

He went to open the bottle of wine, and couldn't recall what he'd done with the corkscrew. Maybe he'd left it upstairs after he'd come back from Marylebone High Street. Upstairs he went. No, not there. He traced back over the early part of the day. The car? Possibly. In fact, almost certainly. Hadn't he driven it straight to the car park before coming back to Lucas Grove? It must be lying there in its brown paper bag on the passenger seat.

Damn.

The bottle sat smug on the table. Of course, he could easily do without, but he'd been looking forward to a couple of glasses of wine to make mellow the solitary hours till bedtime. Not only that, he'd forgotten about the other bottle, the one he'd bought for himself and Nicky, and which was still in the fridge. He couldn't have a build-up of bottles. His thoughts strayed beyond the house. What about neighbours? Ronnie the next-door neighbour would have a corkscrew.

Ronnie didn't answer his bell, so Mark assumed he was out. When he went back into the kitchen, however, he realized that the sound of a lawnmower was coming from next door. He unlocked the double doors and went out into the garden. There was a gap in the honeysuckle hedge, and through it Mark could see an elderly man in a short-sleeved shirt, stooped over an electric mower and plodding up and down his rectangle of lawn.

'Excuse me,' Mark called through the hedge. The elderly man didn't hear at first. He turned on the second shout, startled, peered about, then caught sight of Mark. He switched off the mower and approached the hedge.

'I'm sorry to bother you,' said Mark, 'but do you happen to have a corkscrew?'

'A corkscrew? Most certainly.' Ronnie disappeared into his house, and returned a moment later with one. He handed it over the fence to Mark.

'Many thanks,' said Mark. 'It's the one thing Alice doesn't seem to possess.'

'Now that does surprise me.'

'I'll let you have it back in a moment or two.'

'No, no – that's all right. You hold on to it. I'm sure I have a spare.' There was a hesitant pause. Mark really didn't want to get drawn into conversation. But it seemed rude just to go inside. Ronnie filled the pause. 'How are you settling in?'

'Very nicely, thanks.'

'Take it you have to come up to town on business?'

Mark heard his mobile trilling from the kitchen, its insistent little burble of notes rising on the evening air. Thank God. 'I'm sorry, I can hear my phone. I'd better answer it.' He held the corkscrew aloft. 'Many thanks.'

Ronnie waved the thing away with a large, wrinkled hand. 'Happy to be of assistance.'

Mark fled to the kitchen. His phone stopped. He fished it from his jacket pocket.

'1 missed call'

When he clicked to find the source of the call, it said **'home'**.

Home, thought Mark. Strange how quickly it had become his no longer. He wondered why Paula had rung. Perhaps there was some problem, and she needed him. Perhaps she'd realized how pointless this was. He pressed the recall button.

'It's me. You called me. I just missed you.'

'Oh, yes . . .' She sounded a little distracted. 'I spoke to Gerry today. He said you were taking some time off from work.'

'That's right.' Good, she was concerned, she felt she'd pushed him too far, she wanted to make amends, feel her way to a reconciliation.

'Well, I need an address for you. To send things on.

I can deal with bills and bank statements and immediate household stuff, though we'll need to come to some kind of future arrangement –'

'Paula –'

'Yes?'

'Isn't this jumping the gun a bit? I mean, how long is this separation meant to last?'

'I don't know.'

'I mean, aren't you rather overreacting, talking about future arrangements?'

'Mark, I'm not going to get into all that again. I simply rang to get your address.'

A silence elapsed. 'You can send things on to the office.'

'Gerry said you weren't going to be coming in. Can't you tell me where you're staying?'

It came back to Mark, that moment of elation when he had first discussed the rooms with Alice Kendal, the immaculate sense of anonymity, being nowhere and no one. He wanted to preserve it. That realization took him by surprise.

'No.'

There was a silence, into which suspicion seeped like a stain. Paula's voice was cold and unhappy. 'I suppose you're staying with that girl?'

'That's finished. You read the letter.'

'Really? Why won't you tell me where you are, then?'

'Because I'm not sure you care. I'm gone. Isn't that enough?'

'This is ridiculous. I simply need to send on your mail.'

'I don't want it.'

Further entreaty would involve a loss of dignity. Paula's only option was indifference. She gave a sigh. 'Fine. Have it your way. I suppose I can always ask the boys to pass things on to you. I take it you do intend to see them?'

'Of course. I told Owen I'd try to fix up something this weekend.'

'Good.'

Mark was exasperated by her tone, her insistence on hostility. 'Look, how far do you intend to take this wronged wife bit? We're not going to get anywhere if there's all this antagonism –'

Paula hung up. Mark listened to the soft purring of the line for a few seconds, then switched his phone off. He took Ronnie's corkscrew from the table, opened the wine, and poured himself a glass. It wasn't very good. And it was overpriced. He felt very unhappy. Except for the one unforeseen aspect of his situation which had emerged from his conversation with Paula.

Nobody knew where he was.

The next morning Mark's secretary had to ring him twice about sales contracts which had been mislaid. Clive, too, rang a number of times, now experiencing further problems in Camberwell. In the afternoon Gerry called. He wasn't happy.

'We can't operate like this, Mark. Either you're on the planet or you're not.'

'I'm meant to be taking some time away from the office.'

'That's the point. If you were on holiday for two weeks, we'd all know where we stood. But saying you're just going off for an indeterminate length of time is madness.'

'I don't see the problem. I've been handling things.'

'It's hardly the same as being here in the office, where people can see you and speak to you. We can't run a business indefinitely with you at the end of your mobile.'

'It's been exactly two days.'

Gerry sighed. 'Paula brought some of your mail round to the office. She says you won't tell her where you are.'

'Why should I? She kicked me out.'

'Whatever problems you and Paula have can't affect the day-to-day running of this business. You're out there somewhere, doing your thing, while I'm meant to run the show on my own, without knowing if and when you're ever coming back.'

'I'll be back. I just don't know when.'

'There are limits, Mark. There really are. I have to warn you.'

It was the closest he and Gerry had come to a row in nineteen years, and Mark didn't really care. He ended the call. He switched on his laptop, which he had taken down to the kitchen, and examined his laughing, twenty-year-old image, his faded youth frozen in eternity.

Alice Kendal came back at seven o'clock that evening. Mark was in the sitting room at the top of the house, doing no more than lying on the small sofa, which he had dragged to the other side of the room, and staring out at the sky and the rooftops, when he heard the front door open and close.

His mind spiralled back down to reality. He went downstairs. Alice Kendal was standing in the hall, her case on the floor beside her, leafing through the mail.

'Hello,' said Mark.

She glanced up. 'Hello. Why don't you make us both a cup of tea?'

Mark, diffident in the light of his recent exclusive territorial occupation, went through to the kitchen and filled the kettle.

'On second thoughts,' said Alice, following him through, 'what I'd really like is a drink.'

'There's some wine I bought,' said Mark. 'It's not very good. And there's not a lot left.'

Alice shook her head. She opened a cupboard next to the fridge and took out a bottle of whisky. 'This is more like it. Go on, you sort it out.' She handed the bottle to Mark and sat down at the kitchen table. She seemed exhausted.

Mark fetched two glasses and poured generous measures. Alice lifted hers approvingly. 'Cheers.' She knocked some back.

Mark sipped, feeling like a schoolboy waiting outside the headmaster's study.

'OK.' Alice put one elbow on the table and propped her chin on her hand. She stared at Mark with her large, luminous eyes. 'So, tell me what's been going on in your life. Why the sudden change of circumstances?'

'My wife decided she wanted a separation.'

Alice nodded. She cast her eyes down to her Scotch. 'And you didn't see this coming?'

'Maybe I should have. Please don't think I had any idea it was going to happen when I took the rooms.'

'Of course I don't think that.' Alice drank off the remains of her whisky. 'If that had been the case, you wouldn't have answered my advertisement, would you?'

'Quite. It's an unexpected development.' Mark sipped his drink. 'I'll have to look for somewhere else.'

'Not necessarily.' Alice unscrewed the cap of the bottle and poured herself another drink. Quite a large one. Mark was surprised. She offered to top his up, and he let her.

'I admit that I hadn't envisaged having anyone around at the weekends, and of course it may turn out to be a tiresome inconvenience. But you're here now. Why don't we give it a couple of weeks and see how it goes?'

Mark hadn't really thought ahead to this moment. He had assumed she would politely but firmly insist that he could only stay on the terms they had arranged, or not at all. He wasn't sure he entirely liked even the possibility of being a tiresome inconvenience. He drank a very large mouthful of whisky, and let the fire of it settle in his stomach before answering.

'I'm fine with that, if you are. How much extra do you want me to pay?'

Alice shrugged. 'Another fifty a week? The money was never the main thing, anyway.' She got up and opened the fridge. 'Have you eaten?'

'No.'

She bent to rummage. 'You don't live on much, do you?'

'I tend not to eat a great deal when I'm on my own.'

'Too lazy to cook, like most men. Like me, too.' She closed the fridge. 'If we're going to be cohabiting, we might as well get cosy straight away. I'll order a takeaway, and you can pick it up. OK?'

'OK.' Mark sat sipping his drink while she rang the local takeaway. He was surprised by how straightforward and natural it all seemed.

He said as much a couple of hours later, when the tinfoil curry debris had been cleared away, and they sat sipping more whisky. Mark was getting pleasantly pissed, and knew he would no doubt feel like hell tomorrow, but he wasn't bothered. It was like Friday nights in long-gone flatshares – too much talk, too much alcohol, too late at night. A kind of freedom.

'No, what I meant was – I feel like I've known you for years. That's a cliché, right?'

'Right. Well, you've just about told me your life story, so that's natural.'

'No. It would be natural if *you*'d told me *your* life story.'

'Some other time.' Alice had kicked off her shoes and was resting her leathery bare feet on a chair. 'So, I take it you're not just going to abandon your business?'

Mark had told Alice all that had happened over the last few weeks – all, that is, except the reason why he'd taken the rooms. He had made no direct reference to Nicky at all, merely to the fact of a passing affair which his wife had found out about.

'No. How could I do that? I mean –' He laughed. 'The business is what I'm about. I'm not about much else. Haven't really *known* anything else, for the past twenty-odd years. Except Paula and the boys.'

'And your bit on the side.'

'Oh, Christ . . . That wasn't anything. I don't think.' The small sliver of pain which was Nicky was working its way out of his system. So it had seemed over the past few days. 'No, the business is me. Me and Gerry. I just – I just don't want it right now. I don't want anything of – *that*.' He waved a hand. 'I mean, I'm waking up now, here, in your house, and I'm thinking – what's the point of me? A few weeks ago, the point was my home and my marriage and my sons and my job . . . And I could just about tell you exactly how every sodding day was going to end. And that was good. In a way. I suppose. And then something happened, and it seemed like the worst thing in the fucking world. Sorry.'

'Mmm. Interesting. So, here you are, stripped to the bare essentials.' Alice swirled the remains of her drink. 'With a bit of time on your hands. What a great opportunity.'

'How? How's that?'

'You've just been telling me how you've always been defined by this and that, job and marriage . . . Now that's gone. You can find out what you're all about, can't you? Seek out the inner man. Ha!' She laughed.

He laughed, too.

'It's all rubbish, isn't it? I should probably go back to work, try and sort my marriage out, and get on with it.'

'Probably. On the other hand.'

'On the other hand.'

'On the other hand, you could give yourself a chance.'

'To what?'

'I don't know. I don't know.' Alice rose, and bent to pick up her shoes. 'I'm going to bed. I've had a hell of a week. See you in the morning.'

She padded out of the kitchen. Mark sat with his warm whisky, pondering.

12

The boys came up to town to see Mark the following afternoon. He arranged to meet them in a cafe near Baker Street. They talked about the situation at home. Mark was anxious to know how things stood.

'Mum hasn't said what's going to happen,' said James. 'Just told us these things don't sort themselves out overnight.'

'Where are you staying?' asked Owen.

'I've got a place.'

'Can we see it?'

'There's not much point. It's just somewhere to stay. Until I come back. Until your mother has me back.'

'She talks like she might not. She's all like – "Trust isn't something you can repair", and stuff.'

'Do you hate me?' asked Mark.

'No,' said James.

'Yeah, a bit,' said Owen.

'But I think you're a prat,' added James.

'Mum says you've stopped going into work.'

'Mmm. I want a bit of time off.'

'What do you do all day?'

Mark looked from one son to the other. 'I don't know. Yet.'

The boys gazed at him, trying to work out what could possibly be connecting him to life, if it wasn't their mother, them, the office and peripheral daily minutiae. Mark sat with his coffee and his hangover, saying nothing. He had got himself into this position. From dutiful husband and father, to complete nobody. And in a way, as long as the boys were all right, he was fine with it.

They seemed to be all right. He slipped them each twenty and they floated off in the direction of Oxford Street.

'I can't get you a parking permit,' said Alice. 'Only two per household. My daughter, Lizzie, has the other.' It was Sunday evening, and Alice Kendal was getting ready to drive to Northampton to catch the ferry. 'I'd let you use hers, but she's coming back at the end of the week.' She frowned. 'She only told me last night. She's been living with friends in South Ken, but they're going abroad. So we're going to be something of a busy household.'

Mark read into this.

'I don't have to stay.'

'Don't be silly. You're all paid up in advance. Besides, I said you could.'

'But you wouldn't have advertised the rooms if you'd known your daughter was going to be around.'

'Perhaps not. But there's no guarantee that Lizzie will be around for long, anyway. There's no guarantee of anything with Lizzie.'

*

Monday morning dawned. Mark awoke in the solitude of the house and contemplated the day ahead. The week ahead. Was this an adventure, or an exercise in total futility?

He went downstairs in boxers and a T-shirt, and made himself some coffee. He wasn't hungry. After reading the remnants of yesterday's papers for three-quarters of an hour, he went back upstairs to shave and shower. In the little bathroom he contemplated the array of toiletries which he had gathered up and chucked in his bag the night he'd left. Besides shaving brush, razor and tub of shaving soap, there was cleansing scrub, pre-shave oil, post-shave cream, hydrating lotion and a detoxifying gel. The last two had been bought by Paula, and he'd only used them a couple of times, but the fact remained that they were there. His. He stared at them. What on earth was the point of all this stuff? He hadn't needed any of it twenty years ago.

Mark bunged everything, except for razor, brush and shaving soap in the little pine cupboard underneath the sink. Then he looked at himself in the mirror. He quite liked his stubble. It had defiance. Why shave, anyway, when there was no one to shave for in the day that lay ahead? No one cared what he looked like. No one was going to judge him. He splashed his face with water, cleaned his teeth, and put on jeans and a T-shirt.

He felt good, and quite unlike himself. Whoever that was. Or had been.

The day outside was sunny, promising heat, and Mark went out without any aim beyond buying a paper and seeing what happened.

The paper bought, his steps gravitated towards Marylebone High Street once again. This time its bustle and brightness didn't have the same effect on him as before. Everyone except him seemed to have purpose. He felt aimless. The notion he'd had in the bathroom earlier – that no one would look at him or judge him – seemed less liberating out here on the pavement. He passed the cookware shop and decided to go in and get a coffee. He had found on his last visit that there was something he liked about being surrounded by the paraphernalia of domesticity. It was clean and womanly, spoke of Delia and Nigella. It was comforting.

Mark sat at the back of the shop with his coffee. From time to time he looked up from his paper and surveyed the shop, watching the young, self-consciously cool customers buying poultry shears and oyster clamps and couscoussiers and croquembouche moulds without necessarily knowing what to do with them, and the well-dressed, middle-aged women with set, purposeful faces, cruising among the copper-bottomed saucepans and gravy separators with the same covetous hunger with which they must once have haunted clothes shops and boutiques.

The girl in the oversized apron passed the table. Mark caught her eye as he turned the page of his paper, and they exchanged a brief smile.

Clearing the cups and plates, Morna gave Mark another furtive glance. She'd liked him when she'd seen him last week. Today he was a bit stubbly and unkempt, which made him look younger, but he had that nice worn look that older men got at a certain point. Not old, exactly, but rough around the edges, which she liked. He had an interesting face. She hadn't expected to see him again, but she'd kept the corkscrew which he'd left behind, anyway. It was behind the till.

Mark was deep in the business pages when she touched his elbow, startling him. He looked up.

'You left this last time you were in.' Her accent was northern Irish, gentle. She handed Mark a small brown paper bag. Mark had to look inside before realizing that it contained the corkscrew.

'Oh, right . . . I thought I'd left it somewhere else. Good of you to remember. Thanks.'

'That's OK.'

Mark went back to the business pages. His false assumption about where he'd left the corkscrew made him think about the Welbeck Street car park, where his car was still housed, and how much he was paying to keep it there, and what the hell he was going to do about it. This annoyed him. He didn't want to be thinking about such a thing. He folded up his paper, drained his coffee, and left. The thin girl watched him go.

Buying his coffee had made Mark realize he was running out of cash. He'd have to find a cash machine. It was then that it occurred to him that any withdrawal he made would appear on the bank statement, and Paula would know where he was. Roughly. He felt suddenly jealous of his seclusion.

He found a branch of his bank, and went in. He set up

a new account for himself, and arranged for a transfer from his and Paula's joint account. He hesitated over the amount. He had originally intended to move only a thousand or so, but on impulse – defiance? A sense of exclusion from a home which he had largely paid for? – he transferred twenty thousand. He might be living in a bedsit, but for however long this existence was meant to last, he was buggered if he was going to subsist on meagre drawings from money which was mostly his. He would never spend it, anyway. There was nothing in his new life to spend it on. Still, having that sum of money at his immediate disposal expanded the possibilities. It might shake Paula a bit, too, if she ever came to look at the accounts. Make her wonder. Even though Mark knew that if anyone was entitled to behave in a petty, revengeful way, it wasn't him.

The sun was high and bright, and Mark could conceive of nothing to do except walk about. Little waves of panic kept rolling and curling in his stomach as he thought about home and the office and reality.

He crossed roads, he looked in shop windows, and read posters on the sides of buses and gazed up at the high plane trees and the pigeons and the sunshine, and felt as though he hardly existed. Stray words and phrases, descriptive of all he saw and felt, floated through his mind, threading themselves into tattered skeins of verse. His thoughts hadn't roamed this free, with such melodic abandon, since he was a young man. He tried to shape them into a poem, but he couldn't keep track.

He crossed another nameless road and turned a corner and saw ahead of him a large, leafy square, and office workers sitting on benches beneath the trees with their sandwiches. Mark realized it was lunchtime, and that he was hungry. There was a sandwich shop nearby, so he queued with the rest of the world and bought himself a sandwich and a drink, and went back to the square to sit on the grass and eat it. Looking round, he saw that just about everyone seemed to be solitary. A group of building workers in dusty boots sat laughing and eating together, but all the office people seemed to be on their own. Mark wondered why this was. Some had newspapers or books. They didn't look particularly lonely or unhappy. Maybe they were glad of the solitude and the sunshine.

Morna was sitting on the grass eating lunch when she saw the tall, dark man of the forgotten corkscrew come into the square. For a moment she thought he was coming towards her, but either he hadn't seen her or didn't recognize her. He sat down a few feet away on the grass. She let a couple of moments pass before speaking, taking in the look of him, his dark, thinning hair, his eyes squinting against the sunlight, the way he leaned his arms on his knees.

'Hello again.'

Mark looked to his left, not sure if someone was speaking to him or not. There, sitting with her back against the trunk of a plane tree, was the thin girl from the cookware shop. She looked different without her apron, just her T-shirt and baggy combats. She smiled. She was eating a roll.

'Are you stalking me?' asked Mark.

'Now that's funny,' said the girl in her soft Irish accent. 'I was just wondering the same about you.'

'No. I came here quite innocently. I was just walking around. To be honest, I'm not entirely sure where I am.'

'How ever can that be?' She gave him a quizzical smile. 'You're in Berkeley Square.'

'Right. I don't really know London that well.' He ate more of his sandwich. 'Well, this is something of a coincidence. If you're not following me, how come you're here, too?' He smiled to show he wasn't entirely serious.

'That's a right suspicious mind you've got. I came down in my lunch hour to see my agent.' She gestured, roll in hand. 'Her office is across the way. I ring up, but I have this idea that it's a good idea to go and show my face sometimes. Not that it seems to make much difference.'

'What kind of agent?'

'I'm an actress.'

Mark nodded. He screwed up his sandwich wrapper and drained his drink.

A silence fell between them, and beyond it the city hummed and muttered.

'What do you do?' asked the girl.

Mark said nothing for a moment. 'I don't do anything.'

'Is that right?'

For a moment he thought she had posed a moral question. He floundered, then understood, and searched for a response. 'I've only come to live here recently.'

'And you haven't a job?'

Words were still wheeling in his mind like birds. 'I'm a part-time poet.' He wasn't. Nor ever would be. It was a way of laughing at himself.

'Not much money in that.'

'I'm not too worried about money. I have enough.'

'You're lucky.' She tilted her head back and squinted up at the sunshine dancing in bright patterns through the leaves.

'Tell me what kind of an actress you are. Will I have seen you in anything?'

Morna told him about her small part in *The Bill* a year ago, and various plays and pantomimes. He watched her as she spoke, thinking how skinny she was, and how every part of her being seemed dusted with tints of brown – her hair, her thin, dry mouth, her large eyes with their papery lids. She reminded Mark of an autumn leaf. 'It's hard getting work. We're an overcrowded profession. You take what you can. I do a lot of trade exhibitions, that kind of thing. Pretty deadly.' She wiped her hands on her trousers and held out a hand. 'I'm Morna Hannon.'

Mark shook her hand. 'Mark Mason.'

'Now, that sounds like a better name for an actor than mine. So, what about you, Mark? Have you written many poems?' There was a warmth in her soft accent which invited confidence.

'Remarkably few.' When had he last ventured into verse? All of twenty-two years ago, no doubt. 'Though I was working on one half an hour ago.'

'A friend of mine writes poems. He's had a few things published in poetry magazines. He couldn't make a living out of it, mind.'

'I shouldn't think anyone can.'

'You should meet him and talk to him.' Mark nodded. A brief silence fell, and then Morna stood up. 'I've got to be getting back to the shop.'

'I'll walk with you.'

'So, do you live round here?' asked Morna, as they reached the High Street.

'Yes. I have rooms.'

'Know many people?'

'No.' Mark had to smile. How differently his circumstances appeared through her eyes. She saw him as a newcomer in need of friends, someone who needed to make sense of his situation in the neighbourhood. She didn't know that this was all temporary, a brief illusion grafted on to reality.

'Well, if you're in need of company, you can always come and join me and my friends for a drink some evening. We're usually in the Three Castles around eight.' She pointed. 'Up the top there, last road on your left before you reach the main road.'

'Thank you,' said Mark.

She said goodbye and went into the shop. A strange encounter, no question. He was like some kind of stray. New to the city, feckless, not anchored to anything. Weird, at his age.

She glanced back, and through the shop window

saw Mark take his mobile from his pocket. He strolled off up the street, talking into it. Well, he obviously had friends. He wasn't the stateless creature he made out. She wondered if he'd ever show up in the pub. Probably not.

The phone call was from Craig, very agitated. 'We've got big problems with a whole batch of balers which we've been sending out over the past six months. The power packs for the hydraulic systems are failing. We may have to recall the whole lot.' Mark endeavoured to feel concern as he assimilated this news. He let Craig babble on for a moment or two.

'You'll just have to do the best you can,' said Mark at last. He ended the call, without listening to any more of what Craig had to say. He stood at the edge of the road, thought for a few seconds, then switched his phone off. He carried on walking back to Lucas Grove.

He went straight to the room at the top of the house and switched on his laptop.

'You have 14 unread messages', his computer told him. Mark read none of them. He went straight into Microsoft Word and opened a new document. He sat thus with the blank screen before him for some length of time, occasionally glancing out of the window at the summer sky, and the contrails of jets, and the chimney pots, and endeavoured to summon back the kite tail scraps of poetry which had collected in his mind during his walk to Berkeley Square. At one point he thought he had a few, and his fingers tapped tentatively at the keyboard. But what came up on the screen was not what he wanted, nothing close to the fragments that had skimmed and soared in his heart and mind an hour before.

The medium was all wrong. It wasn't tactile enough. He needed a direct connection from his heart to his head to his hand, for the words to flow through him and on to – paper. He needed paper.

He closed the empty document. There were now eighteen new messages in his email inbox. He clicked, gazed at the list of names. One from Paula, one from his father, the rest from the office, the last four since the phone call from Craig. His father rarely emailed him. Perhaps his parents had heard about himself and Paula. He felt guilty about enough people right now without having to add them to the list. That message could stay unread. Nor had he any intention of reading messages from the office. He read Paula's. The content was to do with the renewal of her car insurance, and the whereabouts of the MOT certificate. There would be a lot more of this, thought Mark. In terms of division of labour, the payment of bills and the sorting out of insurance had always been his task. Domestic paperwork was something Paula hated. A mental picture of her – she was always her most girlish when exasperated – came to him. He brooded for a while, then tapped in a businesslike reply.

Glancing at his watch he saw that it was nearly four. He decided he would do some shopping, go back to that Waitrose on Marylebone High Street and get in some proper provisions, now that he was here for the duration.

Wheeling his trolley round the aisles gave Mark a new

sense of location. He felt the way he had when he had first gone to university. Shopping in the local supermarket was one of those grounding experiences, a way of digging oneself in. When he'd finished his shopping and was waiting in the queue, he noticed the shelves of stationery and remembered his abortive poetic attempts of a couple of hours ago. He added a packet of fibretip pens and two lined notebooks to his trolley.

Back at the house, Mark unpacked his groceries and made coffee. He would go and sit in the garden, he decided, in the warm summer air. His mind felt open and mellow, emptied of its usual burden of work-related worry and detail. A book would be a good thing. He hadn't read in a long time. He remembered the bookcase which stood in the sitting room upstairs. He went up and inspected the titles. *The Collected Poems of Philip Larkin.* That would do. Good and melancholy and middle-aged.

He took the book downstairs and sat on the small patio. After twenty minutes he heard the drilling buzz of the doorbell. For one wild and anxious moment he was fixed with the certainty that it might be Paula. Or Gerry. Or someone who had found out where he was.

He laid down his book, went through the kitchen and down the hall, and opened the door.

A girl was bent over on the doorstep, rummaging in a bag. She straightened up, pushing back strands of long, honey-blonde hair, a key in her hand. She was tall and shapely, with wide eyes and a soft, full mouth, and so lovely that it momentarily astonished Mark.

She stared at him. 'Are you Mummy's lodger?'

The word conjured up a sad, seedy individual of no fixed personality, lurking in dim attic rooms. Mark wished he'd shaved. 'I suppose I am,' he replied.

'I'm Lizzie,' added the girl. 'Can you help me with my bags?'

Mark picked up the suitcase and the overnight bag from the step, and the girl brushed past him and into the hall, where she proceeded to dump the contents of her handbag on to the hall table. She turned to Mark. 'Would you be a darling and pay the taxi? I've almost no money.'

Mark set down the cases, and felt in his pockets. He went out to the cab. A few minutes later, and twelve pounds lighter, he came back in. Lizzie, busy opening her mail, looked up and gave him a sweet smile. 'Thanks. I hope it wasn't much. I'll pay you later. Is there any tea going?'

'I'll make some,' said Mark. And so he did. He hoped she would stay around in the kitchen and talk. He wanted to be able to look at her properly, to sort out whatever it was that made her so intoxicatingly pretty. But Lizzie merely took the mug of proffered tea and said, 'Thanks. See you later.' And she went off upstairs, already answering the chime of her mobile phone.

Mark felt displaced by her arrival. He didn't feel he owned the kitchen any more. He went upstairs to his rooms. The pens and notepads he had bought earlier lay on his bed. He picked them up and went through to the sitting room and sat down at the rosewood table near the window, and opened one of the notepads. He thought for a while, and then he began to jot down a few words.

An hour later he was still there. The few words had grown to several lines, with much scoring out and rephrasing. He would look up occasionally, staring through the window at the world beyond, seeing nothing, fiddling around with images and nuances of words. He was aware of people arriving at the house, of the front door slamming, and female voices, and feet on the staircase below, but the awareness did not intrude beyond into his deeper consciousness, where his poem was being formed.

As the evening settled into dusk, he grew tired and hungry. He came to. He closed his notebook and laid down the pen. He realized that Lizzie had friends in the house, and that the voices and laughter, exclusively female, came from the kitchen. He could not intrude. Lizzie's arrival in the house had reduced his territorial occupancy alarmingly.

Mark picked up his jacket and his keys. He would go out, he would find food and drink and possibly adventure. His few hours of introversion, the effort of honing life and meaning from a collection of words, and turn them into something like poetry, had left him cleansed and awake. His mind felt supple and new, as though reborn from the mind of the old Mark.

As he put on his jacket he patted the pocket in a reflex gesture, checking for his mobile phone. He paused and drew it out, contemplated it, then switched it on. He keyed in his pincode and waited.

Nineteen missed calls, said the screen. The little message envelope winked at him, too. Somewhere out in the stratosphere, kick-stepping away, were little chorus lines of words, ready to dance into his phone and into his life at the click of a button. But he didn't intend to read any texts from anyone.

After a second's hesitation, however, he keyed 121, and put the phone to his ear. For the first time ever, as he listened to the dulcet female voice which relayed his messages, he found himself trying to picture the creature to whom such a voice might belong – a slightly breathless but composed female of twenty-two or -three, with lowered eyes and a kind, gentle expression. 'You have' – the mechanical pause gave her voice a note of sweet uncertainty, he marvelled that he had never heard it before '– six new messages.'

Gerry's voice broke the spell. 'Mark, I need to speak to you urgently. Craig told you about the problem with the balers this morning, and it's beginning to look big. These bloody Austrians claim the contract doesn't cover this problem. I really need you to get over there and see them before the end of the week –'

Mark switched his phone off. He stared at it. He laid it on the table. Then, after a moment's thought, he picked it up again and glanced round the room. A small bureau stood in the corner of the room. He went over and opened one of the empty drawers, and put his phone inside. He unplugged the charger, too, and put it in the drawer. Then he closed it, and went downstairs.

Celebrity interview question. What item do you never leave home without?

For years he had carried a mobile phone around with him, each model more sophisticated than the last, to the point where it was almost an extension of his being. He had experienced flashes of panic in the past if he left it behind. Now he felt light and free.

He walked out into the summer night, Mark III.

13

Paula was sitting in the garden with Samantha, Gerry's wife. It was six in the evening. Two large, cold glasses of white wine stood on the wrought-iron table between them.

'When was he last in touch?'

'A fortnight ago,' said Paula. 'I sent him an email asking something about the MOT on my car, and he emailed me back. And he's seen the boys. He met up with them at some cafe near Oxford Street. That's the last I heard. He seems to have his phone permanently switched off. I don't know what he's playing at. One moment I'm livid, the next I feel it's my fault. What if I sent him over the edge, kicking him out?'

'Don't go blaming yourself. You had every right to do what you did.' Sam took a hearty swig of her wine. It was deliciously cold. This was Sam's idea of a great time – sitting in pleasant surroundings, drinking alcohol and discussing someone else's problems. 'It's a petty gesture, that's all. He probably thinks he's making some sort of point. Mind you, it's driving Gerry nuts. He needed Mark last week to go to Austria to sort out some problem. He's furious at not being able to get hold of him.'

'Honestly, Sam, when I asked him to leave, I didn't think he was going to just – dump everything. I can't believe he's letting Gerry down like this. I'm really sorry.'

Sam thought it politic not to tell Paula about the threats Gerry had made about dissolving the partnership and suing Mark. Not that she entirely believed them. He was just frustrated and upset by Mark's disappearance.

'Don't be silly. He'll be back.'

'Well, that's the stupid part, isn't it? I was the one who wanted him to go. Why should I sit here worrying about where he is?'

'Maybe it's a ploy, like I said.'

'What, to make me take him back?'

'Mmm. Possibly he thinks if he leaves it long enough, then shows up, you'll be so relieved you'll forgive him.'

'In his dreams.'

'Don't you want him back, then?'

Paula sat back in her chair and picked up her glass. 'I haven't a clue. I haven't a clue about anything . . . Look, there I was until a few weeks ago, thinking we were fine – well, as fine as anyone ever is.' She stared at her untasted wine. 'And all the time, it was going on, right in the office. She was there, he fancied her.' Paula shrugged. 'Well, any man can fancy a girl. They do it all the time. Mark, Gerry – they all do. But to decide, in spite of everything you have, and the people who trust you, to do something about it?' She shook her head. 'That's the worst part. There was I, the loving wife, and all the time he wasn't even bothered about me, or the boys, or anything it might do to us. Can you imagine? He wanted her more than he cared about us. I would never have believed it of Mark. So how can I want him back, when I don't even know him? I mean, it changes everything. Everything. Doesn't it?'

'Perhaps.' Sam stroked the stem of her wine glass. She sighed. 'I know this isn't a very fashionable thing to say. Not politically correct, if you like. But there is that thing with men. I mean, I really think their brains are in their trousers half the time. If you come to think about it, it's amazing that kind of thing doesn't happen more than it does.'

'What, with Mark?'

'No,' replied Sam in mild irritation. 'With men in general. Going off the rails. Having affairs. What I'm saying is – you can decide to let it change everything. Or not. As you like. It doesn't have to. Look at it this way. You only found out after it was over. Let's say you'd never found out. Would it have made any difference? Honestly?'

'But that's not the point! I did find out!'

'Yes, but it had ended, hadn't it?'

'Well, *he* didn't end it! She did. For all I know, he might have been planning to leave me and run off with her.'

'Well, from what you've told me, and speaking to Gerry, that's not the way it sounds. I think he made a mistake. And you can make him pay for it in several ways. Kicking him out is one way. Just be careful it's not you who ends up paying the price.'

'God, Sam, I don't know what to do. I'm confused and I'm bloody miserable. And I'm still angry. *And* I don't know where he is.' She sipped sadly at her wine. 'I'm just so tired of thinking about it all.'

'Maybe you should get away for a while, try and get a clearer perspective on things.'

'You think so?' Paula regarded Sam thoughtfully. 'That's what Lorna, my boss, suggested. She has a friend with a house in the Caribbean. They go there each year, just a group of women together. She asked me if I'd like to go along.' Paula leaned her head back and stared at a plane coming in low over Harlow. 'I think I might.'

They talked around, above and below the subject until the wine was finished and a dusky edge was creeping across the garden. Sam's phone bipped. She read the message.

'That's Gerry. He's going to be home in twenty minutes. I'd better get going, put supper on.'

The two women rose and went into the house.

'How are the boys with all of this?' asked Sam.

'They're all right, so far as I can tell. James is hardly ever around. He's at some music studio or his girlfriend's most of the time. Owen's got his exams, of course. Oh, and that's another thing I'm feeling guilty about. Wrecking his tranquil home life when he's got A levels to worry about.'

'You're not the home-wrecker. Mark is. Stop beating yourself up about this. He's bound to be in touch.'

'The point is, Sam, I come out worst in all of this. I'm the one doing the worrying, and having to sort out the bills and stuff, and he's out there doing – doing God knows what. Probably having a great time. Having another affair, probably.'

When Sam had gone, Paula went back out to the garden. She sat down and gazed into the lengthening shadows. She thought about all that she'd said to Sam, and how most of it was an exaggeration, really, a way of getting her feelings out into the open. The anger she had initially felt with Mark had ebbed over the past three weeks, leaving a little scum tide of resentment. She could have handled that. She could have had him back and put his affair behind her. She didn't want her marriage to end, really. Life was too lonely and frightening without Mark. But this disappearing act of his was too much. New, small waves of a different kind of anger came lapping in with each hour that he failed to call, or answer messages.

OK, she had been the one who asked him to go.

And he had gone.

But the understanding had been, surely, that he should remain in sight, abject, supplicant, waiting for her signal. Not just vanish like this.

As she sat there, a horrifying thought bobbed into her mind from nowhere. What if something had happened to him, or he'd done something? No, that was absurd. She would know. Yet why had the thought not occurred until now? How strange that today, really, was the first day when she had had this sense of disconnection from him. Up till now, she had assumed he was out there, sulking, or playing for time, or whatever. And the boys had said he was all right when they saw him. Still, that had been two weeks ago. Paula rose from her chair. Her limbs felt cold.

She went into the house and upstairs to the study, and switched on the computer. A few moments later she was studying the bank statements online. Her hands were shaking lightly as she scrolled through the recent movements on the joint account. All the withdrawals and transactions were hers. Nothing by Mark. Oh, God – why? Then she stopped, and saw why. Two transfers caught her eye. A credit of twenty thousand pounds into the account, then straight out. Straight out to an account in Mark's sole name. Mark didn't have his own account. Nor did she. Their joint finances, both believed, were a mainstay of their marriage. What's mine is yours, and yours is mine . . .

She stared at the figures for some minutes. Her initial apprehension slowly crusted over with a hardening sense of hostility. Mark had moved funds from their deposit account and then out to a new account which he had set up in his own name. It was a new form of estrangement and betrayal. His inaccessibility, his recent silence, was part of it. He wasn't dead. He had stuffed his wallet and tiptoed away from the wreckage of a domestic crisis which he had provoked, and which he should have fought to resolve. And she had no idea where he had gone.

'He's a really weird guy.'

Lizzie was lying on a sofa, eating an apple.

'I don't think so,' said Alice. 'I quite like him. Anyway, you said you hardly ever see him.'

'Do you know what he does all day?'

'No, what?' Alice looked up.

'He watches DVDs on his laptop. He told me.'

'So?'

'Well, the man should get a life, I mean.'

'He pays the rent, and he keeps himself to himself. He's the ideal tenant.'

'Loser, more like.'

'He's a businessman. At least, that's what I understood. Runs a recycling company, or something. He took the rooms initially as a pied-à-terre from Monday to Friday, then had some kind of ruction with his wife. That's why he's here at the weekends.'

'If he's a businessman, how come he never seems to do any business?'

'Oh, I don't know. I'm not that interested.' Alice kicked off her shoes. 'I've got enough to worry about.' From her armchair she gazed thoughtfully at her daughter. 'How long are you going to be staying?'

'Not sure.' Lizzie finished her apple and chucked the core deftly into the wastepaper basket near the window. 'Until I can get some money together. Pamela has an idea she'd like to start a shop.'

'Selling what?'

'I don't know. Clothes and stuff. I said I might be interested.'

'Lizzie, you haven't any money. And besides, the last

time you decided to start a business it was a disaster. All those creditors who never got paid. It was mortifying.'

'You were the only one who was mortified. I didn't see what the big problem was. That's the whole point of a company, for God's sake. You don't have to be personally responsible for the debts. You've got no idea how business works.'

'And you have no moral centre.'

'Just as well. Slows you down.'

Alice got up and went through to the kitchen. She didn't think she could handle another protracted visit from her daughter. It wasn't just the stream of visitors and the endless phone calls. It was the fact of her. Callous and lovely. The loveliness was the worst. It chafed at Alice's soul to see that lithe young body as Lizzie sloped around, yawning, in the morning. Skin still supple and soft, hair that shone, all the effortlessness of youth. Alice would look in the mirror and see decay, fine lines, beauty on the run and almost out of sight. Lizzie, much as she loved her, was a living reproach, and one she could do without. For much of the time Alice felt she looked not bad. Then Lizzie would arrive, and Alice would feel the thickness of her hips and leatheriness of her elbows.

Mark was in the kitchen, making coffee.

'Sorry.' He did a retreating, apologetic thing with his body, though without actually moving away.

'What for? You're allowed to make coffee, Mark.'

'I don't like to get in your way at the weekends.'

'Don't worry, I don't mind. And you're not in the way.'

Alice went to the fridge and took out a half-full bottle of white wine, and poured a glass. 'Want one?' she asked.

'No, thanks. I'm OK. How was your week?'

'Very, very tiring. What about you? Busy?'

'In a way.' He stared down at his coffee, stirring it slowly. 'Busy escaping.'

Mark left and went upstairs, his mind skimming the content of his days and hours. For two weeks he had done almost nothing except go on long walks and watch films. He was a daily visitor to the local video store, and was now on pretty familiar terms with the young Cypriot guys who ran it.

He had started off with films which he had always meant to see, but had never got round to. *Judgement at Nuremberg. Serpico. Manhattan. Once Upon a Time in America. Brazil.*

Then he'd moved on to modern European: Polanski's *Knife in the Water*, Fellini's *Roma*, *Cinema Paradiso*, *Il Postino*. He watched the complete five-hour version of *Fanny and Alexander*. After a few Chabrol films he got a taste for thrillers, and he advanced to Hitchcock, watching *Frenzy*, *Vertigo*, *Suspicion* and *Rear Window* in one mammoth after-noon-to-evening session.

Then came British comedy: *The Ladykillers*, *Kind Hearts and Coronets*, *Passport to Pimlico*; Peter Sellers films, *I'm All Right Jack*, *Trial and Error*, *Two Way Stretch*. Glutted with Britishness, and needing a change, he switched to modern American films. In the past two days he had watched *Pulp Fiction*, *Mean Streets*, *Raging Bull* and *Get Shorty*.

Now Mark lay on his side on his bed, head propped on one hand, mug of coffee cradled against him with the other, and resumed watching his latest DVD. The experience reminded him of scuba-diving, immersion in a world of light and colour, with occasional returns to surface reality. He pressed the remote and dived back down into the beautiful depths. This evening he was watching *Leaving Las Vegas.* As he followed Nicolas Cage on his drink-driven slide to annihilation, it was as though the man's middle-aged despair and isolation flowed like a miasma from the screen and into Mark's soul. He lay motionless, riven, as the film played out.

As the credits rolled, he switched off his laptop and lay on his back and cried.

He cried for a long time, and when it was over, he felt softened and clean, like a tired child after a bath. He lay and stared at the ceiling and listened to the sounds of the street.

He sat up and looked at his watch. It was only half past eight.

Half past eight on a Saturday night. Roll away the years, and he would be getting ready to go out with friends, footloose, fancy-free. The ache of recollection of a youth that had flickered past and out of sight was almost physical. A whole city beyond his window was living out a Saturday night as it should be lived, and he was sitting here in this room, alone. He needed company. He needed people.

He thought about the mother and daughter downstairs.

Living with them, yet scarcely knowing them. He and Alice got on well enough. For a moment he thought about asking her to go for a drink, but there was a danger there of misconstruction. Best not.

Three times he had ventured out for a meal in the evening, and each time had ended up spending it alone. How could it be otherwise? People in London were contained, shut off, moving in their own exclusive nebulae of friends. It was hard to make contact. Mark was not adept at approaching people. He never had been. He had a sudden memory from years ago, seeing out of the corner of his eye a blonde girl sidling up, smiling tentatively, in the student union bar. Paula. He shut his eyes. Then and now, it was all so different. She didn't want him. She had made that manifest.

He stood up. This was no good. He had to go out. He couldn't face another evening within these rooms, living endless vicarious lives through a series of movies.

A light drizzle was falling as he stepped out into the street. Dusk was only just touching the edge of the sky. He walked without purpose. He paused outside the little Turkish restaurant where he had eaten a few nights ago. But he didn't really feel hungry. And that had been a lonely experience. He kept walking. He came to the High Street, and hesitated outside a noisy, bright pub. He glanced through the windows, and couldn't go in. The rain fell more heavily.

People drifted past him, couples, knots of friends, human beings with a purpose. Cars splashed by on the wet road. A Tom Waits song came into his mind, 'Looking for the Heart of Saturday Night'. That was him, but without the feel-good factor. He felt like the most solitary being on the planet.

He kept on walking, and had almost reached the end of the street when he saw the pub on the corner, the Three Castles. A sudden recollection of the girl from the cookware shop, the one he had talked to in Berkeley Square, came to him, igniting him with anxious hope. This was where she and her friends drank. They wouldn't want a sad, middle-aged bloke joining them. Would they? He could see.

He pushed open the door and went in. He glanced around the jumble of faces and figures that filled the pub and couldn't see the girl. He'd even forgotten her name. He went to the bar and ordered a drink. The barman was polite but cursory, too busy to chat. A sea of sound filled Mark's ears. Everyone knew everyone. He knew no one. He drank his drink.

Morna was on her way back from the ladies when she saw Mark. He was half-turned away, leaning on the bar. She went up and touched him on the shoulder.

He turned. A look she didn't understand broke across his features.

'Hi,' she said, and gave him her biggest smile. 'I thought you might have been in before now. Are you on your own?'

He'd forgotten how nice the soft, warm brogue of her voice was. 'Yeah. I just looked in. You know – quick drink.'

'Why don't you join us?' She indicated with her head the group of people occupying two tables in the corner. They looked young, noisy, happy.

'Are you sure?' He felt glad, but uncertain.

'Of course! Mind you get your round in, though.'

A few seconds later he was seated in the midst of a group of people. They accepted him without question. Morna made introductions over the babble of conversation. A couple of the men stretched their hands out across the table to shake his. The girls gave him a smile. Someone said Morna's name in passing, and his mind grabbed it gratefully. Of course. Morna. Morna, Morna. Mountains of Morne.

The man next to Mark, who had moved his chair round to make room, said, 'I was just telling Dave here that France have no chance against Italy. Absolutely no chance.'

And there he was, in a conversation. Football, the great leveller. He entered the debate about the current European Championship – with more diffidence than the others, since he was a newcomer – but contributed all the same. He studied the men throughout the conversation. They weren't all young. A couple were in their mid-to-late thirties, at least. He began to feel better, playing his part. After a bit he bought a round, which took two trips to the bar and left him little change out of a twenty.

The man on his left broke out of the general chat to say to Mark, 'So you're a friend of Morna's?'

'You could say that. We've only met a couple of times.' Seeing that elaboration was expected, Mark added, 'I haven't been in London long, don't know many people. Morna said I should drop in one evening.'

A hand touched his arm. Morna had come round to his side of the table, a tall, thin man in tow. 'Come on, shove up. Mark, this is my friend I told you about – Patrick the poet. Patrick, this is Mark Mason.' Patrick, who had a thick moustache and sad, amiable eyes, nodded and smiled. 'Mark writes poetry, too.'

Mark's mind flitted over the notebooks, the couple of pages of ragged verse untouched for days. 'Well, I –'

'Patrick's a great one for poetry evenings and that stuff.' She smiled at Patrick. 'Aren't you? Mark doesn't know many people hereabouts, so there you go.'

Well satisfied with her introduction, she went back to her seat at the other side of the table.

Seconds of strained silence ticked by. Patrick stared mournfully at his beer. 'So,' said Mark, 'you write poetry full time, do you?'

Patrick turned his beer glass slowly with long, bony fingers. 'No, I work at the V and A. I write in my spare time.' Patrick looked at Mark with spaniel eyes. 'What about you?'

'To be honest,' said Mark, feeling like a complete fraud, 'I haven't written a great deal.' Patrick nodded. 'I'd like to, though.' This was true. If he could hang the sky with all the images and feelings which slipped formlessly in and out of his mind through these demented days, he would be a poet indeed. 'But it's hard. Sometimes I feel as though I haven't got the heart.'

These last words seemed to animate Patrick; he looked at Mark with new interest. 'You need that. Heart.' After a moment he added, 'You should come along to one of our poetry workshops.'

A vision rose in Mark's mind of a roomful of earnest wordsmiths hewing out their verses, carpeting the floor with woodchip words and spiralling shavings of rhyme. He smiled. Patrick caught the smile, and gave Mark an anxious, enquiring look. 'I was just thinking,' responded Mark. 'Workshop. I mean, it sounds like woodwork. Crafting things.'

Patrick smiled, too. Mark felt with gratification that in some obscure way he was making a connection with Patrick. Patrick nodded. 'It's a bit like that.' He lifted his bony hands and shaped the air. 'You can feel them taking form, like a carving beneath your hands.'

They both sat nodding; the silence lengthened. Mark somehow had the feeling that conversation with Patrick involved lots of silences, so to fill it he said, 'Yeah, I'd like to come to one. To a workshop. I don't seem to be getting a lot done. I mean, I started something two weeks ago, a poem, and it went really fast at first. But now . . . you know, nothing. I can't finish it.'

'I know. That happens. It can take me a month to write just one decent verse.'

Mark could believe it. 'So, what kind of thing do you do at the V and A?'

They talked about Patrick's job, which seemed to involve humidity levels and the preservation of paintings. Eventually Patrick drained his glass and said he had to go.

'I don't know when the next poetry workshop will be. I'll find out and tell you next time you're in.'

'Thanks.' Mark raised a hand and smiled as Patrick left.

Morna slipped into Patrick's empty seat. Her large eyes were shining, as though she'd had quite a bit to drink. 'So, how are you getting on?'

'Fine.' Mark nodded, glancing around. 'Yeah, good. You have nice friends.'

'I'm glad you like them.' She sat with her chin on her hand, apparently studying Mark. 'So, what have you been up to the past couple of weeks?'

'I've been hibernating.'

'Wrong season.'

'Hiding.'

Morna sipped her Guinness. 'You're a man of mystery, right enough.' Mark hoped she wasn't going to start probing. She didn't. She said, 'You want to come in more often, now you know a few people.'

Mark nodded. Suddenly he didn't want to stay. He got up. 'Thanks. I will. I have to be off now. I'll see you soon. Thanks again.'

Morna watched him go. She couldn't work this one out at all. He was the most detached being she'd ever met. Was it right that he just spent his days making poems and walking about, like he'd said? She couldn't imagine such an existence. It was like he'd come from nowhere and was going nowhere. Yet he struck a chord. He both intrigued and touched her.

Mark felt reborn as he walked home. Three pints, a baptism. He was alone no longer. He thought about poetry workshops, about standing up in front of serious, intelligent people and sharing his poems. He imagined a world far removed from shredders and compactors, a world without the likes of Clive Pinsent and Neil Gregory, with their cheap ties and oversize watches and dodgy shoes and 'I'm mad, me!' socks. It would be a new beginning, fulfilling some of the promise of the idealistic youth on his laptop.

He put his key in the lock and went into the house. Hungry, he went into the kitchen and made himself cheese on toast. Alice came in. 'Oh, that looks so good! Put some on for Lizzie and me, and we can all watch Parkinson together. I'll open some more wine.'

So he did. With new serenity and lightness of heart he cooked everyone supper, and sat with Alice and Lizzie in their living room and watched television and shared their wine.

Alice and Lizzie were curled up on the sofa, and Mark sat in an armchair. Alice glanced at Mark and nudged a footstool in his direction. He propped his feet on it. 'Thanks.'

Both Alice and Lizzie gave him an appraising look as he sat with his long legs stretched out, his empty, crumb-strewn plate in his lap. Then they turned their gaze to the television, and sat thinking their own thoughts, while Mark fantasized about being the first poet to appear on Parkinson. Unless Betjeman or Andrew Motion had been there already.

14

The news of Mark's disappearance trickled through the corridors of Emden Environmental Services, and reached Nicky in the week before she was due to leave. How she was counting the days. She might have known someone would get wind of what was going on – *had* been going on; had *hardly* been going on – between her and Mark. That was offices for you. She couldn't take much more of the sidelong sexist banter of her male colleagues, hinting at but never quite touching on.

It was Clive Pinsent who told her. Clive the runt, anxious and insecure, always hunting on the fringes of the pack, had picked up the scent from the bigger beasts. Now he came to Nicky in her lunch hour and dropped his morsel at her feet.

'You heard the news? The boss has gone awol.' He settled his backside on one corner of Nicky's desk and swung a foot. Nicky stared dispassionately at him, thinking how stupid his hair looked, spiked up and gelled like that. 'Absent without leave.'

'I know what awol means, Clive. And I haven't a clue what you're on about.'

'Disappeared without trace. Mark. Seems Gerry's expecting to find a pile of clothes on the beach any day now.

The official story is he's on holiday, but he's completely incommunicado. Not answering his mobile or his emails. Hasn't done for a fortnight.'

'People often do that when they go on holiday, Clive. It's what a holiday's for.' Nicky, when she'd originally heard that Mark was taking some time away from the office, had assumed he was taking tactful leave of absence till she'd worked out her notice.

'No, you don't get it. He told Gerry he'd be away from the office, but he'd still be around, sort of. You know, if Gerry needed him. Then when that baler business went pear-shaped the end of the week before last, Gerry was going fucking ballistic because he couldn't get hold of Mark. Pardon my French. Even his wife hasn't a clue where he is. It's like he's vanished off the planet.'

'So, why do you think I care? I'm going to be out of here in a week, thank God.'

'Yeah, well, that's it, isn't it? Everyone knows you had a thing going with old Mark. Knocking off the boss. So, are you two running off together? You and him got some little love nest planned?'

Nicky's considering gaze rested on Clive for a long moment. 'Clive, you are such a prat. D'you know that?'

'Thanks.'

'No, really. I've been wanting to tell you that since day one. Now, get your fat little arse off my desk and fuck off.' She rose and took her jacket from the back of her chair. 'Pardon my French.'

Poor Clive.

Nicky picked up her bag and left the office. Clive might be an idiot, but she didn't doubt the truth of what he'd said. Clive didn't pick up information like that unless it was out in the general domain.

So Mark had disappeared. Was it because of their affair? She felt a chilly ripple of excitement at the thought that it had been too much for him, her ending it the way she had. She remembered the last conversation they'd had, the one in the restaurant. The way he'd looked at her. Like it was the end of the world. What if he'd gone off and done something really stupid? For the most fleeting of moments, real fear and horror gripped her empty little heart, and squeezed. The result was not guilt or anxiety. Just a pleasant twinge of vanity.

Was she to blame if Mark had fallen insanely in love with her? He'd got the entire relationship out of proportion. He should have known it was just a bit of fun, not going anywhere. She couldn't help it if she had that effect on men.

Helen of Troy, she sailed off to the sandwich bar.

Lizzie Kendal was bored. Lizzie was often bored. She led a life of almost total vacuity, though she herself would not have recognized this description. So far as lovely Lizzie was concerned, she lived a life full of meaning and significance. In the first place, almost since infancy, Lizzie had understood that to be beautiful was a kind of sufficient purpose in itself. She was not one of those women who looked in the mirror and saw a reflection of her imperfect humanity. When Lizzie looked, she saw only her own beauty, and was well satisfied.

This was Lizzie's story.

She had grown up in a world of expensive private schools, largely inhabited by creatures as lovely and as shallow as herself. Had she been born a hundred years earlier, Lizzie would have been a deb, and had a season, and broken a dozen hearts, and married well. As it was, after leaving school she spent a year in Florence ostensibly studying art history, idled a year away in a gallery in Bruton Street owned by a friend of her mother's, went to lots of clubs and parties full of rich young people, and ingested a conventional array of recreational drugs. Possessed of few emotional depths and a very high sex drive, Lizzie found her fleeting relationships with men perfectly satisfactory. She was too busy with herself to be concerned about anyone else.

Then Lizzie had made a horrid discovery. This was that her mother, contrary to Lizzie's childish assumptions, was not wealthy. Not even moderately rich. Lizzie's expensive education and peripheral pleasures had been paid for by her father, whom Alice had divorced when Lizzie was an infant. When Lizzie reached twenty-one, he regarded himself as relieved of his financial obligations, and told Alice so. Alice told Lizzie. Lizzie was appalled.

'Who's going to pay for my things?' she had asked her mother.

'No one. I certainly can't. Get a job, like everyone else.'

Lizzie had never really looked long and hard at her mother and her domestic circumstances. She did now. And she felt very bitter. She had been deceived into living a life that she had assumed was hers by right. All the other girls had money, trust funds, wealthy parents with lovely homes. Not she. What was she to do now? She couldn't just go and get an ordinary job and be a horrible, ordinary, boring person.

Nothing if not resourceful, Lizzie examined the situation and saw that she must turn her best assets into the tools of a trade. She began to seek modelling work. To her friends she pretended it was just for fun, something to keep her from being madly bored. No one knew how hard Lizzie worked at it. Her looks and natural hauteur struck a certain fashionable chord, and she was successful very quickly. She earned enough to maintain a very pleasant lifestyle, which was gratifying. It also enabled her to assume, briefly, a kind of moral high ground, from which she could pour vague scorn on the idlest of her idle rich friends. Without attaining any kind of supermodel status – being not quite skinny or ruthless enough – Lizzie enjoyed minor celebrity as an 'it' girl, and still managed to maintain her posh image.

So far, so good.

For four years Lizzie spent freely, and saved nothing. She rented an outrageously expensive little flat off Sloane Square. She bought heaps of designer clothes and shoes and bags and jewellery. She took holidays with wealthy friends that she could barely afford. In short, she behaved exactly as though money would never be in short supply.

Things began to go wrong. She put money into a disastrous night-club venture, which folded after a few months. With scrupulous amorality and the good guidance of an accountant friend, she managed to avoid her creditors, but her financial standing was badly damaged. At the same time fashion, which had once thrown a brief, kind glance in her direction, turned its gaze to the new, fresh faces of sixteen- and seventeen-year-olds. Work began to dry up. Her position was not good. In fact, it was precarious, teetering on the brink of disaster. She was forced to give up her flat and return home for a spell. And since Lizzie carried on her life in a hedonistic, late-night, car-door-banging fashion, this was hard on Alice, nursing her mother through the last stages of terminal illness.

Respite came for both Lizzie and Grandma. On her death Grandma left her only granddaughter enough money to regain her independence and move out again. Not so much money, however, as to enable Lizzie to assume her former Sloane Square lifestyle. She moved in with friends who owned a house in Redcliffe Gardens. This lasted for nine months. Then the friends, with the carelessness of easy wealth, decided to move to Monaco for a while, and Lizzie couldn't afford to rent the house alone. So back she came to Marylebone, Grandma's inheritance almost spent.

Here was she was, at the height of summer, stuck in her mother's house, with little money and scant work, while all the worthwhile people frolicked and laughed in the sunshine far away. No wonder she was bored.

The last thing Mark expected was the knock on the door. He was so immersed in the words sketched on the page before him that he literally jumped. He got up and opened the door. There stood Lizzie.

'Hi.'

'Hi,' said Mark.

Without invitation, Lizzie sauntered in. 'I haven't been up here since Grandma died.' As though that qualified her intrusion.

Mark wondered what she wanted. At least, a part of his mind did. The other, larger part was preoccupied with taking in details concerning her golden skin and soft hair. He watched as she moved round the room with a springy step, glancing at everything in a proprietorial way. 'Still spend your time watching films?'

'No. I got bored.'

'I should think you did.' She glanced at the notebook open on the table. 'What are you writing?'

It struck Mark that it was rather like having a mildly impertinent and very beautiful child break in on one's solitude. 'Nothing. Personal things.'

She looked directly at him with lustrous hazel eyes. 'You don't mind my coming up here, do you? I was just so bored downstairs.'

With instinctive good manners, Mark said he didn't

mind. Nor did he. Now that the initial irritation of the intrusion had passed, it was near to wondrous to watch her settle her lithe young body in one of the armchairs. She crossed her legs and smiled.

'You're a very strange kind of lodger.'

'Am I?'

'Mmm. Spending all day up here. What do you do?'

'I write. A bit.'

'Really? A writer? I thought you were a businessman.'

Hearing this description of himself was peculiar. It seemed to belong to some other, vaguely distant being. 'I am. Sometimes.'

'What kind?' ·

Mark sat down on the hard-backed chair next to the table. 'I run a company that provides environmental services.'

'My. I haven't a clue what that means.'

'Waste compactors. Things like that. Very boring.'

'I've no doubt.' She sighed and glanced around. 'So, what do you write about? When you're being a writer.'

Mark leaned forward, resting his forearms on his knees. He hoped his smile was polite. 'Are you really so bored that you need to come up here and interrogate me?'

'Oh, yes. Absolutely. I want to know all about you. I really am that bored.' She turned her gaze on him again. 'Alice tells me you've split up from your wife.'

Mark gave up. He was also momentarily distracted by Lizzie referring to her mother by her Christian name. 'Yes.'

'Did you just fall out, or what?'

'Why do you need to know?'

She shrugged. 'I'm curious.'

'Well, I don't really want to tell you.'

She nodded. Then, after a silence she said, 'D'you want to buy me lunch?'

Mark looked at her in surprise. 'You still owe me money, actually.'

'Do I? You should have mentioned it.'

'Hardly.'

She raised her eyebrows. 'Anyway.'

'All right. I don't think I can take much more of this.'

For a moment Lizzie thought he was talking about her, then Mark closed his notebook and she understood.

'Go on – tell me what you were writing.'

He hesitated. 'Poetry.'

Lizzie's smile was wide and beautiful. She looked genuinely thrilled. Either that, or she thought it was very funny. Mark wasn't sure which. He looked at her for a moment, then stood up. 'Come on.'

They went to a pub a couple of streets away and sat at a pavement table. Lizzie's manner was so presumptuously forthright that Mark found it easy to behave similarly. It lent everything the air of a companionable stand-off.

'You're going to have to pay for me,' said Lizzie, inspecting the menu. 'I haven't brought any money.'

'Don't you ever have any?'

'Now and again. But I spend it really fast.' She looked at Mark. 'You own your own company. You must be doing all right.'

'The two don't follow. Anyway, it's a partnership.' Thoughts of Gerry and the office flowered in his mind and then dwindled, without quite vanishing.

'Let's have a drink. I feel like some wine.'

'It makes me fall asleep in the afternoon,' said Mark, in the shadow of his last thought.

'So?' Lizzie stretched slender arms above her head, narrowing her eyes like a cat. 'I love sleeping in the afternoon. Don't you?'

Her soft lips curved in a smile. Mark looked back at the menu.

They had lunch, and a glass of wine each. Mark paid. Lizzie talked about herself, sketching her marvellous vanity and complacency with frowns and smiles and staccato movements of her hands and shoulders. It was quite ridiculous how much self-regard she had, but Mark found he didn't care. Somehow her loveliness excused it. Perhaps someone who looked the way Lizzie did couldn't help being like that. Perhaps beauty, unquestioned and accepted, corrupted in the same way as power. In fact, perhaps it *was* power. Mark thought about these things, only half-listening, not very interested in the vicissitudes of modelling life.

To Lizzie it seemed that his mute gaze betokened the usual masculine admiration. In fact, Mark was con-templating her sloping cheekbones and luminous eyes and wondering if Alice had once looked like her daughter. And whether Lizzie would one day look like Alice.

'I'm interested in your mother,' said Mark. The glance Lizzie gave him forced him to add, 'I don't mean I'm not interested in you. I was just wondering about Alice. I don't know a great deal about her.'

'Not much to tell,' said Lizzie, looking bored. 'She does this job in Brussels, or somewhere. I don't know why.'

'Earning a living, presumably.'

'She made a complete mess of her divorce from my father. I mean, if she'd done it properly, she wouldn't have to worry about a thing now. I don't understand her.'

'Who is your father?'

'My father,' said Lizzie, 'is Peter Kendal, the musician.'

'Really? Well, well.' Mark was truly astonished. 'A rock legend.'

'Rock has-been. I don't honestly like him. Not at all.' Lizzie smoothed back her hair, then spread it out, the silky strands slipping over her fingers. 'He's incredibly tight-fisted. And he has this stupid West Coast accent now. And his music sucks.'

'A lot of people would disagree with you.'

'A lot of dinosaurs might. I mean, prehistoric, or what? God.'

'So Alice was once married to Pete Kendal? That does surprise me.'

'Why?'

'Oh, I don't know. It just does.'

'She was fantastic-looking when she was young,' said

Lizzie, defensive of the credentials of her own looks. 'She was a model in the sixties. Worked with everyone – Bailey, Terence Donovan . . .'

'So that's where you get it from.' Mark smiled at her.

'Of course, the business has changed a fantastic amount since her day . . .'

Lizzie launched again into an exploration of her fascinating self, as Mark sat reflecting on Alice's life. What must it be like, he wondered, to have burned such a bright star, your youth and loveliness celebrated, and now to be middle-aged and tired and faded? And never saying a word about it. To Mark she simply was who she was. Alice didn't talk about whatever glamorous past she had once inhabited, or how she had once been married to a rock icon. Mark contemplated Lizzie, selfish and self-absorbed Lizzie, and wondered if she ever paid any heed to the possibility that she, too, would one day be like her mother. He imagined not. The young, he knew, never paid any attention to the prospect that one day they would no longer be young.

Lizzie must have realized that Mark wasn't really listening to what she was saying. She fell silent, and sighed, glancing at the people at tables nearby. Finding nothing of interest there, she returned to Mark.

'So, how long do you plan on being our lodger?'

'I have no idea. I'm not thinking ahead.'

'I can't imagine why you're there. I mean, there must be more exciting places you could be, than stuck at the top of our house.'

'I've no doubt. But it's where I am.'

'I think you're really strange. Let's have another glass of wine.'

'No. I'm going back.'

'To do what? Write more poems?' Mark didn't reply. 'I think you should write one for me.'

'I'll bet you think someone should write an entire symphony for you.'

'You're so rude, d'you know that?'

'And you're so –'

She waited. 'What?' she asked at last. He could tell from her eyes that she thought she already knew the answer.

'Good to look at.'

'Put it in a poem.' She picked up her Gucci sunglasses from the table and put them on, tilting her lovely chin complacently.

Lizzie was going shopping, so Mark walked back to the house alone. He welcomed the solitude of his rooms. On the table lay his notebook, and within its pages his poem, like a precious secret. He had never before realized how much effort it could cost to create a thing of apparent spontaneity and delicacy. As the words and lines accumulated daily, as he worked and reworked and added and subtracted, he began to feel they might actually amount to something remarkable and worthwhile.

But he didn't open the notebook. Lunch with Lizzie had chased away the muse. Instead he switched on his laptop. He went into his emails without wanting to, without knowing why. He scrolled through the accumulated messages which he had left unread for the past few weeks, all the unopened little envelopes. He looked at the list of names. They were all out there, clamouring, agitating, trying to find him and bring him back. Just two taps on the touch pad and it would all roll in on him, engulfing him with guilt. The urge to do so, brain to muscle, actually sent a tremor through his fingers and he pulled his hand away. His heart began to thud thickly in his chest, and he could feel sweat spring out on his skin. He told himself it was just the wine, and sitting out in the sun over lunch. But he knew it wasn't. He felt the familiar panic rising, and clenched and unclenched his fingers. Every muscle in his body felt unbearably tense. He got up and went through to the bedroom and lay down on the bed.

Eventually the sensation passed, and the panic subsided, and Mark lay inert and a little nauseous. He closed his eyes and slept.

He slept for over three hours, until the screeching of children passing in the street below his window woke him up. He lay listening to the shrill voices as they receded, then slowly he got to his feet and went through to his sitting room. The laptop sat open, its screen now urging him to switch to mains power to avoid losing work. He clicked out of the endless screed of emails, and back to the picture on the desktop. He contemplated his young self for some time, mind dislocated and blank. A tune crept into his head. And words. Something about a buck-toothed girl in Luxembourg. He groped for the connection and retrieved a line from a Smiths song. What a strange thing the mind was. You looked at a picture of yourself as you were back in the eighties, and the brain jukebox began a quick flick and shuffle through the archives before dropping the record on the turntable. Not even a conscious act.

He suddenly had a great longing to listen to The Smiths, to hear Morrissey's plaintive voice singing those songs about yearning and disappointment, echoing every single thing he'd felt and thought back then. He thought about his shelves of CDs back home, neatly sectioned off – pop, rock, jazz, classical – and the sub-sections placed in alphabetical order. Sad, or what? And yet he hardly ever listened to them. Not any more. Not since life and family and work had crept like ivy round his heart and choked him near to death. He hadn't even thought to cart them off with him when he left Paula.

He went out. He walked the length of Marylebone High Street but found no record shops. He walked all the way to HMV on Oxford Street. There he spent an hour combing the racks, and came out with a carrier bag of CDs. He went back to his room and emptied them out on to the bed. The Smiths, The Jam, The Pretenders – he had always fancied Chrissie Hynde, even though that kind of woman scared him – and The Specials. He turned the CD case over and examined the list of tracks. 'What I Like Most About You Is Your Girlfriend'. They weren't writing songs with titles like that any more. His heart felt warm and sad at the same time.

He slipped The Smiths disc into his laptop and lay back

on the bed, listening with closed eyes to song after song. He felt transported, light, approaching happy for the first time in weeks.

The CD ended and silence filled the room. The present rolled in on him. It was only music. It was a part of him, or had been once, but it had nothing to do with the way things were now. He thought about Morrissey, after years in the LA wilderness, asking his audience, 'Where did the years go? Why did they have to go?'

Even Morrissey no longer had the answers.

Mark lay there for a while, the past unreclaimed. He tried to shift his focus to the present, wondering how long he could go on in this limbo. He thought about Paula and the boys, and how much he missed them. Wasn't this reason enough to go back, even if Paula tried to shut him out again? But he found, as he contemplated this, that the thought of returning was a physical impossibility. The very idea tightened his limbs and set his nerves flickering once more. The music hadn't cleansed him. He felt his stomach fold in and his breathing rise. It might sicken and stifle him to go back into that office. To breathe that air and know that this was it, this was all and for ever. Or to go back to his house and let it enfold him, doors closing around him, life closing around him. To watch his sons go off into an exciting new world which was soon to discard him, and accept that it was all downhill from here on in.

He closed his eyes and concentrated on breathing deeply. His mind felt as though it was tipping like a seesaw. Gradually it came to rest.

He opened his eyes. At least here, in this shiftless, timeless state, in these silent rooms, he was in a kind of melancholy limbo. He should be feeling guilty about cutting himself off from work and his family. Well, yes, maybe he should. But guilt didn't touch him. He was numb. This isolation worked like an anaesthetic. In fact, it was like the stuff they gave you, a pre-med, that made you hope death would be like that, all woolly and soft and easy. He need make no decisions. Anything he did was of little consequence, really. And that was fine.

He lay for a long while in this vacuous state. At last he roused himself, glanced at his watch, got up and put on his jacket. He would get something to eat and go to the pub. He went just about every night. He knew people now. They knew him.

Day by day, his new existence was growing around him like a delicate shell.

15

Even though he had no intention of communicating with anyone, and despite the panic it had brought on last time, Mark found himself clicking on to his email site once more. It was a way of testing himself. The longer the list, the greater his disengagement. It was the sight of Owen's name in the list of unanswered emails that gave him pause.

He hesitated over Owen's message, then opened it. Whatever else he did to the rest of the world, he couldn't ignore his son.

'Hi, Dad. Howya doin? Have form I need you and Mum to sign for gap year trip. Can you ring or email me so I can give it to you? Really important. All the best, O.'

The message touched Mark profoundly. The tone was so careless, so devoid of anxiety or particular concern about Mark's whereabouts or doings. It was simply expressive of the blithe trust of a child – which Owen still was, even at eighteen.

Mark went to the bureau, opened the drawer, and took out his mobile phone. He placed it on the table while he plugged in the charger, and there it lay, full of reproach, his little exiled friend. Mark actually felt apologetic.

Strange, the intimacy one created with pieces of technical equipment. My buddy, the mobile phone.

He sat down and keyed in Owen's short-dial number. Owen answered. He sounded no more surprised nor relieved to hear his father's voice than if they had spoken just the day before. Mark said he'd got his message, and did Owen want to come up to town and get together, and Mark would sign the form. Owen said that would be cool. Mark told him where the Three Castles was, and they arranged to meet that evening.

Owen was already there when Mark arrived. He was sitting at a table with a pint, dark head bent over his mobile, doing a bit of texting. Mark experienced a rush of intense and exhilarating love when he saw him.

Owen looked up. 'Hi, Dad.' He put his phone in his pocket. 'Pint?'

'Don't worry, I'll get it.' He had to resist the temptation to reach out and touch Owen, stroke his hair, rub his cheek.

When he came back to the table with his drink, Owen already had the gap year form spread out on the table. His father might have been listed officially missing for a month, but Owen had his priorities.

'So, where do I sign this?'

'Here.'

Mark scribbled his name next to Paula's. The sight of their two signatures side by side, once symbolic of every joint enterprise, gave him a pang, an acute reminder of their present separateness.

Owen put the form away. He looked at his father. He noticed he was thinner, his hair somewhat longer, his chin stubbly. That, plus the T-shirt and jeans he was wearing, made him look younger. Different.

'How are you? Everyone's really worried about you. You're not answering your phone. Or your emails.'

'No.'

'How come you answered mine?'

'How come you emailed me?'

'Because I knew you'd answer.'

'There you are, then.' Mark sipped his pint. 'How did the A levels go?'

'OK. Thanks for your card.'

'Oh, you got it? Good. How's James?'

'He's fine. He's worried about you, too. Everyone is.'

'So you said.'

'So, what's going on, Dad? When are you coming back?'

'I don't know. I don't know the answer to anything right now, so don't ask me. Just tell everyone I'm fine.'

'Can't you at least let Mum know where you are?'

'Did she ask you to find out?' asked Mark. If Paula was ready to make a move, maybe that would be the best way forward. Or back. Whatever.

'No. I told her I was seeing you. She didn't say anything.'

Fine, then. She wasn't bothered. She'd wanted this separation, and now she had it. He need feel no compunction.

Mark had no idea of the bitter resentment he had aroused by moving money from the joint account.

Father and son sat silent for a moment, sipping their drinks. Then Owen spoke. 'Mum said Gerry's talking about dissolving the partnership.'

This went through Mark like a low-voltage shock. He said nothing.

Owen, his eyes on Mark's face, registered the effect of his words. 'Couldn't you just give him a call?'

Mark rubbed the stubble on his chin. He felt bad, bad, bad about Gerry. He had put the business so resolutely from his mind. Isolation had made it easy. It was remote, far away, something he had put by for a while. The idea that Gerry felt so betrayed was painful, more painful than anything to do with Paula.

'It's not something I want to talk about, I'm afraid.' There was an awkward silence. Mark swiftly changed the subject. 'So – what's the news from deepest Harlow? Give me the local gossip.'

Owen told Mark stuff about neighbours, and James's girlfriend's brother wrecking his father's car, then added, 'Mum's talking about going on holiday.'

Mark found he was mildly offended. 'Really? Where?'

'The Caribbean. With Lorna and some other people.'

It had once been a plan of Mark and Paula's to go to the Caribbean for a second honeymoon. Something they had talked about in sweet and intimate moments. They'd had those once. They really had.

'I see.' Mark brooded briefly. Then he looked at Owen. 'So, you all set for your trip? Got everything together?'

They sat talking about Owen's gap year venture to

Australia. Ten minutes later Mark saw Morna come in. She passed the table on her way to the bar, smiled and said 'hi'.

'Who's that?' asked Owen.

'Just someone I know.'

'Are you – you know, is she, like, a girlfriend, or something?'

Mark met Owen's apprehensive gaze, somewhat surprised. He and Morna often went for long walks and talks, but it was all strictly platonic. Still, what else did he expect Owen to think, after what had happened? 'No. Just a friend. One of the regulars, if you like.'

Owen absorbed this. Mark could tell he was trying to make sense of his father's existence. He shook his head. 'This is such a strange situation. You living up here. New friends, and stuff. I mean, I don't get what you do all day.'

'I write a bit. I do a lot of thinking.'

'Are you OK, though? I mean, is it, like – I don't know . . . a nervous breakdown, or something?' Owen looked suddenly anxious, like a child.

'I don't think so. I don't know what it is. But essentially I think I'm OK.' Mark leaned back in his chair. How did you explain to an eighteen-year-old what it was like to be middle-aged and look back over the trackless waste, the years of work and children, and wonder where your youth had gone? No point in trying to explain. Owen would find out soon enough.

Morna appeared at their side, drink in hand. 'Mind if I join you?' she asked Mark.

He pulled back a chair. Morna sat down and gave Owen a smile. Mark introduced them.

'Owen's going off on his gap year at the end of summer,' explained Mark.

'Is that right?' Morna sipped her lager. 'So, where are you off to?'

'Australia. Sydney first.'

'I've been to Sydney. It's fantastic. You'll have a good time.'

There was talk of Sydney, which flowed freely enough and just about disguised the unease of the situation. Then Owen drained his drink and said, 'I've got to be going. I'm meeting Bill this evening.'

'OK.' Mark got up at the same time as Owen. 'Back in a second,' he said to Morna, and walked with Owen to the door.

Outside on the pavement, Mark said, 'Tell your mum I'm fine.'

'I think you should speak to her, Dad. She doesn't let on, but I know she's – well, worried or angry, or something. I mean, I don't think you're making things any better, frankly.'

Mark said nothing for a moment. 'The point is – she doesn't want me around.'

'Yeah, but I don't think it was meant to be permanent. I don't think she meant –' Owen was at a loss. 'I mean, this is weird.' He lifted his hand in a gesture that encompassed the pub, the street, Mark's appearance, his disappearance, the whole situation.

Mark laid a hand on his shoulder. 'OK, I'll speak to her. Why don't you and James come up to town for a meal? Maybe Saturday?'

'Sure. I'll tell him.'

'I'll give you a ring.'

'OK. See you.'

Mark watched him as he walked down the High Street. Then he went back into the pub, feeling raw and anxious.

Morna was sitting, chin on hand. Her expression was gentle and considering. 'I never knew you had a son.'

Mark lifted his drink. 'Two. And a wife. You never asked.'

'When have I ever asked you a thing about yourself?'

He looked at her. 'Who or whatever you think I am, I'm not. No man of mystery. Much more boring than that.'

'Well, you know what? You're whoever you want to be. You just get on with it.' She smiled and sipped her drink. 'He's a lovely boy.'

'Yes, he is.' He glanced at Morna. 'Have you eaten?'

She shook her head. 'Just a sandwich at lunch.'

'There's a good Turkish place a couple of streets away. Come on. My treat.'

They had supper together, and talked randomly, mainly about films and a little about poetry and Morna's theatrical career and ambitions. It pleased Mark to take Morna out for a meal. Because she had been the one to rescue him, to lift him out of his solitude. He had no real understanding of how much he had grown to depend on her undemanding and gently stimulating company.

Morna had a rather clearer perception. She wasn't a girl given to easy romantic inclination, but within her lay a natural female instinct to develop empathy and affection into something stronger. Each time she was with Mark, especially alone and talking like this, the attraction grew stronger. Old he might be – anyone over forty was pushing it – but there was something in his candour, and in the displaced sense of him, which made him seem younger. Ageless. Watching his face and listening to his voice, she began to hunger for some touch, some contact.

They were talking about his poetry.

'I don't know how you can do it,' said Morna. 'Just sit alone for hours on end, you and a bit of paper. I'd be climbing the walls.'

'It doesn't feel like hours. It doesn't feel like any time at all. I'm not sure I could do it just anywhere. The place I live in – it's just a couple of rooms – they have a special quality. I don't know. I can't describe it.'

'Why don't you show me? Come on. Make us a cup of coffee. Show me the place where the muse visits you.'

Mark was momentarily nonplussed. The rooms, his refuge from reality – he couldn't imagine being there with another person. Yet Morna – Morna would be all right. Besides which, he didn't see how he could gracefully refuse.

'OK. There's not much to see.'

He took her back to number eleven, Lucas Grove. He knew Lizzie was out. He took Morna upstairs.

He flicked a switch on the wall of the sitting room, and

soft light sprang up from lamps around the room. 'Make yourself at home. I'll sort out some coffee,' said Mark.

He went down to the kitchen.

When he came back up with the coffee, Morna was sitting on the sofa. That was all. Just sitting, hands clasped, as if considering. Not that there was much else to do in that room, he realized.

'I think I see what you mean,' said Morna. 'It's a very tranquil place. It has a good atmosphere.' She looked round. 'There's not much of *you* going on in it.'

'That's the point. None of it has anything to do with me.' He sat down near her on the sofa, unselfconsciously so, but close enough to make her heart beat a little harder.

She sipped her coffee. 'So, tell me what it is you write about in your solitary hours.'

'Anything that occurs to me. Things I see in the day. People. Situations. Not everything works. Most of what I start goes nowhere. Still, it's not as though it matters. No one's paying me.'

'Is that how you rate creative output, then? Whether you'll get good money for it?'

'I suppose so, in terms of significance. Anyway, that's not quite what I meant. I do it more as a kind of therapy. Not necessarily for public consumption.'

'So you're not going to show me any of your poems?' Mark shook his head.

'What about Patrick and his poetry evenings? There must be something you're prepared to put out there.'

'Perhaps. I don't know. I probably won't, if it actually

comes to it. It's all rather personal, you see. My poems are a way of dealing with –' He paused uncertainly.

'Issues.'

'Issues. I really hate that word. I can't think of a better one right now. Yes, personal issues.'

'Such as?'

Mark looked at her, studying her gently smiling face. For a moment he considered telling her everything there was to tell. She might have answers. Morna – Morna of the brown eyes and lilting voice – was a person to confide in. But if he did that, if he let his two worlds come together, Mark knew he would be in danger of losing something before he had even found it. So he held his peace.

In the silence, with his eyes on hers, Morna thought he might reach across and touch her, kiss her. Anticipation tipped her heart.

But he did neither of those things. He simply glanced at his watch. 'Only just gone ten. We could finish this and go back for a quick drink at the Castles. What d'you think? This place is fine for writing bad verse, but not much else.'

'Yeah, OK.' She ducked her head and drank her coffee. Why could she not put out her own hand, offer herself as she wanted to? She wished she were a bolder girl.

They finished their coffee and went downstairs. Mark took the cups through to the kitchen, and as he came back along the hall to where Morna waited, the front door opened and Lizzie came in.

She regarded them both with a cool smile.

'Hello, Mark. Just off out?' Her eyes slid to Morna,

rested there for a brief, appraising moment, and then went back to Mark's face.

'Morna, Lizzie. Lizzie, Morna. Yes. We're just going down to the pub. Want to join us?'

'Love to, but no. Thanks.'

'OK.' As they passed on the way to the door, Mark added, 'You couldn't let me have the twelve quid you owe me, could you?'

She said nothing, but opened her bag, found her purse, and handed him a tenner and two pounds coins.

'Thanks,' said Mark, and smiled before closing the door behind him.

The encounter that evening, while of no apparent special significance, marked a shift in Lizzie's attitude. In the days that followed, a certain emotional pattern evolved between her and Mark, woven between points of domestic contact. They met occasionally in the kitchen, or coming and going from the house. Sometimes they talked, sometimes they indulged in mildly unkind banter, but mostly their encounters held a casual wariness.

At such moments the threads of communication lay slack.

It was when they were in the house together, but apart, that those threads grew taut and strangely vibrant.

One day as Mark sat upstairs, Lizzie broke into song in a room below, the sound sudden and careless, off-key. Mark listened, bemused. Then her voice fell silent. He knew that it was the thought of him which had made her stop. His mind seemed to connect with hers, and their thoughts lay pooled for a moment, before drifting apart. It was a while before Mark could focus properly on what he had been doing.

Another time, when Mark was coming downstairs, he stopped on the landing which overlooked the garden and saw Lizzie sunbathing on the little patch of lawn. He watched as she unhooked the top of her bikini. She put it to one side, turning, and picked up some suncream. A fractional pause in the movement told him that she had picked him up in her peripheral vision. She sprayed some lotion on to her palm and began slowly to rub it into her breasts. Mark didn't move. He couldn't have, even if he'd wanted to. The past weeks had been monastic; sex had been far from his mind. Now a heavy weight of desire filled his limbs and rooted him to the spot. He knew with utter certainty that she was aware he was watching. She stroked the skin of her breasts with slow, splaying fingers, the gentle, circling movements lifting her nipples. Everything was reduced to a lazy, erotic tableau. Mark watched. Her head was turned away, one slim brown arm raised as she performed, making a delicious pretence of being unobserved.

Mark knew, without a shadow of a doubt, that she was smiling.

He had to go upstairs and masturbate. The need was urgent and intense. Even at the instant of his solitary climax, he knew she was thinking of him. And he of her. And that she was still smiling.

He lay on the bed in the moments afterwards, and tried to give a name to the atmosphere in the silent house.

Mark met Owen and James that weekend, on Saturday evening. He took them to the Turkish restaurant in Marylebone Lane. The boys observed that the waiters greeted Mark with smiling recognition. It perplexed them that their father inhabited a new world, and inhabited it without them.

The three of them ate dinner and talked about England's progress against the West Indies at cricket, and the fallout from the European football championships. Not in the manner of circuitous small talk, but because these were serious subjects which had to be dealt with. It was only towards the end of the meal that the conversation turned to Mark's betrayal and defection. Mark could tell that the boys had already discussed the matter between themselves in depth. They spoke now with detachment and a lack of censure that impressed him. They weren't interested in moral rights or wrongs. They simply wanted to sort things out. They wanted Mark to come home.

Mark reminded the boys of the terms in which their mother had ejected him, and the fact that she had indicated the separation was indefinite, so far as she was concerned.

'Yeah, but, Dad, these things are all about negotiation,' said James. 'She was really angry with you. She had a right to be, and she had to show you. But I honestly don't think she wants you gone for good. You were meant to try and put everything right. Not disappear.'

Mark contemplated his sons, saying nothing.

'When it happened,' said Owen, 'when you left, she was all, like, it's up to your father, not me, kind of thing. We both said it was really bad, what you did, but that she should let you try to show you were sorry. And we both reckon that would have worked, if you'd given it time. But when you went off without saying anything, jacked in the business and stuff, it was like you kicked her in the teeth twice.'

Mark said nothing for a long time. Both boys studied his face anxiously, waiting.

Mark wondered if he should try to explain to them that his affair with Nicky, such as it had been, had merely been a random manifestation of something far deeper and more complex, and not the catalyst they imagined. He wondered if he should try to draw a picture of his world as it was at present. And he decided there was little point. It wasn't what they cared about. They were troubled by his desertion. They were clearly perturbed by evidence of his new and separate existence. They wanted him home.

'The thing is,' said Mark at last, glancing first at James, 'you're off to art school this autumn.' He looked now at Owen. 'And you're off on your gap year at the end of summer. Why do you care whether I come back or not?' A little part of him wondered why he was being so unnecessarily cruel.

They both looked bewildered. 'Dad,' said James, 'It would just be really stupid if you didn't. We don't want you and Mum to mess things up like this.'

'It's been really shitty without you.' Owen was fighting off tearfulness. 'Mum doesn't like it. I know she doesn't.'

Mark shrugged. 'She's happy enough to go off on holiday.'

James stared at his father, angry and exasperated. 'Oh, come on, Dad. What's she meant to do? She's had a miserable time the past few weeks.'

'She told me she never wanted to live in the same house with me.'

'That's just what she said. She'd have you back. I'm sure she would. But she can't make any moves. It's up to you now.'

'Yeah,' said Owen, 'it is.'

Silence between the three of them.

'Will you ring her?' asked James.

'I'll see,' said Mark. 'I'll see.'

In the aftermath of that conversation, Mark felt it his duty to ring Paula. If only to keep faith with the boys. As soon as he got in he took his mobile from the drawer and switched it on. He left it on the table while he crossed the room to take off his jacket and open a window. From behind him came a sudden thrumming buzz which made his heart leap. He turned and saw his mobile moving in a slow, trembling gyration on the table; he must have left the answer mode switched to vibrate. It spun to the edge and fell to the floor, where it continued its agitated buzzing like an angry insect. Trembling with panic, Mark bent to pick it up, and pressed the answer button to put it out of its misery. Even from that distance he could make out the metallic, seductive voice saying: 'You – have – twenty – one – new – messages.' He could hear in his mind the clamour of those twenty-one voices raised in rebuke and demand. He switched the phone off, and threw it back in the drawer.

The boys were one thing, but the rest of that world had to be kept at bay.

One evening the following week Mark came into the kitchen in search of his house keys. Lizzie was busy dicing and slicing.

'I'm making salad niçoise. Want some?' She seemed in a good mood, swaying and humming to music on the radio.

'No, thanks. Kind of you, but I'm going out.' Mark spotted his keys next to the radio and scooped them up.

'Not that sad pub again.'

'No, not that sad pub. A poetry workshop.'

'God, you know how to have fun. So, what do you all do? Sit around and read one another your poems?'

'I don't know. This is the first one I've been to.'

Lizzie turned, pieces of chopped tomato in her palm. She lifted one towards Mark's mouth, and he dutifully ate it. It was a small act of unconsidered intimacy, and one he found oddly arousing. He watched as she turned back to her work, hips lifting to the music.

'I'll see you later, then.'

'Bye,' said Lizzie, without looking round.

About fifteen minutes after Mark had gone, Lizzie padded upstairs to the top of the house. She tried Mark's door. He hadn't locked it. She turned the handle and went in. She stood for a few seconds looking round, savouring this secret intrusion.

She began to go through Mark's things. She did it slowly and with interest. Lizzie had been doing this kind of thing ever since boarding school. She was one of those people who always investigated her host or hostess's bathroom cabinet, or her guest's suitcases. She had to look. She had to know.

Along with trousers and jackets, she found eight suits hanging in Mark's closet. Good suits. She fingered them. She examined the ties and shirts, inspecting the labels. Designer stuff, shirts from Jermyn Street. She'd never seen him wearing any of these. Only jeans or chinos, and T-shirts or sweatshirts. Who was he kidding? More to the point, why?

And golf clubs. Golf clubs?

The bedside table was disappointing. Only a copy of poems by Philip Larkin next to a travel alarm, and nothing in the drawer. She moved on to the chest of drawers beneath the window. Socks, boxers, a few T-shirts, a couple of belts. All very boring.

She went into the sitting room and strolled around. There was almost no evidence of his inhabitancy, beyond a coffee mug and a little stack of CDs on the mantelpiece. She looked at each of these, but they told her nothing. Then she saw the laptop on the table by the window. She opened it and switched it on, but she needed his password to go any further. She switched it off and closed it, then pulled open the right-hand drawer of the rosewood table. This was more interesting. She pulled out a notebook and opened it, feeling a ripple of sly excitement. After a moment she sat down. It wasn't easy to decipher the scribbled verses, with all the scorings-out and amendments. One was about trees in a park, and another about a solitary hat in a shop window. She knew this shop; it was round the corner from Lucas Grove, on the way to Marylebone High Street. She flipped the pages, glancing at his efforts with fluctuating interest. One she came across was more arresting than the others. She read it twice. It was entitled 'Posterity'.

What do you ask of posterity, or it of you?
That words you utter now might echo in another voice
some day
in unimagined centuries,
or some small deed or thought resound in the lives of
    strangers
decades hence,
for good or ill?
Men strive and fight to outlive death,
and reach beyond the boundaries of infinite time and
    endless space
to worlds as yet unknown.
A vanity reflecting God's own pride imbues us,
lifts us,

makes us wonder
whether some watcher at the highest window of oblivion
sees our spirit cross the sky,
a tiny, tail-less comet,
sparking its brief light,
then falling black and far into the silence.

She thought it a little pretentious, but the glimpse it gave her into Mark's mind interested her. She tried to imagine Mark sitting thinking all this stuff, up here in this room. There was something sexy and intriguing about uncovering his most private thoughts. The invasion had a stealthy intimacy. She wondered what he'd be like to fuck. It wasn't the first time she'd wondered this, but something about seeing his innermost mind revealed made the whole notion more erotic and interesting. Poet-fucking. Maybe he'd write a poem about her.

She flipped slowly through the rest of the notebook, pausing now and again, then put it back. She opened the left-hand drawer, and fished through the various items it contained. Pencils, another notebook with nothing written in it, a cheque book – new, only two cheques torn out, the stubs blank – and a cash withdrawal receipt. She looked at this with considerable interest. The mini statement printed on it showed a balance of nineteen thousand, seven hundred and fifty pounds. Well, well. Someone kept a serious amount of money in their current account. Lizzie smiled. She put it back with the rest of the things and closed the drawer.

She looked round the room once more, then got up and crossed to the bureau. She opened the drawers one after the other, and found them all empty, except for the one with the mobile phone in it. Lizzie picked it up, looked at it, then returned it to the drawer.

Then she left and went downstairs.

16

At roughly the same time that Lizzie was taking the note-book from the drawer, Mark was nervously preparing to read his poem 'Posterity' aloud. He and twelve other would-be poets were seated in a semicircle on plastic chairs in the children's section of a local public library. On Patrick's instructions Mark had photocopied his poem in advance, and each member of the group had a copy.

Mark stood up. His hands were shaking. There came to him a fleeting recollection of a sales conference in Llandudno eighteen months ago, where he'd had to give an address. He'd felt scarcely any trace of nervousness then. Balers and compactors – his world. Not much imagination or effort needed there. His audience had con-sisted of assorted salesmen up for the weekend – or down, depending on how you looked at Wales – who weren't particularly bothered what Mark said to them, regarding seminars and speeches as parenthetic to their socializing and drinking.

He looked around at his audience now. Not so large, but much, much more intimidating. For a start, unlike his sales conference audience, they were listening. Mark had envisaged the poetry workshop as a loose, friendly bohemian gathering. The little group now seated in the library, ranging from young and scruffy to elderly and smartly dressed, regarded him with beady-eyed, critical intentness. Mark cleared his throat and loosened his grip on the paper to lessen the trembling, and began to read.

When he had finished, the woman who was the workshop mentor – a poet with a minor reputation, according to Patrick, and of whom Mark had never heard – nodded and smiled. Her manner was nervous and earnest, but encouraging, for which Mark was grateful. She and others had been making notes.

'So, can I invite some comments on Mark's poem? Starting with the title, perhaps?' She glanced brightly round.

A thin, grey-haired man in a denim jacket volunteered. 'I feel the title is too grand a concept – posterity. I don't see how a poem as brief as this can adequately address it. How can you possibly ask something of the future? The question, surely, is how will the future deal with you?'

Mark stared at the man. He had no idea what to say in response to this, or whether he was even meant to. An elderly woman at the end of the row leaned forward with a keen expression.

'I found everything in the poem too ethereal. There's nothing I can smell or taste, or hear or touch. Perhaps if you used the word "red" somewhere it might make it less sterile.'

The thin man glanced at his notes. 'And why does God have to come into it? Does God really have pride?'

'Perhaps he's the Old Testament God,' said Patrick.

'Possibly, but how does God advance the poem?'

The elderly woman went on, 'If not red, then perhaps some warm colour. This poem has such a cold feeling about it, except for the word "light". Perhaps you could give the light a colour, maybe a phosphorescent colour?'

A young man with an enormous beard had been staring at the photocopy of Mark's poem. He shook his head. 'The problem for me is that the poem reveals no sense of the poet. I mean – who is he? We don't know.'

Am I bloody invisible? wondered Mark.

'Well, it's obviously written from a purely male perspective.' This was a plump, middle-aged woman sitting next to Mark, dressed in combat trousers and a crop top that revealed a roll of midriff. 'Women don't obsess over notions like this.'

The man next to her tapped his lip with his pen and frowned at his copy of Mark's poem. 'If this were my poem, I would put the "Men strive" section at the beginning.'

'If this were my poem, I wouldn't have written it,' said the plump woman.

Mark felt blood surge up and into his face.

The elderly woman's musings continued. 'Perhaps if you added a smell of some sort – like sulphur, or creosote?'

A woman further along the row spoke. 'I'm sorry, but "tail-less comet" is a non-sequitur. If it doesn't have a tail, it isn't a comet. So where does the light come from?'

'It might be an asteroid,' said someone thoughtfully.

'I don't understand the reference to "our spirit". "Our"

is plural, so it should be "spirits, and comets, and lights".
Shouldn't it?'

'Well, "spirit" is obviously a religious reference.'

'It's strange you should say that, because I don't find anything religious about the poem. Sexual, yes. But nothing religious.'

Mark sat staring at the floor, his arms folded, willing this to come to an end. But the voices continued.

'I think the words are too promiscuous for the metre.'

'Well, I don't even see any metre here. I can't make the stresses fall into any pattern.'

'I feel the whole thing could do with tightening up,' said the young man with the beard. 'The progress of the poem is towards the image of this mysterious watcher and the spirit that goes out. So you could really do away with, probably, the first eleven lines and still accomplish the same thing.'

The mentor interrupted. 'Well, those are all very interesting observations. Would you like to take any of them up, Mark?'

Mark looked up. 'No.'

'Perhaps about the religious nature?'

'No, really, it's fine.' He looked round at the group. 'It's just a poem.' He thought with some longing of the vacant, bored faces of the salesmen at the conference in Llandudno.

'Well,' said the female poet tentatively, 'the purpose of the group is comment and response, to help you work on your poem. Is there nothing that's been said . . . ?'

'No. I'm not interested in changing it.'

'Perhaps if you were to consider some of the ideas that others have expressed –'

'I don't see how you can write a poem by committee.'

The group sat in silent hostility. The mentor looked uncertain.

'Very well. Thank you, Mark. We'll move on.'

'Can we do my poem next?' said the plump woman. 'I have to leave in ten minutes.'

Two hours later – two long, long hours for Mark – the group broke up. It appeared it was their custom to repair to the pub next door for a convivial drink after their workshops.

'I don't want to go for a drink,' said Mark to Patrick. 'Not with them.'

'OK,' said Patrick. 'There's another place up the road.'

They left their fellow poets and walked up the street.

'Are they all like that, these workshops?' asked Mark.

'No,' said Patrick. 'That's quite a good one. I mean, Lena's method of critique is quite kind. The focus is on response, as opposed to criticism.'

'I'm not sure I appreciate the difference. It was like being back at school. With a bunch of very savage, sophisticated kids. I honestly don't know why people subject themselves to that. Why do they?'

'Why?' They had reached the other pub, and Patrick pushed open the door. 'A variety of reasons, I suppose. Pint?'

'Thanks.'

Patrick fished out his wallet and ordered the round. He leaned on the bar as their pints were being pulled. 'The people that run the workshops are mostly poets in need of a fix of adoration. Well, esteem or deference, at any rate. As for the group, the participants –' He handed Mark his pint. 'Some of them are there to learn and improve. Others are out to impress, or to reaffirm to themselves that they're better poets than the rest. Some are just there to network.' They took their drinks to a table and sat down. Patrick pulled out a tin of rolling tobacco.

'But nobody's very good. I mean, I'm not saying my poem was that good, but some of the stuff that got read out tonight was total crap.'

Patrick smiled his sad smile as he threaded wisps of tobacco into a Rizla paper. 'Most of the people there aren't trying to get anywhere.'

'How do you mean?'

'They'll never get published. The group is just a way of being heard. No one's ever really going to succeed. That's not the point. They just want to say things, and for people to listen.' Patrick shrugged. 'And if they can pick someone else's stuff to bits at the same time, so much the better.'

'Never, ever again.' Mark took a long drink. He looked at Patrick. 'Why do you go? Why put yourself through it? Your poem was excellent, and that old bag went on about how it was too non-specific and didn't work for her. Work for her? After the load of garbage she came out with?'

'I see it's getting to you – the competitive spirit.'

'It's not what poetry should be all about.'

'What should it be about?'

Mark was silent for a moment. 'I don't know. About speaking from the heart. One's own heart. It's a personal thing. I think poetry works on a strictly adolescent level for me. It's a way of working out feelings.'

Patrick licked the edge of his roll-up, stuck it, then lit it. 'So – what was your poem all about?'

'Oh, I don't know . . . Well, yeah . . . about me, I suppose. About being an individual. What it's all about. Life. Wanting to do something significant. Not just fade away.'

'Like a burned-out star.'

'Like a burned-out star. Quite.' Mark was silent for a moment. He was thinking about all the jokey text exchanges he and Nicky had had about mid-life crises. 'I suppose I'm reappraising a lot of things. My life is in a bit of a mess at the moment, you see. I don't generally talk about it . . .' He looked up at Patrick, met the gaze of those mild, benign eyes, and realized how deeply he needed to talk about his predicament. Patrick was a chance encounter, a free-floating friend in a world which Mark had never intended to inhabit. Above all, he had not the remotest connection with Mark's past. Who better to confide in? Over the next fifteen minutes he told Patrick everything which had brought him to this point, about the affair, and Paula, and his sense of alienation from everything which had given his life momentum over the past twenty years.

By the time he had finished, he was acutely aware of his accumulated sense of desperation.

'I don't know where I want to be any more. I don't know what I want to do. I don't even know who the hell I am.'

For a moment or two Patrick was silent, absorbing all that Mark had told him. Then he spoke. 'I felt like that when I broke up with my wife. It wasn't quite the same thing, though. We had a daughter who died, and everything just fell to pieces.'

'Oh, Christ, Patrick – I had no idea. I'm so sorry. When was this?'

'Eight years ago.'

Mark's woes felt suddenly marginal in the face of such tragedy. 'And what happened? How did you sort yourself out?'

Patrick smiled sadly. He had been staring at his pint, and now he looked up at Mark. 'I don't think I did, really. It just sort of goes on for ever.'

A silence fell, and Mark considered the bleakness of what Patrick had just told him. Poor guy. To lose a child, have your world fall apart. And for everything to stay that way. With selfish inevitability, he turned these thoughts to his own predicament. What if it was to happen to him? What if it really was all over? What if Paula was going to divorce him? What if he'd pushed Gerry to the point where the partnership broke up?

What if, like Patrick, he had no world to return to?

*

When Mark got back to Lucas Grove, a taxi was waiting outside number eleven with its engine running. The driver, when he saw Mark put his key in the front door, leaned his head out and suggested that he might want to tell the young lady she'd already clocked up over eight quid in waiting time, and would she like to get a move on.

Mark went in. From the hallway and through the darkness of the kitchen he could see light glimmering in the garden. He went outside. Candles were placed around the little patio, moths fluttering in and out of their light. Lizzie was pacing the lawn, talking on her mobile. She was wearing a short dress of ethereal chiffon, and sandals of teetering delicacy which made her sway as she walked up and down. In the candlelight the skin of her arms and face had the sheen of silk. After a few moments she flipped her mobile shut.

'Your taxi driver's growing restless,' said Mark.

Lizzie turned to him with a look of cool satisfaction. 'I don't think I'll be living here much longer. Thank God.' She slipped her mobile into her bag. 'Now you can have the house all to yourself. Except for mother on weekends.'

'It won't be the same without you,' said Mark. And meant it.

'Sweet.' She picked up her bag, about to go to her taxi. As she passed Mark she paused. She put up her hand, cupped his chin in her fingers, and kissed him. The soft pressure of her mouth was startling. She took her lips from his and looked into his eyes. Then she kissed him again, and this time she opened her mouth, and the taste was of clover, honeyed and fresh. He returned the kiss. She moved away, the layers of her gauzy dress lifting like moth wings, and with a smile she slipped through the French windows into the darkness of the house.

Mark stood stock-still, his mouth tingling. He heard voices, and then the front door closing. He sat down in one of the garden chairs.

Alice's voice startled him. 'Was it really too much to ask her to make sure she doesn't wake the entire place up when she comes in later?' She stepped out on to the patio. 'Candles! How very pretty.' She sat down, pulling a chair and slipping off her shoes. She seemed tired. She said something else, but Mark didn't hear, his mind still in small pieces.

'I'm sorry?'

'I said – why don't we break out the Scotch I brought back with me? It's on the kitchen table. You get it. I'm exhausted.'

Mark went to the kitchen and fetched the duty-free Scotch and two glasses.

Lizzie had kissed him. Since the debacle of Nicky, Mark had thought that no woman would ever want him again. And this one, beautiful and young and callous, had kissed him once, and then again, with real and interested desire. Or so he had thought.

He took the bottle into the garden and poured a drink for himself and Alice.

Alice returned to her complaint. 'That girl. She bites my head off when I merely ask her to behave considerately. I wish she'd find somewhere else to live.'

'I think she has. She said something just before she went out.'

Alice paused, glass halfway to her lips. 'Has she? Oh, well.' She drank, sinking back into her chair. 'And what about you, Mark? How long are you going to hide away in my house, fighting reality?'

'Reality? I don't know what's real any more.' He thought about his poems, and the workshop earlier. Nothing was really an escape. Every escape became an existence, if you let it. If you stayed for long enough.

'What about your wife? How are things between you two?'

'Much as I left them. I haven't exactly given things a chance to change between us. She doesn't know where I am.' He thought about what Owen had said. 'She doesn't want to.'

'What about your business?'

'The same.'

Alice frowned at him over the rim of her glass. 'What have you been doing all the time you've been here?'

'As you say – hiding. Thinking. Waiting. Walking – I walk a lot. All over the place. You can just about cover London on foot, if you want to. And I've written a bit. Poems.'

'Well, it's a way of passing time. But you can't go on like that for ever.'

'I know.'

They sat in silence. Mark suddenly remembered something.

'You never told me you were married to Pete Kendal.'

'Ha. That was a long time ago. At least, it seems like a long time ago.' Alice sipped her Scotch. The expression in her eyes grew distant. 'It's hard to believe the sixties are history. They were so –' She plucked at the air for words. 'So *now*. I mean, nower than anything now.' She laughed. 'You think it's going to last for ever when you're young, don't you? I did. Lizzie does.'

Mark wasn't so sure about that. He could just see hard-hearted Lizzie, with one eye on the main chance, taking a slide rule to destiny, bringing on the nips and tucks and deftly staying one step ahead of her fate. Which, ultimately, was to be her mother. To wither and grow out of beauty like a shrivelling peach.

'She's so like me,' went on Alice, 'you wouldn't believe it.' She smiled wryly, then glanced at Mark. 'You wouldn't, would you?' Mark realized she was getting drunk quite quickly. Perhaps she'd had a few on the plane. 'I'll show you. Wait there.' Alice put down her glass and went into the house.

Mark sat among the glimmering candles. Alice came back with a large album. She sat down and hefted it between her knees, taking another greedy swig of her Scotch before starting to turn the pages.

'There.' She lifted the album, put it on the table and pushed it towards Mark. 'Nineteen sixty-six. I made the cover of *Nova*. You won't remember it. Big magazine at the time. Radical. Made *Vogue* look staid.'

Mark drew the album across the table. The girl that looked out of the picture was like Lizzie, but not like her. The shape of the face was the same, the velvety cheekbones, the full mouth and fine brows. But the eyes were full of expectancy, charged with confident hope. Lizzie's eyes were quite different. Mark gazed at the long-limbed beauty, marked out for her era by silken hair parted straight in the middle, the eyes painted with black eyeliner, the lips pearly pale. 'Wow,' he said.

'Yeah,' said Alice. 'Wow.' She gazed sadly at the photograph, then turned the pages. 'Bailey,' she remarked. 'Antonio . . .' Different images of Alice's young and fragile beauty flickered before Mark's gaze. 'I loved being beautiful. It was absolutely the point of my being. Not in a proud way, you know. Not for myself. I just loved the look on men's faces. Not men in the street. Artists, musicians. I met lots of them in the sixties. I wanted to inspire them. I wanted to make something out of my beauty, for it to last and be remembered. Modelling didn't quite do it. Not unless you were Twiggy, or Shrimpton. And even then, fashion magazines weren't exactly immortality.' She closed the album and sat back. 'When I married Kendal, I thought he might write something for me, something inspired by me, that would last for ever. Like *Layla*. I wanted to be his Patti Boyd. But Kendal didn't write anything for me.' A moth danced on the rim of her glass. Alice flicked it clumsily, and it stuttered to the table with a damaged wing.

Gold moth dust coated one side of her finger. She brushed the dying moth from the table and into the darkness, then lifted her hand to wipe whisky tears from her face, leaving a smear of moth dust on her cheek. 'I just wanted to be someone's muse, that was all. Not much to ask, would you think?'

'I don't know,' said Mark. 'I don't think you can direct inspiration.'

'It's like – It's like when I go to the National Portrait Gallery, and there are all these people, all immortalized, all painted. Modern people. Some of them I grew up with. A girl I knew was painted by Lucien Freud. And I think, why couldn't someone have painted me? Why couldn't someone just have captured what I was, and made me immortal? I knew I would never be beautiful for ever, but that way I could have been. It was all I was about, you see. Just a song, or a portrait, or a poem – just so it wouldn't all have been wasted. Loveliness is so quickly wasted. The awful thing, the most unfair thing about growing old is that inside you're still you. You're still eighteen.'

Mark knew exactly what she meant. He watched forlornly as tears trickled down her face. She didn't bother to wipe them away. 'Oh, God,' she said at last. 'I'm so stupid. Don't mind me.' She gave a gasp of sad laughter and drained her glass.

Mark closed his eyes. The Scotch was getting to him, on top of the three pints with Patrick earlier. 'I think I have to go to bed.'

He opened his eyes to find her gazing at him ruminatively over the rim over her glass. Her tears had left smudges of mascara beneath her eyes. 'You know,' she said, 'I worry about you – up there in those lonely rooms. Day after day. Night after night. What's that all about?'

'I don't know, Alice.' He was silent for a moment. 'But yes, it is lonely.'

She sighed. 'We're all lonely, though, aren't we? Lonely, lonely . . . All lonely together.' She laughed and patted Mark's hand. 'You're good company, Mark. I like you. I like finding you here when I get back.' She held out her glass. 'Come on, top me up.' Her voice was gravelly with whisky. Mark picked up the bottle and poured some into her glass. She raised it. 'Here's to you and all your problems. I hope you solve them.'

'Thank you.'

'Won't you have another?'

'No, thanks,' said Mark. 'I haven't your stamina. What I need is sleep.' He stood up. On impulse, he bent down and dropped a brief kiss on her forehead. 'Goodnight.'

She gave a murmur. 'Goodnight, Mark.'

After he had cleaned his teeth and turned off the tap, Mark stood in the bathroom and gazed at his reflection. His own moderately attractive features looked back at him – worn around the edges, a little heavy on the chin, hair receding, but not bad. He smiled in wistful amusement. He couldn't kid himself. It wasn't his looks which had inspired this sudden surge of interest in Lizzie. Maybe it was the fact that he didn't belong anywhere.

The mysterious stranger who just rode into town. The rover, the drifter. Clint Eastwood. Gary Cooper. Mark Mason, cowboy of the world of waste disposal.

Who was he kidding? He switched off the light, and went to bed.

Paula and Gerry had lunch together, to discuss Mark's disappearance. Until now there had been speculation and anxiety, telephone calls, deep and meaningful conversations between Sam and Paula, but this was a kind of summit meeting. Paula knew it was to do with the business.

'The situation's giving me serious problems, Paula. I can't carry on indefinitely like this. I need to know Mark's intentions regarding the partnership. I don't know what to tell clients, and it's bad for staff morale.'

'I know. I can imagine. But I don't know any better than you how to get hold of him. He hasn't vanished off the planet. I told you the boys saw him a week or so ago, and Owen had to get him to sign a form.'

'Why didn't you ask Owen to try and find out where he's living?'

'I'm not going to grovel, Gerry. I asked him once and he refused to tell me. All I know is he's somewhere in London. Near Regent's Park, apparently.'

'That's no good to me. He could be sitting at the next table and it wouldn't make any difference, not while he's cutting himself off completely from the business.' Paula said nothing, simply gazed at her scarcely tasted food.

'The point is, I have to start thinking about protecting the firm's interests.'

'What do you mean?'

'Well – look, under normal circumstances, when a partnership goes off the rails like this, you try and talk. But I can't talk to Mark. He doesn't answer his phone. He doesn't reply to emails. So' – Gerry drew a heavy breath – 'I may have to instruct a solicitor.'

'To do what, exactly?'

'Whatever has to be done. To go through the necessary formalities. I can't run a business with a partner who isn't there. Who may never come back. What I'm saying is – I may have to look at dissolving the partnership. It's the last thing I want, believe me.'

'Isn't that a bit drastic?' Paula felt a beat of panic in her breast. This was all becoming close and real. Her marriage, Mark's livelihood, their world, all ending. What would happen? What would she do?

'I'm not sure I have much choice – not if things go on as they are. A partnership is like a marriage. If one person walks out of it, then the other person has to decide at some point whether it's over, and if so, how to move things on, provide for the future.'

'Sounds like Mark and me.'

'I'm sorry. That was insensitive. I was just trying to make a point about the business. The point being that things can't carry on in a state of uncertainty.'

'It just seems so extreme, involving lawyers.'

'I couldn't agree more. I would like nothing better in

254

the world than to sit down with Mark and sort things out face to face. We go back a long way. He's going through a tough time, I know – you both are. I want him to see that walking away from things isn't the answer.'

'I sent him away.'

'You did what most wives would have done. You can't blame yourself.'

Both sat in sad silence. Gerry ate the remains of his lunch. Then Paula said, 'He replied to an email Owen sent him. Maybe if you sent an email from Owen's email address, he'd read it. You might be able to persuade him to talk to you.'

'I could try, but I doubt if it'll work. If he was prepared to speak to me, he'd have answered my emails, or taken my calls.' Another silence, at the end of which Gerry, with a frown of embarrassment, said, 'Look, I know this isn't a question I should be asking, but it could make a big difference to all of us. To everything. Do you plan to divorce Mark?'

'I don't have any plans where Mark's concerned. Until he comes back, until he makes contact, everything's on hold. I don't even know how I feel about him, or about us.'

'I don't want you to think my main concern is for the business, Paula. It's not. It's only part of it. I'm as worried about Mark as you are. The problem is not knowing what his mental state is. The way he's acting may have been brought on by a serious breakdown, something we don't know about.'

'According to the boys, he's perfectly fine. They said he

was a bit scruffy, and rather preoccupied, but that was all.' Paula, who had been prodding absently at her salad, laid down her fork. 'I can tell you this for free. He moved twenty thousand out of our joint account. It tells you something, doesn't it? Hardly the act of someone in the throes of a breakdown.' Her eyes filled with tears.

Gerry gazed at her in concern. 'Come on. It may mean nothing.'

'Oh, the whole thing is bloody ridiculous! He's too cowardly to face up to the mess he's made, so he runs away to hide somewhere.' Paula dabbed her eyes with her napkin. 'I don't know why I'm crying about the stupid bastard.'

'I think you do.'

Paula's brief tears subsided. 'He can't stay away for ever, Gerry. We both know that. Let me ask Owen to email him, see if he'll just talk to you, or to me, or to anyone. Don't do anything about lawyers till then. Please. OK?'

Gerry sighed. 'OK.'

Gerry sat at his desk. Neil Gregory sat opposite, bulky and concerned.

'I think Mark has some kind of problem,' said Gerry. 'I don't want to do anything drastic, but I think I'm going to have to if I can't get hold of him.' He sat back, sighing. 'I've sent an email from his son's email address. Maybe he'll answer that. But I doubt it. Here' – he slid a sheaf of sales figures across the desk to Neil – 'you'd better look at these in the meantime.'

The following day Neil visited the south-east sales office. Nicky was clearing her desk.

'Last day?'

'Yeah,' said Nicky. 'Finally. I'm having a drink round the corner at half five, if you fancy coming along.'

'Can't say I blame you for leaving. There'll be others following suit soon enough.'

'How d'you mean?'

Neil gave a sigh. 'Partnership problems. Gerry's just about given up on Mark. No sight nor sound from him in weeks. God knows what it means for the firm's future. You're probably getting out at just the right time.'

Nicky paused in the act of clearing her belongings. Information from Clive was one thing, but it was quite another for Neil to talk in this way.

'Anyway,' said Neil, 'see you later for that drink.' And he left.

Nicky sat at her desk, pondering. She felt responsible, in a way. Something had pushed Mark over the edge, and she'd been part of it. He was a silly sod. She thought about the last time they'd been alone together, lying on the bed in that funny house, listening to him talk, while she wished her godawful period pains would go away. And it came to her. That was where he was. Nobody else knew about those rooms in that house, except her.

After a few seconds' doubt and hesitation, she picked up the phone, and with a bravery that cost her some effort, rang Mark's wife.

17

A few days later, midweek. Mark woke. It was eleven twenty. He had spent the previous evening in the pub with Morna and others, drinking and talking. He lay watching the curtains shift in the mid-morning air, feeling lousy. Too old to be drinking like a teenager.

The house was quiet. Alice was with her school of businessmen in Luxembourg. And Lizzie? Perhaps she had already packed her bags and gone wherever it was she was going. He hoped not. She wasn't the most harmonious companion he had ever had, but he liked her vexing presence. He thought maybe he was a little in love with her.

He got up and went through to the sitting room. The contrast between his inert world and the busy life that lay somewhere in the streets beyond was profound. To fend off his hangover melancholy he switched on his laptop. The desktop image of himself in his student days was no longer inspiring. It was deeply depressing. He went into his messages. The flow of new messages had dried to a trickle. Only one in the last two days, and that was from Owen. He opened it.

It wasn't from Owen. He read it before he could help himself.

'Mark, bugger the business. Just talk to me. Gerry.'

The pathos of this hit Mark hard. He could just see Gerry, eyes anxious behind the big glasses, agonizing over what to say, the way he always did when some client was being difficult or there was some tricky problem. 'Oh, fuck it, Mark, I don't know how to write this.' And Mark would suggest, and Gerry would tap it out, and together they would find whatever words were needed. Poor Gerry, all on his own, could do no more than this.

Mark couldn't face it. He shut down the computer, pulled on his jacket, and left the house. Long walks were now habitual with him. Mostly they helped to free his mind, the pavements and the railings and shop fronts and trees slipping past while his thoughts floated into a realm of poems and fantasies. Up, up and away. Not today. His conscience was stuck fast to Gerry's text.

He trod the streets for some time, thinking back over the years, starting up the business, their first, cramped offices, the bank loan they thought they would never pay back, their early successes, their near-disasters, their gradual ascent from small to big, from modest beginnings to their present success. He realized he had never really given much thought, in all these years, to his feelings towards Gerry. He took him for granted. Everything about him. His energy, his ambition, his frequent outbursts of exasperation and ebullient good humour. Above all, his industry. His assumption that Emden Environmental Services was worth a lifetime's work and devotion. Gerry's loyalty to the business, and to Mark, had always been unquestioning. Gerry, in the office come what may, making the same assumptions about Mark.

Only Mark had let him down.

All the guilt and remorse which he had seemed incapable of feeling now flooded him. He stopped on the pavement and stood still. Though neither of them would ever have used the word, a lot of love existed between himself and Gerry. He only saw it now, and the enormity of his betrayal hit him hard.

He looked up at the sky. It didn't necessarily mean anything if he rang Gerry. It didn't take him back there. It was simply the least he could do.

Mark returned to the house and went upstairs. From the bureau drawer he took out his mobile phone. He plugged in the charger and, after a moment's hesitation, keyed in Gerry's number. When Gerry answered, Mark almost hung up. But didn't.

'Gerry,' he said.

'Mark.' Gerry's voice was poised between astonishment and relief. 'Mark, hi.'

'Hi.' Mark sat down in an armchair and turned his gaze to the window.

Gerry's voice was tentative, careful. 'How are you?'

'So-so.'

There was a silence. 'I think,' said Gerry in the tone of one not wishing to alarm, 'that we need to talk.'

In Mark's mind the structure that was the last five

weeks grew suddenly fragile, almost non-existent. 'You want to dissolve the partnership,' said Mark.

'No,' said Gerry at length. 'No, I don't. Quite the opposite, in fact.' Mark's eye traced the line of the rooftops beyond the window. 'I think the same goes for Paula. I don't know what's been happening with you, Mark, but you've really got to start talking to us.'

Long seconds ticked by.

'OK.' He owed Gerry that much.

'I have to come up to London tomorrow. I'm seeing Barry Cooper from Maybrick's. I could come across when I've finished. Paula says you're somewhere near Marylebone.'

'No,' said Mark quickly. 'That's OK. I'll come to you.' He knew Maybrick's, a retail outlet over in Elephant and Castle. He knew Barry Cooper. Part of the other world. No saying he would go back there. 'There's a hotel near the War Museum.'

'Where they had that health and safety seminar? Yeah, I know the one. The Bedford.'

'I'll see you there about six. In the bar.'

'OK.' Gerry was hesitant. Such a straightforward arrangement. He'd thought it would all be more difficult. 'See you then.' He put down the phone. He thought he knew why Mark's manner had been so direct. Mark wanted no further part of the business. That was probably what he was going to tell Gerry tomorrow. Gerry reflected on this with a heavy heart. End of an era. At least he would know where he stood. If it were true, he wondered what it would mean for Paula.

Mark went for a walk. He went to Marylebone High Street, and to the cookware shop. 'When do you get off for lunch?' he asked Morna.

'Ten minutes.'

'Come for a walk. I need to talk to you.'

They walked together to Berkeley Square. 'What did you want to talk about?' asked Morna.

'Let's get some lunch. Then I'll tell you.'

'You pay and I'll get it,' said Morna.

Mark gave her a tenner. He lay on the grass beneath the shade of the trees and closed his eyes. He opened them a few minutes later to find her standing over him.

'What's that?' He raised a hand to shade his eyes.

'My digital camera. I thought I'd take some photos of the sleeping poet.'

'Yeah, right.'

He sat up and she tossed him a packet of sandwiches. 'Come on, then. Let's hear what you've got to say.'

They sat in the dappled sunshine, and Mark told Morna about Paula and Nicky, and the business, and Gerry – all that he'd done.

'I'm not a poet. I sell waste compactors. That's all I've ever done in my stupid fucking grown-up life. I'm a boring businessman.'

Morna, who had listened in silence, said bleakly, 'You're a coward, is what you are.'

'Yeah.' Mark nodded. 'That's right.'

'You abandoned everyone.'

'My wife has no idea where I am.'

Heartsore, thought Morna. This is what it means. She didn't want Mark to be married, or part of anyone else. She'd realized there was a wife somewhere around the day she'd met Mark's son, but she'd hoped it was somewhere dim and distant. All this had happened in a mere matter of weeks. He was that close to going back, she could tell.

'Do you love her?'

Mark glanced at Morna and chucked another piece of his sandwich at a pigeon, trying to hit it.

'Yes. But things change. She changed. She *really* changed.'

'How?'

A surprising image came to Mark's mind. 'She got bigger.'

'What? You mean, like, fat?'

'No. In every way except that. She got this job, and her personality sort of – expanded. She used to be Paula, my wife, looking after us all – me, the boys, the house, all that. Now she's Paula the businesswoman. Everything about her is much larger. Her hair, for instance' – Mark was warming to his analogy – 'every morning she blow-dries it, and it's all –' He made an inflating gesture with his hands. 'And nails. She's started wearing false nails. Why? Why does she feel she has to grow wildly in every direction?' He realized Morna had begun to giggle, rolling over face-down on the grass, and he laughed, too. 'No,

I'm serious. Heels. High heels. All the time. Well, most of the time. She's even expanding upwards.'

'Honest to God, you make it sound like one of those old sci-fi movies. Oversize, rampaging woman stalks the streets, terrorizing the populace, and her husband in particular.' Morna began laughing helplessly again.

'She's always so – so perfectly turned-out, and so bloody *busy*, tearing around the place. I feel like I'm caught up in the slipstream.' He plucked blades of grass. 'Bobbing along in her wake.'

Morna's laughter died away to a smile. Lying on her stomach, she looked up at Mark. 'Do you like the way she looks? Is it sexy?'

'Sexy? In a way, I suppose. But it doesn't really matter what I think. It's not done for my benefit. She's doing it for the world at large, not me.' Mark crumpled up his sandwich packet. 'Sunbeds. That's another thing.'

'Did you like the way she looked before? I mean, did you prefer it?'

'It's not so much to do with the way she looks. That's just part of it. But – yes. I suppose I did. She looked sort of – simpler. She didn't do stuff with her hair that much, or wear make-up, unless we were going out somewhere. Everything about her seems to have got more complicated. That's the only way I can put it. More extreme. She's all out there' – Mark gestured towards the wider world – 'instead of –'

'At home for you.'

'That's not what bothers me.'

'OK, let's look at this objectively. How old is she?'

'Forty-three. Same as me.'

'And your sons are – how old? Eighteen? Nineteen?'

'About that. James is twenty in October.'

'So, all your wife – what's her name? Paula? All Paula's ever done, since she was twenty-one or so, is marry you, have your children, and look after you. And now your boys are grown up, she wants to make something more of her life. And you don't like it. You feel you're losing control of her.'

'I never did control her. I'm not that kind of man.'

'You may not think you are, but you are. You feel threatened by what's happening. You want her to go back to the way she was, so you can be in control again.'

'Psychobabble. Total crap.'

'My God, but you need a good slap! Do you never talk to the woman? Do you ever tell her you don't like the way she's changed?'

'I've tried. I've told her she doesn't need to do all this. She doesn't even need the job. I earn more than enough for all of us.'

'Not in the last five weeks you haven't. And for God's sake – weren't you the one who had an affair? Now, how secure does that make any woman feel? You could be off with some piece of totty, and bang, there goes everything. What makes you think any woman nowadays is going to sit around relying on her husband to bring in the money?

The way marriages are these days, every woman has to look out for herself.'

Mark couldn't help smiling at the way Morna's northern Irish brogue grew stronger the more heated she became.

'And what in God's name are you smiling for? She's proved she was right to go out and get a job. She can't trust you, can she?'

'So, what are you saying? That I feel emasculated by the fact that she goes out to work, and I want her back in the kitchen so I can feel better about myself?'

'Something like that. Have you never thought that maybe one of the reasons you had this daft affair, or whatever it was, is that you felt sexually threatened? She's done a bit of growing up, and you feel sidelined. So off you go and screw your secretary.'

'Not my secretary.'

'Whatever.'

Mark stared into the distance, thinking about Nicky. She seemed nothing more than a cipher now. But perhaps there was some truth in what Morna said. Mixed up with the desire to rediscover his romantic, lost youth there had been a definite sense of resentment, of his displacement in Paula's world by other things.

'I am a pathetically weak individual,' said Mark at length. 'Amn't I?'

'You are, right enough. But I love you.' She uttered the words mildly, a joking aside to exasperation. And Mark took them as such.

'No, you don't. You despise me. I despise me.'

There was silence for a moment. Morna lay staring at the blades of grass, while Mark continued to chuck bits of sandwich at the pigeons. Morna looked up and said with simple suddenness, 'I'm leaving London soon.'

'Oh?' Mark was disconcerted.

'I'm joining a theatre group, travelling round England. Compact History, it's called. Saul and Liam are coming, too.' These were people Mark knew from the pub, actor friends of Morna's.

'I'll be sorry to lose you.'

'You make me sound like I work for you. Anyway,' she sighed, 'you'll be off home to your wife, see if you won't.'

'Will I?' Mark squinted up at the sky through the shifting layers of foliage. A gust of wind stirred the air, and all over the square large, curling leaves drifted down from the plane trees, the first of late summer.

'If you've any sense.'

'I think I've lost most of that.'

'Or,' said Morna quietly, not looking at him, 'you could carry on your wild adventure. Your voyage of self-discovery.'

'How would that be?'

'You could come with Saul and Liam and me.'

Mark laughed. 'I'm not an actor. In fact, I'm really bad at it.'

'You can drive a van. You can shift scenery. You can do lots of things.' She looked at him now. He met her gaze.

'You mean, I can keep on running.'

'If you like.'

He shook his head at the impossibility of it. But he felt in his stomach a little twist of excitement. The idea of moving on . . . No money, but how much money did he need, anyway? His solitary existence of the last few weeks had cost him little, except in rent, and that bloody car park. He could sell the car. Paula could have the house, have half of everything, have her life.

He didn't know what he felt, or what he thought. He looked back at Morna.

'You're a true friend, you know that?'

'What? You think I've got your best interests at heart?' She smiled wryly. 'If that was the case, I'd be packing your bags for you and sending you off home.'

She stood up. 'Come on, I need to get back. And you' – she looked down at Mark, still sitting on the grass – 'you need to work out where you're going.'

Mark stood in front of the closet, contemplating the row of suits hanging there. They hardly seemed part of him any more. Nonetheless, he would wear one today. He couldn't turn up at the Bedford in jeans and T-shirt. However things might turn out, this was still a business meeting. He selected a light grey Armani suit which he had always liked, and a blue silk tie, and laid them on the bed.

He would need to iron a shirt. In the weeks he had lived in the house, he had never had occasion to iron anything. He had grown accustomed to, and rather fond of, his rumpled and creased existence. He went downstairs.

He was banging through cupboards, building up the same amount of frustration as he had over the corkscrew, when he heard the front door open and close. He looked out into the hallway and saw Lizzie.

'I thought you'd gone.'

Lizzie did two things – two careless and curiously arousing things. She reached down and slipped off her high-heeled sandals, and kicked them aside, and then lifted a hand to unpin her hair, letting it slide softly to her shoulders. She shook her head back and looked at Mark with her beautiful, heedless eyes.

'No. I'm moving out tomorrow. Why?'

'You've been gone for three nights.'

'Who's counting?' She brushed past him on her way to the kitchen. Mark resumed his search in the cupboard under the stairs.

'What are you looking for?' asked Lizzie.

'An ironing board.'

'It's in my room.' She opened the fridge and took out a bottle of mineral water, and swigged straight from it. She stood in her bare feet, looking at him. 'What do you want it for?'

'I need to iron a shirt.'

She shrugged. 'You can come and take it away. The iron's not very good.'

They went upstairs to her room, and Lizzie folded up the ironing board and gave it to Mark.

'Can you lend me some money?' she asked, as he was about to leave.

Mark turned. 'How much?'

Lizzie looked indifferent. 'A few thousand. Ten would be nice.'

Mark just managed not to laugh. 'What do you need it for?'

She turned away. 'Forget it. I don't know why I asked.'

Mark took the ironing board away. He ironed his shirt. Then he had a shower and washed his hair. He considered shaving – he had left it two days – but decided not to. Whatever other concessions he was making, he liked to feel this sad edge of defiance. As he tied his tie, fingering the embossed silk, he realized he had missed the cool gratification of slipping into a freshly ironed shirt and a smart suit. Feeble but cherished pleasures. Shoes, instead of trainers, were a bit of a relief, too.

He went downstairs, and was standing in the hall checking through his wallet when Lizzie sauntered out of the kitchen, eating a peach. She contemplated him.

'You scrub up nicely.'

'Kind of you to say so.' Mark didn't look up. Thirty-five quid, enough for the cab fare and a couple of rounds.

She came down the hall towards him. She put out her hand and he glanced up, expecting her to pick some unseen thread or fluff from his suit, but instead, in one of her strange, intimate gestures, she lightly brushed the hair back from his temples. She was so close that he could

270

smell peach on her breath. For a moment, as he looked into her eyes, he thought she was going to kiss him again, but she merely surveyed him critically.

'What's the big occasion?'

'Business.'

She turned away. 'Have fun.'

Mark went out. It had occurred to him that he could drive to meet Gerry, but he found he had no wish to get into the Jag. Or even go near it. The idea had been to take a taxi, but as he walked down the street he decided, since he had time in hand, to walk instead. He had done plenty of walking over the past few weeks, and found it soothing and mind-emptying.

He strode out in a south-easterly direction through Cavendish Square, across Oxford Street, and down Regent Street to Piccadilly Circus. He walked to the National Gallery, through Trafalgar Square and down to the river, across Hungerford Bridge, then followed the grim, grimy Waterloo Road all the way to the War Museum. During his perambulations of the past weeks he had become pretty well acquainted with the central topography of the city, and only had to ask twice for directions.

His mind did not empty itself as easily as he had hoped. He found himself thinking, as he walked, about his conversation with Morna. He wondered if there was any truth in all the stuff she had said about controlling. He tried to think back to his feelings in the time leading up to his defection. His betrayal. His affair. His adventure. His folly. Yes, he had tried to re-establish contact with Paula, to summon back an intimacy which he felt they had lost. He could fairly say that. But at the same time he had been complaining, in an oblique way, about the amount of attention which her job diverted away from him. He found it hard to work out exactly what it was he wanted, then or now.

The Bedford, which he had last visited over a year ago, was a seventies hotel with all the decade's seedy strivings towards smartness. It should have been depressing simply to step inside, but Mark had been in so many hotels of the same kind that it was rather like coming home. He wasn't aware of this. He made his way to the bar on the first floor. His walk had made him a little late. Gerry was already there, sitting at a table, polishing his glasses with a tissue, his briefcase on the floor beside him. The bar was busy, full of men in suits enjoying the end of a working day.

Gerry saw Mark crossing the bar, and got up.

'Hi,' said Mark. They shook hands. 'Drink?'

'I'll have a Scotch. Thanks.'

Gerry kept an uneasy eye on Mark as he bought the drinks. Mark looked somewhat different, and it wasn't just the longer hair and two-day stubble. He had a detached quality about him, as though he wasn't properly part of his surroundings.

Mark sat down with the drinks.

'Cheers,' said Gerry.

'Cheers.' Mark didn't drink. He sat staring at his drink, turning the glass slowly on the beer mat. Then he looked up at Gerry. 'What happened about the baler problem? I'm sorry I landed you with that.'

Gerry shrugged. 'Craig went out to Austria and sorted it out. In the short-term, at least. They've accepted liability. It's still a bit of a headache, though.' There was silence for a few moments. 'So – what's been going on, Mark?' Gerry asked at last. His eyes behind his thick glasses were strained and anxious.

'I don't know. I just needed to get away from everything. I haven't got a good explanation.'

'What the hell have you been doing all the time you've been away? Where are you living?'

Mark took a large swallow of his Scotch. He put down his glass, folded his hands, and told Gerry, as exactly as he could, what he had been doing – the isolation, the poetry, the endless movies, the walking, the nomadic contacts. It took ten full minutes to describe the entire circumstances of his present existence.

'Why did you just vanish? What was it for?'

'I thought maybe I'd find some kind of answer.'

'To what?'

'To things. To the feeling I had that wherever I was in life wasn't where I wanted to be. That I'd missed something.'

'And?'

Mark looked up from the bowl of peanuts which he had been contemplating. 'What? Did I?' He looked back at the peanuts, picked up a small handful. They tasted slightly stale. 'It's been different.' His thoughts moved at glancing speed across people and moments of the past few weeks. Different could quickly become the same, if you let it. He looked back at Gerry. 'How's the business?'

As he asked the question, Mark realized that the idea of the office wasn't setting off the usual queasy panic. He felt anxious, but it was because he genuinely wanted to know. He needed to find out how bad he'd made things.

'Not – not great,' said Gerry, looking down at his drink. 'To be honest, sales figures should be much higher. Much higher.' He shook his head.

Mark said nothing. He was to blame. Unless he did something about it, things would continue to get worse.

Gerry stared sadly at Mark. 'What I think,' said Gerry, 'is that you've been suffering some kind of depression.'

'What?'

'Depression, Mark. It's an illness, you know.

'Is it?'

'You had an affair – why, I don't know.'

'Fun. Excitement. I thought I owed myself a bit of –. Oh, shit, I don't know why. It would take a long time to explain.'

'And Paula found out, and threw you out. And I think that triggered a depression. I think you should see some-one. Above all, Mark, I think you should come home. Paula had every right to kick you out after what you did, but she wants you back. That's how I read it. Come back and sort everything out. I can't run the business without you.'

Mark said nothing. A sudden burst of laughter from a

group of businessmen at the end of the bar made him glance up. Back to that, he thought. Doing deals, taking calls, selling, managing, meeting deadlines, drinking in crap hotels at the end of the day. He thought about Morna and her friends, going on the road. He thought about the people at the poetry workshop.

'If you don't,' went on Gerry, suddenly moved to impatience by Mark's vacant expression, 'I have to tell you that I'm going to have to start considering my options.'

Mark's eyes shifted to Gerry's face. 'Tell me what's been happening while I've been away. Tell me the worst. Sales figures, the lot. I think I should know.'

After all, he had put the suit on.

18

It was almost half ten when Mark got back. He and Gerry had had a few drinks at the hotel, then gone on to a tapas bar near Waterloo, where they discussed life, and being forty-something. They talked about the business as well. They returned, by way of reminiscence, to the firm's beginnings, and moved gradually to the present. Gerry was careful to say nothing about tomorrow, or the day after that. He decided he could wait a little while, and see what happened.

In the taxi on the way back to Marylebone, Mark realized he felt better. About what? He had no idea. He let himself into the house. Its established familiarity, its sense of being his home, had been addled by the conversation with Gerry. Life in Harlow, and every-thing that belonged to it, was real and present in his mind. He went to the kitchen and filled a glass with water, and drank it. He didn't switch on the light. He unlocked the French windows and looked out across the garden, ghostly in the moonlight. He thought about Lizzie moving like a beautiful moth among the candles, and the way she had kissed him. A space seemed to open up in his heart.

After a few minutes he heard the front door open, and

the purr of a taxi pulling away in the street, then the front door closing.

Lizzie came into the kitchen, and stopped, seeing Mark's silhouette. He turned.

'Why are you standing in the dark?' she asked.

'I was looking at the garden in the moonlight.'

'Very romantic.' She went to the fridge and poured herself a glass of apple juice, then strolled to his side. 'Not much to look at.'

'When you were out there the other night, surrounded by all those candles, it seemed very beautiful,' said Mark. 'I don't think I'll ever forget that.' She smiled, gratified, serene. 'Or the fact that you kissed me. For some reason.'

'Don't let it prey on your mind. There doesn't have to be a reason.'

'No?'

'Your generation really gets off on sexual tension. Personally, I can't stand it. What's astonishing is that we haven't been to bed together, all these days alone in this house.'

Mark said nothing for a few seconds. 'I didn't know you wanted to.'

'Well — something to do.' She sipped her juice and gazed at the garden. 'Sex without hang-ups, that's the thing. I'm not sure you could handle that.'

'You're probably right,' he answered.

'Still.' She looked at him with eyes devoid of feeling. Then she put her mouth to his. Mark kissed her. He kissed her with passionate absorption, tracing with his fingers the silky skin of her arms and shoulders. Her body moved against his, the pressure languorous and sensual.

He drew his mouth from hers and studied the perfection of her face, the way the ghostly light from the garden lit the soft planes of her cheeks and the curve of her brow and upper lip. How empty her eyes were. With sincere objectivity he said, 'You are the loveliest woman I've ever seen.'

'I don't need all that. Let's go upstairs.'

'No. No, hold on.' He gazed at her in silence for some seconds, then asked, 'Where are you going tomorrow?'

'A flat in Knightsbridge. Why? What makes you ask that?'

'I don't know. You asked me for money earlier.'

'It would have helped.'

'How can you afford a flat in Knightsbridge?'

She tilted her head back slightly. 'I don't have to. I'm letting someone else do that.'

'What's that all about?'

She ran a hand over his shoulder and pressed her hips against his. 'Don't you want to go to bed?'

'Tell me.'

She said nothing for a moment, combing her fingers lightly through her hair. 'It's a man I know. A boyfriend, if you like. Well, he's forty-eight. He's rich, something in finance. He's been on at me for ages to come to some sort of arrangement.'

'You're moving in with him?'

'God, no. It's my place. He pays. He pays for me to live in a penthouse in Knightsbridge. He pays for my time. That's the point of the arrangement.' She drew away and picked up her glass of apple juice from the table. She glanced at Mark, reading his eyes. 'I knew I'd have to do something like this some time. Don't look at me as though it's something terrible.'

'Why do you need to do that? Why don't you just go on living here? Why resort to that?'

'I'm not resorting to anything. Plenty of girls I know do it. How much do you think it costs someone like me to live, Mark? Most of my friends couldn't live in London on less than ten thousand a month. Granny's money hardly paid for half a year's clothing, and I'm talking Dior and Cavalli, not Topshop.' She sipped her juice. 'He's taking me to New York next weekend, to shop at Barneys. He thinks it's every girl's heart's desire. He'll give me a credit card.' She tilted back her head, letting the moonlight paint beautiful shadows beneath her cheekbones and throat. 'He'll take me to the Riviera in summer and St Moritz in winter. Not very imaginative, but men who manage hedge funds generally aren't. He likes spending money on me, so – why not?'

'And in return –'

'In return I keep him amused, captivated, keep the excitement high.' She put down her glass and came to Mark. She kissed him lightly. 'I keep him in a state of electrified suspense.'

'A high-class call girl.'

Lizzie merely smiled. 'There you go with that genera-tion thing again. Girls don't think like that any more. Sex is one thing. Financial security is another. All relationships are transactions of some kind.'

They stood in wary stillness. Then Mark put his arms around her and kissed her again. He wondered how often people knew they were doing something for the last time. Probably not that often.

At length he took his mouth from hers. 'If I were to give you the money you asked for,' he said, 'would it make any difference?'

She laughed softly. 'Hardly. You'd have to put more than twenty thousand to good use if you wanted to keep me.' She rocked slowly against him. 'Why don't you?'

'I couldn't afford you.' He thought about Nicky, and how he had rented these rooms. 'I wouldn't know what to do with you. Not my world.'

'Ah. And what is your world?'

He let his hands slip from her shoulders. 'One of fantasies, I suspect.'

'Then put me in a poem. Why don't you do that, Mark? Why don't you write me a poem?'

He gazed at her. 'I honestly haven't the words for you, Lizzie.'

Lizzie could tell from the way he spoke that they would not sleep together. She slipped from his embrace with a glance of smiling indifference. 'Night,' she said, then went to the French windows and stepped out into the garden.

*

Mark lay on his bed, still in his suit. Was he mad? He had just turned down – or failed to capitalize on – an offer of sex from a young and incredibly beautiful woman. There would come a time when it would probably rank as one of the biggest regrets of his life. Like John Betjeman, not sleeping with more women would probably be up there in his top five. But no, he wasn't mad. Someone like Lizzie would probably drive him mad. Heartless, soulless women were always the ones it was easiest to fall in love with. Sandra and the lifeguard. Lizzie and the hedge fund broker. One night with Lizzie and he would be a lost soul. And she wouldn't care. What woman did?

Paula did. The realization broke over him like a wave. Paula loved him to the point where betrayal by him was the worst thing that could happen to her. She had shown him that. She had wanted so badly to punish him, and now he was punishing her. Like Gerry's constancy, he had taken the depth of Paula's feeling for granted, and was doing it even now. She had found a job because she wanted to make her life and herself more interesting, and all he could think about was how sidelined he felt. With every justification in the world she'd thrown him out of their house, and instead of trying to make amends, he'd sulked and sequestered himself.

The truth of these things was stark and unavoidable. Life changed, things changed and had to be faced. No good trying to escape, when all you were doing was discarding people who had done their best for you. He felt bleakly ashamed. He thought back, with deliberate effort, to the days when he had first known Paula. He knew it had been happy and exciting, but couldn't remember how it had felt to be in love with her. That was because she had woven herself so quickly and naturally into his very existence and being. That was love. Sometimes people could become so much a part of you that you couldn't even see or feel them any more. Not in the way he'd thought he needed to see and feel. The kind of thing he had been looking for, the kind of heartbreak that Lizzie had offered him just a short time ago, was a response to impossibility, longing borne out of unattainability, and pain. If not here, then somewhere else. If not her, then someone else.

He wondered if these weeks on his own had done him any good at all. What had he found that he could not have expected? Kindness, perhaps. He thought of Morna, mournful Morna of the wispy hair and dry, chapped lips, and big brown eyes. Kind women offered possibilities in a way that Lizzie's type, and Nicky's, did not. He could imagine himself on the road with Morna, going like a gypsy from town to town, building sets, shifting scenery, driving vans. Writing poetry. Verses and verses, for posterity. That could have happened twenty-three years ago, when he was still the boy on the desktop, untouched and unafraid. But he was the sum of his parts now. No escaping that.

Suddenly, unbidden, came a recollection of being in France with Paula and the boys when they were just toddlers. A holiday on a shoestring, an escape from a relentlessly difficult year with the new business. They were in Paris, a mistake with the boys at that age. They'd all gone to a cheap restaurant for lunch. James, refusing to eat anything on the menu. Owen, continually throwing his juice beaker on the floor. Paula, in the wake of one of those bickering exchanges that young couples have over the innocent heads of their offspring, barely speaking to him. Rain outside. Mark remembered how his entire situation had, in that instant, seemed hateful.

Their waiter was young – kind, detached, busy. To him they were just another family. Mark had watched him moving among the tables, bringing dishes, clearing up, taking orders, calling out to the kitchen in rapid French. He could just imagine the waiter at the end of the day, hanging up his apron, pocketing his tips, slipping out into the busy Paris streets. He conjured up an image of the kind of place the waiter lived in, where he went with his friends. He saw him going to clubs, bars, movies, living at ease with the language and the people and himself in the freedom of this fantastic city. The more Mark watched the young waiter, the more he'd had a sense of the closure of his own life.

Bang – the beaker on the floor again.

Mark remembered picking it up, and at the same time thinking how it would feel if he could just get up, walk away, and disappear. Just reinvent himself, be like that waiter, start again in some foreign city and never look back.

Now he knew. It felt lonely, and strange, and after the initial sense of liberation it didn't really work, because all the people who mattered were a part of you, and you couldn't leave them behind any more than you could leave yourself.

No, really, there was no room for reinvention.

Paula stood outside Marylebone tube station, and looked up from her *A–Z* at the mid-morning traffic. She really hated the fact that she was doing this. When that girl from sales had called her to tell her where she thought Mark might be, she had received the information coldly, no intention clear in her mind. Gradually she realized the situation couldn't go on indefinitely, that she must find him. Despite what the boys said, Mark might really be having some sort of crisis. Someone had to do something.

She found Lucas Grove, and rang the bell of number eleven. That Mark should be living in this house, in this street, seemed so wildly improbable that she didn't really expect him to answer the door.

He did.

He stood barefoot in his jeans, unshaven, looking at her in utter surprise.

'Hello,' said Paula.

After a pause of some length, Mark said, 'Come in.'

She closed the door behind her and followed him into the house, down the hall and into the kitchen.

'This is where you've been living.'

'Yes.' He filled the kettle and switched it on. 'Sit down. I'll make some coffee.'

She watched in silence as he made the coffee. It was

curious to see him move with familiar ease around these strange surroundings. It gave him an air of remoteness. He didn't look like someone having a crisis. It suddenly struck her, with cold sadness, that perhaps he might not come back.

Mark handed her a mug of coffee. 'How did you find me?'

'That girl Nicky rang and told me.'

'Did she say —'

'She just gave me the address. We didn't discuss anything.'

Mark sat down. 'I should apologize.' He rubbed his hands across his face as though tired, very tired. 'I should apologize for a lot of things.' He drank his coffee. The situation made him feel more ashamed than he could ever have anticipated.

'I almost didn't come. When I found out a few weeks ago that you'd moved all that money, I made certain assumptions.'

'I needed to live.'

'That much? How far away did you mean to go?'

'How far away did you want me?'

She was silent for some time. At last she said, 'I want you to come back. That's really hard for me to say, after what you put me through. But I was the one who wanted the separation, and I was the one who kicked you out. So I'm the one who should say it. I want you to come back.'

Mark said nothing. Paula got up and walked to the French windows. She looked out. 'Perhaps you don't want to.

Perhaps you've found somewhere you'd rather be. Something you'd rather do. Someone you'd rather be. Or be with.'

There was a long silence. 'No,' said Mark at last. 'I've found none of those things.'

'So what's it all been about? Why here? This house?'

'I answered an advertisement. You know – rooms to rent.'

'Show me. Show me the rooms.'

'Why?'

'I want to know. I want to see how you've been living.'

He took her upstairs to the top of the house, and showed her the rooms. Paula walked around them, trying to see Mark's life here.

Mark sat down at the rosewood table, and as he watched his wife move around the room, a feeling that was like snow on a landscape seemed to settle on his soul. It was a revelation. It seemed perfectly right that she should be here. She was everything that was familiar and consoling and accepting, and all that he had almost lost. He marvelled that he should not have understood any of this before.

He said softly, earnestly, 'Christ, I am so glad you came.'

She turned to look at him. Her eyes were sad. 'I had to. I mean, what was going to happen to you?'

'I don't know,' said Mark. 'I don't know.' She moved towards him, and he put his arms around her, leaned his head against her like a child.

'Come back, and we'll sort things out,' she said gently.

'I thought you couldn't forgive me for what I did.'

'Mark, I really hated you. I had every right. But I still love you.' She fought against rising tears, and failed. 'I don't want to be without you.'

He held her tight. 'I'm so, so sorry.'

'I know you are. I think I've been unfair, too. I've let certain things take over. I was so anxious about the boys going. I couldn't imagine how life would be, what I'd do with my time. The job was a way of preparing myself, I suppose. I didn't realize how little time it would leave me for everything else. For you. For us. I've told Lorna I need to cut down the number of hours I work. She's fine with that. And you know what? Now the boys are going away, I don't see why we shouldn't take a bit of time off. Go away somewhere together.'

'I think Gerry may feel I've had enough time off.'

'Maybe not now. After Christmas, perhaps. The Caribbean?'

The smile she gave him, looking in his eyes for his heart, touched him, wrecked him. That she should try so hard, when he had done so little. She traced his brow with her finger. 'It's been a really strange few weeks without you. Not knowing where you were, or what you were doing. What *have* you been doing all this time?'

'Oh, I don't know . . . Trying to find out if there was something I'd missed.' He held her, glad to smell her familiar perfume. 'Which is about as stupid as anyone can be.'

They sat and talked for a long while. In the end, with

all the tender anxiety of two people needing to be reconciled, they made love in the small bedroom.

Afterwards, in the early afternoon light, Mark watched as Paula dressed. 'I don't want you to go,' he said. 'Stay here.'

'I have to get back. The man's coming to service the boiler.' She smiled at him over her shoulder as she fastened her bra. The sight was familiar and warm. 'I know. But that's how it is. That's what we bought into.'

'You're right.' He propped himself up on one elbow. 'I could pack and come with you.'

Paula took a comb from her bag and ran it through her hair. 'What about that woman – your landlady? You can't just leave without saying something. It'd look a bit odd, surely.'

'I suppose so. She doesn't get back till tomorrow evening.'

Paula sat down on the edge of the bed. 'I don't mind. You've spent a small part of your life here. Maybe this is something you should take a little time over. Just so long as you mean it.'

'Just so long as you do.'

'Oh, yes.' She kissed him.

'I love you,' said Mark. 'Thank you for coming.'

Paula gazed into his eyes. 'Tell me something. If I hadn't come here today' – she paused, almost afraid to ask the question – 'would you have come back? Ever?'

'Yes,' said Mark. Even if he wasn't sure that this was true, no other answer mattered any more.

*

Mark passed several hours the next day in the room at the top of the house, sitting like a monk in his cell, writing. He wrote all morning, and into the afternoon, while the sun trailed slanting shadows across the floor. In the end he copied all that he had written in his notebook on to the laptop. At the end of the afternoon he went to the PC shop a couple of streets away and printed it out. Just one copy. He read it through, folded it up, and put it in his pocket. Then he went back to the house and packed.

It didn't take long. He closed the empty drawers and went into the sitting room, looking round. He thought about the brief life he had lived here, and wondered if it would have made any difference if it had never happened at all. What had he wanted or expected? He remembered that revelatory moment in the garden in Harlow weeks ago, when desire for the unnameable and unimagined had gripped him, and he had thought that something waited for him out there, something to bring his heart alive. He knew now that everything became mundane in the end. Everything except possibilities. They always remained exciting, elusive.

He thought of Lizzie, and was grateful for that much enchantment.

He sat down at the rosewood table near the window and opened the drawer. He took out the notebooks and other odds and ends. He would keep the notebooks. He would keep the poems and show them to no one. He might read them from time to time just to remind himself that there had been possibilities, once. He opened the notebooks and began to read, slowly and carefully, through the poems which he had invented and written down.

It was after nine when he roused himself from his thoughts. He packed the notebooks away with his other things and went to the Three Castles in the hopes of seeing Morna and Patrick, so that he could say goodbye.

Morna was there with other people. Mark stood with his drink at the bar, knowing she would come over. She did.

'Aren't you coming to join us?' she asked.

'No,' said Mark. 'I'm not staying long.'

She studied his face, thinking he looked different, distant. 'The theatre company's heading off to Birmingham next week,' she told him. When he said nothing, she added without any real hope, 'You can still come if you want.'

Mark smiled.

'You won't though, will you?' said Morna.

'No, I don't think I will. I'm leaving tomorrow.'

Morna nodded, eyes cast down. After a moment she said, 'I've got something for you.' She dug in her bag. 'There you go.' She handed him a photograph.

He looked at it and smiled. 'Thank you.'

'I had the feeling I might not be seeing you after next week.'

No, well . . . I wish you luck. With the theatre, and things.'

'You, too.'

He leaned forward and kissed her, and she closed her

eyes for an instant. 'Thank you for being my good friend,' said Mark. 'And say goodbye to Patrick. Tell him not to go to any more poetry workshops. They're bad for him.'

'I'll tell him.'

She watched him leave. The way people walked into your life, then out again. So casual, not knowing.

Mark went back to Lucas Grove. The house was silent and dark. He went down the hall to the kitchen, about to turn on the light, when he saw candles guttering and flickering in the garden. Someone was sitting at the table. Lizzie.

He went outside. She was sitting in the chair with her back to him, and for a heart-stopping moment the angle at which she sat, the tilt of her head, made her real. Then as she turned her head and lifted the glass at her side, he saw it was Alice.

'Hello,' she said. 'Come and join me.'

Mark sat down at the table, letting the fantasy subside. After a few moments he asked, 'How was your week?'

'Tedious as ever. How was yours?'

'My wife came to see me. I'm moving back.'

Alice nodded. 'That's probably a good thing.' She was silent for a while. 'When will you be leaving?'

'Tomorrow.'

'Tomorrow? That soon?'

'Don't worry – the rent's covered for the next month. Until you find someone else.'

Alice sipped her wine. 'I don't think I'll be looking for anyone. I'm sick of this job. I don't like the travelling. I think I'll find something closer to home, so I won't need a house-sitter. Anyway, where would I find another tenant as good as you?'

'I'd hardly say that.'

'You're sweet. You pay the rent. You don't make a mess. And you're companionable. Speaking of which – go and fetch yourself a glass.'

'No, I won't – thanks all the same.' He dug in his pocket. 'I have something for you. A sort of leaving present.'

He handed her the sheets of paper. Alice unfolded them. She leaned forward, drawing a candle nearer to read by. Mark sat watching her face as she read. When she had finished she looked up at him, her wide eyes distilled with tears.

'Thank you.'

'I don't think it's going to guarantee you immortality.'

'It's beautiful. It's very sad, and very beautiful. No one has ever written me a poem before.' She looked back down at the pages. 'It makes me feel better about a lot of things. You have a gift. You have insight.'

'Everyone knows something about leaving the past behind. About looking back.'

'You shouldn't be doing that yet.'

'Neither should you.'

'No. Well.' She smiled. 'Thank you again. I have enjoyed having you in my house. The weekends won't be the same.' She looked up at Mark. 'Is it going to be all right – for you, I mean?'

'I don't know. I'd like to think so. I've found out certain things, so maybe . . . yes.'

'I hope so.'

Mark stood up. 'I think I'll go to bed. I'm going to make an early start. Beat the traffic.' He thought about his car in the Welbeck Street car park, undriven for weeks. 'So, goodnight. And goodbye. And thank you.' He stooped to kiss her lightly.

'Nothing to thank me for,' said Alice.

He went to bed, leaving her among the candles. And a part of his heart, too, with Lizzie, her ghost shimmering like a moth across the lawn.

In the morning Mark walked to Welbeck Street and drove his car out into the early sunshine. It was strange to be behind the wheel again after all these weeks. He parked outside the house and fetched his cases, being careful not to wake Alice. He left the keys on the kitchen table. As he was going out he noticed the corkscrew lying beside Alice's empty wine bottle from last night. He thought for a moment of taking it. A memento. He decided not to. Every house needed a corkscrew.

With Morrissey belting out on the CD player, Mark drove back to Harlow. The closer to home he got, the clearer his sense of relief and certainty.

Later that afternoon Mark was finishing unpacking. At the bottom of his overnight bag he found the photograph which Morna had given him, slightly dog-eared. He stood looking at it for a moment, then went into his study. He switched on his laptop, connected it to the printer, laid the photograph on the scanner, and scanned it in. His laptop screen still held the picture of himself at twenty, last in the series which had begun with Little Mark on his trike. In its place, he brought up Morna's picture. He gazed at the image of the man lying in his jeans and T-shirt on the grass, eyes closed, caught for ever in the shifting sunlight of Berkeley Square.

He looked quite young, he thought. He really looked quite young.